# ON THE Rocks

## KANDI STEINER

D0802308

Published by Kandi Steiner
Edited by Elaine York/Allusion Graphics, LLC/ Publishing & Book Formatting, www.allusiongraphics.com
Cover Photography by Perrywinkle Photography
Cover Design by Kandi Steiner
Formatting by Elaine York/Allusion Graphics, LLC/ Publishing & Book Formatting, www.allusiongraphics. com

# ON THE Rocks

# SCOOTER WHISKEY
# DISTILLERY

*To those who love whiskey and sunshine,*

*long summer days and front porch sittin',*

*dips in the river and never taking life too seriously —*

*this one's for you.*

SCOOTER WHISKEY
DISTILLERY

# Chapter One

## NOAH

When you hear the word *Tennessee*, what do you think of?

Maybe your first thought is country music. Maybe you can even see those bright lights of Nashville, hear the different bands as their sounds pour out of the bars and mingle in a symphony in the streets. Maybe you think of Elvis, of Graceland, of Dollywood and countless other musical landmarks. Maybe you feel the prestige of the Grand Ole Opry, or the wonder of the Country Music Hall of Fame. Maybe you feel the history radiating off Beale Street in Memphis.

Or maybe you think of the Great Smoky Mountains, of fresh air and hiking, of majestic sights and long weekends in cabins. Maybe you can close your eyes and see the tips of those mountains capped in white, can hear the call of the Tennessee Warbler, can smell the fresh pine and oak.

Maybe, when you think of Tennessee, all of this and more comes to mind.

But for me, it only conjured up one, two-syllable word.

1

Whiskey.

I saw the amber liquid gold every time I closed my eyes. I smelled its oaky finish with each breath I took. My taste buds were trained at a young age to detect every slight note within the bottle, and my heart was trained to love whiskey long before it ever learned how to love a woman.

Tennessee whiskey was a part of me. It was in my blood. I was born and raised on it, and at twenty-eight, it was no surprise to me that I was now part of the team that bred and raised the most famous Tennessee whiskey in the world.

It was always in the cards for me. And it was all I ever wanted.

At least, that's what I thought.

Until the day Ruby Grace came back into town.

My ears were plugged with bright, neon orange sponges, but I could still hear Chris Stapleton's raspy voice crooning behind the loud clamor of machines. I wiped sweat from my brow as I clamped the metal ring down on another whiskey barrel, sending it on down the line before beginning on the next one. Summer was just weeks away, and the distillery swelled with the Tennessee heat.

Being a barrel raiser at the Scooter Whiskey Distillery was a privilege. There were only four of us, a close-knit team, and we were paid well for doing a job they hadn't figured out how to train machines to do yet. Each barrel was hand-crafted, and I raised hundreds of them every single day. Our barrels were part of what made our whiskey so recognizable, part of what made our process so unique, and part of what made Scooter a household name.

My grandfather had started as a barrel raiser, too, when he was just fourteen years old. He'd been the one to set the standard, to hammer down the process and make it what it is today. It was how the founder, Robert J. Scooter, first noticed him. It was the beginning of their friendship, of their partnership, of their legacy.

But that legacy had been cut short for my grandfather, for my family. Even if I had moved away from this town, from the distillery that was as much a blessing to my family as it was a curse, I'd never forget that.

"Hey, Noah," Marty called over the sharp cutting of another barrel top. Sparks flew up around his protective goggles, his eyes on me instead of the wood, but his hands moved in a steady, knowledgeable rhythm. "Heard you made the walk of shame into work this morning."

The rest of the crew snickered, a few cat calls and whistles ringing out as I suppressed a grin.

"What's it to ya?"

Marty shrugged, running a hand over his burly beard. It was thick and dark, the tips peppered with gray just like his long hair that framed his large face. "I'm just saying, maybe you could at least shower next time. It's smelled like sex since five a.m."

"*That's* what that is?" PJ asked, pausing to adjust his real glasses underneath the protective ones. His face screwed up, thick black frames rising on his crinkled nose as he shook his head. "I thought they were serving us fish sticks again in the cafeteria."

That earned a guffaw from the guys, and I slugged our youngest crew member on the arm. At twenty-one, PJ was the rookie, the young buck, and he was the smallest of us by far, too. His arms weren't toned from raising barrels day in and day out for years, though his hands were finally starting to callous under his work gloves.

"Nah, that's just your mama's panties, PJ. She gave them to me as a souvenir. Here," I said, right hand diving into my pocket. I pulled out my handkerchief, flinging it up under his nose before he could pull away. "Get a better whiff."

"Fuck you, Noah." He shoved me away with a grimace as the guys burst into another fit of laughter.

I shook the handkerchief over his head again before tucking it away, hands moving for more staves of wood to build the next barrel. It took anywhere from thirty-one to thirty-three planks of wood to bring one to life, and I had it down to a science — mixing and matching the sizes, the width, until the perfect barrel was built. I hadn't had a barrel with a leak in more than seven years, since I first started making them when I was twenty-one. It only took me six months to get my process down, and by my twenty-second birthday, I was the fastest raiser on our team, even though I was the youngest at the time.

Mom always said Dad would have been proud, but I'd never know for sure.

"Seriously, though," Marty continued. "That's three times now you've creeped out of Daphne Swan's house with the cocks waking up the sun behind you. Gotta be a record for you."

"He'll be buying a ring soon," the last member of our team piped in. Eli was just a few years older than me, and he knew better than anyone that I didn't do relationships. But that was where his knowledge of me ended, because just like everyone else, he assumed it was because I was a playboy.

They all assumed I'd be single until the end of time, jumping from bed to bed, not caring whose heart was broken in the process.

But I wanted to settle down, to give a girl the Becker name and have a few kids to chase after — maybe more than anyone else in Stratford. Only, unlike all my friends, I wouldn't just do it with the first girl who baked me a pie. There were plenty of beautiful girls in our small town, but I was looking for more, for a love like the one my mom and dad had.

Anyone who knew my parents knew I would likely be looking for a while.

"Daphne and I are friends," I explained, stacking up the next barrel. "And we have an understanding. She wants to be held at night, and I want to be ridden like a rodeo bull." I shrugged. "Think of it as modern-day bartering."

"I need a friend like that," PJ murmured, and we all laughed just as the shop door swung open.

"Tour coming through," our manager, Gus, called. He kept his eyes on the papers he was shuffling through as his feet carried him toward his office. "Noah, come see me after they're gone."

"Yes, sir," I replied, and while the guys all made ominous *oooh's* at my expense, I wasn't nervous. Gus had nothing but respect for me, just as I had for him, and I knew maybe *too* confidently that I wasn't in trouble. He had a job that needed handling, and I was always his go-to.

The door swung open again, and the teasing died instantly, all of us focusing on the task at hand as my brother led a group of tourists inside.

"Alright, remember now, this is another area where no pictures are allowed. Please put your phones away until we venture back outside. Since we're one of the last breweries that still makes its own barrels, we don't want our secrets getting out. We know at least half of you were sent from Kentucky down here to spy on us."

The group laughed softly, all of their eyes wide as they filtered in to get a better look at us. Marty hated tours, and I could already hear his grunts of disapproval, like the group was sent with the sole purpose of ruining his day. But me? I loved them, not only because it meant Scooter Whiskey was still a household name, and therefore — job security — but also because it meant a chance to rag on my little brother.

I had three brothers — Logan, Michael, and Jordan.

Jordan was the oldest — my senior by four years. Mom and Dad had adopted him before I was born, and though he might not have *looked* like the rest of the Becker clan, he was one of us, through and through.

Michael was the youngest of us at just seventeen, only one summer standing between him and his senior year of high school.

And Logan, who just walked through the door with the tour, was the second youngest. He was two years younger than me, which meant he was my favorite to pick on.

He was my first little brother, after all.

Once the entire group was inside, Logan gestured to us with a wide smile.

"These are the fine gentleman known as our barrel raisers. You might remember learning about them from the video earlier. As it mentioned, each of our barrels is crafted by hand, by just four upstanding gentlemen — Marty, Eli, Noah, and PJ."

We all waved as Logan introduced us, and I chanced a smirk in the direction of the hottest girl in the tour. She was older, maybe mid-thirties, and looked like someone's mom. But her tits were as perky as I imagined they were on her twenty-first birthday, and she was looking at me like a hot piece of bread after a month of being on a no-carb diet.

She returned my smile as she twirled a strand of her bright blonde hair around her finger, whispering something to the group of girls she was with before they all giggled.

Logan continued on, talking about how the four of us as a team made more than five-hundred barrels every single day before sending them down the line for charring and toasting. He explained how Scooter Whiskey is actually clear when it's first put into our barrels, and it's the oak and charring process that brings out the amber color and sweet flavor they're accustomed to today.

Even though my hands worked along on autopilot, I watched my brother with a balloon of pride swelling in my chest. His hair was a sandy walnut brown, just like mine, though his curled over the edges of his ball cap and mine was cut short in a fade. He stood a few inches taller than me, which always irked me growing up, and he was lean from years of playing baseball where I was stout from years of football before I became a barrel raiser.

If you grew up as a boy in Stratford, you played at least one sport. That's just all there was to it.

Though we had our differences, anyone who stood in the same room with us could point us out as brothers. Logan was like my best friend, but he was also like my own son. At least, that's how I'd seen it after Dad died.

Just like there were only a handful of barrel raisers, the same was true for tour guides. They were the face of our distillery, and on top of being paid well for their knowledge and charisma, they were also tipped highly by the tourists passing through town. It was one of the most sought-after jobs, and Logan had landed it at eighteen — *after* Dad died, which meant he didn't get any help getting the position.

He got the job because he was the best at it, and so I was proud of him, the same way I knew our dad would have been.

It was no surprise to our family when he landed it, given his rapt attention to detail. He'd been that way since we were kids — nothing in his room was ever out of place, he ate his food in a specific order, and he always did his homework as soon as he was out of school, exactly as it was supposed to be done, and then did his chores before he even considered playing outside.

For Logan to be comfortable, everything needed to be in order.

The poor guy had almost made it through his entire spiel when I kicked the barrel I was working on and dropped the metal ring to the floor, creating a loud commotion.

"Ah! My finger!"

I gripped my right middle finger hard, grimacing in pain as the rest of the crew flew to my side. The tourists gasped in horror, watching helplessly as I grunted and cursed, applying pressure.

"What happened?"

"Is he okay?"

"Oh God, if there's blood, I'll pass out."

I had to strain against the urge to laugh at that last one, which I was almost positive came from the hot mom with the great rack.

Logan sprinted over, his face pale as he shoved PJ out of the way to get to me.

"Shit, Noah. What'd you do? Are you okay?" He thwacked PJ's shoulder. "Go get Gus!"

"Wait!" I called, still grimacing as I held up my hand. It was in a tight fist, and with everyone's eyes fixed on it, I slowly rolled my fingers of my free hand beside it like I was coaxing open a Jack in the Box, and I flipped my little brother off with a shit-eating grin.

The guys all laughed as my brother let out a frustrated sigh, rolling his eyes before grabbing my neck in a chokehold. I shoved him off me, stealing his hat and tossing it on my own head backward as I raced toward his tour group.

"Sorry about the scare, folks," I said, playing off the charm of the drawl I was given naturally from being born and raised in Stratford. "Couldn't pass up the opportunity to give my little brother here a hard time."

There were still some looks of confusion aimed our way, but slowly, they all smiled as relief washed over them.

"So, you're okay?" I heard a soft voice ask. "You're not hurt?"

It was the mom, and I leaned against one of the machines on one arm as I crooked a smile at her.

"Only by the fact that I've gone my whole life without knowing you, sweetheart."

Her friends all giggled, one of them wearing a BRIDE TO BE button that I hadn't noticed before. The mom was still blushing as Logan ripped his hat from my head, shoving me back toward the barrel I'd abandoned.

"Alright, Casanova. Leave my group alone."

"Just making their tour of Scooter Whiskey Distillery one they'll never forget, little bro," I chided, winking once more at the mom before I got back to work.

Logan was already continuing on with the next part of his tour as he walked the group out, and I held the mom's eyes the entire way until she was out the door.

I imagined I'd find her at the only bar in town later tonight.

Marty griped at me for being stupid, as PJ and Eli gave me subtle high fives. They were all used to my pranks, especially at my brothers' expense. When you grow up in the same town, with the same people, all working at the same place and doing the same damn job, you learn to make the most of what little fun you can slip into the everyday routine.

"Noah."

Gus's voice sobered me, and I dropped my cocky smirk, straightening at his call.

"My office. Now."

He hadn't even risen from his chair, but I knew he'd heard the commotion from the prank. My confidence in being untouchable as a Scooter employee slipped a little as I peeled off my work gloves and made my way to his office.

"Shut the door behind you," he said without looking up.

My ears rang a little at the sudden quietness, and I let the door latch shut before taking a seat in one of the two chairs across from him.

Gus eyed me over the papers he was still running over his hands, one brow arching before he sighed and dropped the papers to his desk. "First of all, even though I appreciate you bringing some laughter into this place, don't play around when it comes to job safety, okay?"

"Yes, sir."

"I know Logan is your brother, and I don't mind the occasional prank. But slicing a finger off is no laughing matter. Our founder is proof of that."

The story of our founder passing away from a minor finger injury was one we always told to the tours that passed through. Here was this healthy man, older but not suffering from any illnesses, and in the end, it was his pride that got him. He'd cut his middle finger right where it connected at the base of his hand, but rather than telling someone, he just wrapped it up and went about his normal routine.

Infection took his life well before it was time.

"I understand, sir. It won't happen again."

"Good." He kicked back in his chair, running a hand over his bald head as his eyes fell to the paper again. "We've got a potential buyer here who wants one of our single-barrels. But, the situation is a little precarious."

"How so?"

It wasn't strange for Gus to ask me to show one of our rare barrels to potential buyers, mostly older gentleman with too much money to know what to do with it anymore. Each barrel sold for upwards of fifteen-thousand dollars, most of that money going to good ol' Uncle Sam.

"Well, the buyer is only nineteen."

"That's illegal."

"Thanks for stating the obvious." Gus thumped a hand on the stack of papers he'd been staring at. "She's a Barnett."

I whistled. "Ah. So, we can't say no."

"We can't say no."

"But we also can't let it get out, especially since Briar County is just looking for a reason to shut us down again."

"You catch on fast."

I nodded, scratching at the scruff on my jaw. The Barnett's were one of the most influential families in the town, right next to the Scooters and, at one time, the Beckers. The Barnetts had a long line of mayors in their family line, and if they wanted a single-barrel of Scooter Whiskey, there was no saying no — regardless of the age.

"When's this girl coming in?"

"She's here now, actually. Which is why I called you in. I need you to show her the barrel, but keep it low key. Don't do our normal tasting, just to be safe. Show her the room, give her the fluffy breakdown of what her money's getting her, and get her out of here."

"Are her parents going to pick up the barrel at the ceremony?"

Every year, we hosted a big ceremony — better described as a backwoods party — to announce the different barrels, their distinct notes and flavors, and their new owners. We also cracked open one of the single-barrels for the town to indulge in. It was the only barrel not sold to the highest bidder.

"Apparently, her fiancé is. He's twenty-four, so he's legal."

"Why can't he be the one to check it out, then?"

Gus pinched his brow. "I don't know, the girl wants to give it to him as a wedding gift, I guess. She's waiting, by the way, and I just want this taken care of. Can you handle it?"

"I'm on it."

Without another word, Gus dismissed me, more than happy to let me do his dirty work.

I slipped into our one and only bathroom in our little share of the distillery, washing my hands and face the best I could with short notice. Not that it mattered. The kind of people who could afford to spend what I'd pay for a good car on a barrel of whiskey didn't give a shit what I looked like when I told them about it. They only cared about the liquid gold inside.

So, I dried my face and hands, rehearsing the words I'd said to hundreds of rich men and women before this one as Gus' sentiment rang true in my own mind.

"Let's get this over with."

# Chapter Two

## NOAH

Anytime I had to go to the welcome center, I always garnered more than a few curious looks.

There were several small groups of tourists milling about the welcome center, taking pictures with our founder's statue and reading about the transition of our bottles throughout the years as they waited for their tour slot. As I made my way through, heads turned, brows arching as they took in my appearance. It made sense, seeing as how I was always dirty, and a little smelly. My mom would argue that the reason they stopped to stare was because I was "handsome enough to make a church choir stutter in unison."

She said I got that from my dad, too.

I still said it was the whole smelly thing.

I smiled at a pair of older women near the ticket desk who weren't the least bit ashamed as they ogled me. Their husbands, on the other hand, glared at me like I was a bug that needed to be squashed. I just smiled at them, too, and kept my head down.

"Noah Becker," a loud, boisterous, and familiar voice greeted as I neared the ticket desk. "To what do I owe the pleasure?"

"Came to beg you for a date, of course." I leaned over the desk casually, cocky smirk in place. "What'dya say, Lucy? Let me spin you around on the dance floor this Friday?"

She cackled, her bright eyes crinkling under her blushing cheeks. Her skin was a dark umber, but I always caught the hint of red when I flirted with Lucy. She was my mom's age, a sweet woman who had a reputation for fattening all of us at the distillery up with her homemade sweet potato pie.

"You couldn't handle me."

"Oh, don't I know it." I tapped a knuckle on the desk, looking around the seating area. "I'm looking for the potential barrel buyer. She was supposed to be waiting up here."

"Ah," Lucy said, her lips poking out as she tongued her cheek. "The Barnett."

"That bad, huh?"

Lucy nodded toward the front doors. "Too pretty for manners, I suppose. But then again, can't really blame her, considering who her mother is."

Lucy kept talking, but my gaze had drifted to the fiery-haired girl pacing outside. The sunlight reflected off her auburn hair like it was the red sea, her eyes shielded by sunglasses too big for her face as her all-white stilettos carried her from one edge of the sidewalk to the other. She had one arm crossed over her slim waistline, accented by the gold belt around her crisp white dress, and the other held a cell phone up to her ear. Her lips moved as fast as her feet, the swells painted the same crimson shade as her hair.

She was nineteen, dressed like she was at least thirty, with a walk that told me she didn't take any shit.

"She stepped outside to take a phone call a few minutes ago," Lucy said, bringing my attention back to her. "Want me to let her know you're ready?"

"No, no," I said quickly, my eyes traveling back to the girl. "I got it. Thanks, Lucy."

When I pushed out into the Tennessee heat, squinting against the glare of the sun, the first thing I noticed were her legs.

I'd seen them from inside, of course, but it wasn't until I was right up on her that I noticed the lean definition of them. They were cut by a line of muscle defining each slender calf, accented even more by the pointy-toed heels she wore. She was surprisingly tan, considering her hair color and the amount of freckles dotting her nose and cheeks, and that bronze skin contrasted with her white dress in a way that made it hard *not* to stare. The skirt of that dress was flowy and modest, but it revealed just a little sliver of her thigh, and I had to mentally slap myself for checking out a fucking teenager.

"Mama, I don't care if the flowers are dust pink or blush pink. That sounds like exactly the same shade to me." She paused, turning on one heel as she reached the far end of the sidewalk.

I kept watching her legs.

"Well, I'm not Mary Anne." Another pause. "Why don't you just call her, then? She'd be happy to argue with you about which shade of pink is better, I'm sure."

"Ms. Barnett?"

She stopped mid-stride, slipping her sunglasses down her nose just enough to flash her haunting, hazel eyes at me before the shades were back in place again.

"I have to go, Mama. I think the..." She hesitated, assessing my appearance. "I think the *fine gentleman* who will be showing me the barrel is here."

I smirked, crossing my arms over my chest. If she thought I was going to back down from her *I'm-better-than-you* attitude, she was mistaken.

"Yes, I'll come right home after. Right. Okay, okay." She sighed, tapping her foot before she pulled the phone away from her ear. "Okay, gotta go, BYE."

When the call was ended, she let out another long breath, pulling her shoulders back straight as if that breath had given her composure. She forced a smile in my direction, the phone slipping into her large handbag as she stepped toward me.

"Hi," she greeted, extending her left hand. It dangled limply from her dainty wrist, a diamond ring the size of a nickel glimmering in the sunlight on her ring finger as it hung between us. "I'm Ruby Grace Barnett. Are you showing me my barrel today?"

"I am." I took her hand in my own, her soft skin like silk in my calloused, dirty palm.

Her nose crinkled as she withdrew her hand, and she inspected it for dirt as she reached into her bag, pulling out a small tube of hand sanitizer.

"I've been waiting forever." She squirted a drop of the cleaner in her hand and rubbed it together with the other. "Can we move this along?"

I sniffed, tucking my hands in my pockets. "Of course. My apologies, ma'am."

I started off in the direction of the warehouse that stored our single barrels, not checking to see if she was following. I heard the click-clack of her heels behind me, her steps quickening to catch up.

"*Ma'am*," she repeated incredulously. "That's what people call my mother."

"I'm sorry," I said, not an ounce of actual apology in my voice. "Would you prefer *Miss*?"

"I would," she said, sidling up to my side. Her ankles wobbled a little when we hit the gravel road. "Is there... are we walking the entire way?"

I eyed her footwear. "We are. You going to make it?"

The truth was, we had a golf cart reserved specifically for showing our clients the single barrels. In the back of my mind, I knew I should grab it. Miss Barnett *was* a potential buyer. But the way Lucy had responded to my mention of her name, and the way she'd practically curled her lip at the sight of me was enough to make me conveniently forget about the cart.

Little Miss Ruby Grace could walk in those heels she loved to tap so much.

She narrowed her eyes at my assumption. "I'll make it just fine. I'm just surprised you don't have... *options* for your clients. Especially considering the price of the product I'm here to inquire about."

The words were strange as she spoke them, holding a level of arrogance but softened by the lilt of her Tennessee twang. It was like she was still a little girl, playing dress up in her mom's heels, trying to be older than she was.

I stopped abruptly, and Ruby Grace nearly ran into me before her heels dug into the gravel.

"I could carry you," I offered, holding my arms out.

Her little mouth popped open, her gaze slipping over my dirty t-shirt. Even though she was eyeing me like a mud puddle she had to maneuver around, I noted the slight tinge of pink on her cheeks, the bob of her throat as she swallowed.

"I don't need you to *carry* me, sir." She adjusted the bag on her shoulder. "What is your name, anyway?"

"Does it matter?"

I started walking again, and she huffed, hurrying to catch up.

"What's that supposed to mean?"

*It means, I know you don't give a rat's ass what my name is and you'll forget it as soon as you walk out of this distillery and back into your little silver-spoon world.*

I sighed, biting my tongue against the urge to be an asshole.

"Noah."

"Noah," she repeated, rubbing her lips together afterward, like she was tasting each syllable of my name. "Nice to meet you."

I didn't respond, reaching forward to unlock the warehouse door, instead. Once the lock clicked, I tugged it open, gesturing for Ruby Grace to enter.

She stepped through the doorframe, pushing her glasses up to rest on top of her head as her eyes adjusted to the dim lighting. The distinct smell of oak and yeast settled in around us, and when the door closed, Ruby Grace's eyes found me, wide and curious.

"Wait," she said as I flipped on a few more lights. "You're Noah *Becker,* aren't you?"

The skin on my neck prickled at the way she said my last name, as if it said more about me than my dirty clothes in her mind.

"What about it?" I turned on her, and she was so close, her chest nearly brushed mine. She was still a few inches shorter than me, even in her heels, but her eyes met mine confidently.

"Oh, I'm sorry," she said, taking a tentative step back. "I didn't mean it in any way. It's just, I used to sit behind you in church. When I was little." Her cheeks flamed. "We would play this game… oh gosh, never mind. I feel so silly."

She waved me off, stepping even farther away as her head dipped. She clasped her hands together at her waist, waiting for me to speak, to lead us through the towering rows of barrels, but I just stared at her.

It was like seeing her for the first time.

That one apology, that awareness of herself, it was genuine and true. It was the young girl she actually was, slipping through the façade she'd painted so well.

And I smiled.

Because I did remember.

I wasn't sure how I hadn't put two and two together, but then again, how could I recognize the stunning, classy woman before me as the same freckle-faced kid who used to kick the back of my pew? She'd been just a girl then, and I had been eighteen, fresh out of high school and just as bored in church as she was. I couldn't even remember what the game was that we played, only that it used to make her giggle so hard her mother would thump her on the wrist with her rolled-up program.

I smiled at the memory, and then it hit me.

I'd just checked out a woman who used to be the annoying little kid behind me in church.

*New low, Becker.*

"You were a little shit," I finally said.

Her eyes widened, a small smile painting her lips. "Says the Becker. You boys are notorious for causing trouble."

"We like to have fun."

She laughed. "That's one way to put it."

Her eyes twinkled a bit under the low lighting as she assessed me in a new way. She didn't look at me like I was dirty and beneath her, but rather like I was an old friend, one who reminded her of youth.

She was only nineteen, but the sadness in her eyes in that moment told me she lost her innocence a long time ago.

I didn't realize I was staring at her, that we'd gravitated toward each other just marginally until she cleared her throat and stepped an inch back.

"So," she said, eyes surveying the barrels. They were stacked thirty high and a hundred back, each of them aging to the perfect taste. "Which of these beauties is mine?"

"The single barrels are back here," I said, walking us down one of the long rows of barrels.

Ruby Grace's eyes scanned the wooden beasts as we walked, and I opened my mouth to spout off the usual selling points of a single barrel — how limited they are, how no one else would have a barrel of whiskey that tasted like hers, how each barrel was aged differently, for different time periods, and at different temperatures. But the words died in my mouth before they could come out, a question forming, instead.

"So, you're buying a barrel for your fiancé, huh?"

Her eyes were still on the barrels, the corners of them creasing a little as a breath escaped through her parted lips.

"That's right."

I eyed her ring again.

"When's the big day?"

"Six weeks from Sunday," she sighed the words, fingers reaching up to drag along the wood as her heels clicked along in the otherwise-silent warehouse.

I whistled. "That's pretty soon. You ready?"

Ruby Grace stopped, her fingers still on the wood as she eyed me under furrowed brows. "What?"

I arched a brow. *Did I say something wrong?*

"For the wedding? To be married? You know, commit yourself to someone for the rest of your life, that little thing you said yes to?"

She swallowed. "I... Well, no one has asked me that."

"No one asked you if you were ready to get married?"

She shook her head.

Somehow, the rows of barrels felt smaller, narrower, like they were moving in on either side of us, pushing us together centimeter by centimeter.

There was so much wrong with the fact that no one had asked her that pivotal question — at least, in my mind. Here was this young girl, not even twenty years old, not even *close* to her prime years, and she was settling down. It wasn't unheard of in Stratford, or anywhere else in Smalltown, USA. Plenty of my friends got married right out of high school. Most of them had kids before they could even have a legal drink.

But something told me that wasn't what Ruby Grace had pictured for herself.

"Well, I'm asking. Are you ready?"

She blinked, and it was as if that blink stirred her from the thoughts she'd been tossing around. She started walking again, folding her arms gently over her chest. I watched her try to slip on the same disguise she'd been wearing when she introduced herself to me. She wanted the world to believe she was poised — a polished woman, a dignified lady who didn't take shit.

But the truth was, she was still a girl, too. She was still nineteen. Who made her feel like that wasn't okay? To just be a nineteen-year-old girl who doesn't have it all figured out yet?

"Of course," she finally answered. "I mean, Anthony is great. He's older than me, twenty-five to be exact, and he's so mature. He just graduated with his master's in Political Science from North Carolina. That's where we met," she said, her head leaning toward me a bit on that note. "At a party on campus. He said the first time he saw me, he knew I'd be his wife one day. Which is so sweet. And he's on track to be in politics for life." She smiled, but it didn't mask the slight shake of her voice. "The engagement happened a little faster than I expected... I mean, we've only known each other a year. But I think when you know, you know. You know?"

I smirked in lieu of answering.

"And Mama was so excited when we announced our engagement, she wanted to do the wedding right away. It's crazy, knowing we have what usually is about a year's worth of work to do in six weeks. But, she's been taking care of a lot of it... Lord knows that woman loves a project." Her voice trailed off on a soft laugh before she spoke again. "And Anthony, he's exactly what my family had in mind for me. And we get along, you know? We have so much fun."

Why did it feel like she was trying to convince me? Or maybe, it was *herself* she was trying to convince.

"And you love him," I pointed out.

She paused, eyes flicking to mine as she tucked a strand of hair behind her ear. "Right. And I love him."

I could have stared at her all day, deciphering her like a riddle that had an obvious answer if I just thought about it long enough. But she shifted under my gaze, and one glance at the rock on her finger reminded me that she was someone else's puzzle to put together — not mine.

"Well, here they are," I said, tapping one of the barrels on the back wall. They were stacked just as high as the rest of the room, each barrel stamped with a batch number and an exclusive, gold-plated plaque that had all the details about when it was distilled, barreled, what rows it's been aged in over time, and more.

"There are so many," she said, eyes scanning up. "How do I choose? I mean, should I be looking for something specific?"

I scratched at my jaw. "I mean, there is incredible whiskey inside each and every one of these barrels. Part of what makes buying a single barrel so enticing is that you'll have a one-of-a-kind whiskey," I said, finally remembering to give her the spiel I'd put off before. "Usually, we let our potential buyers taste a few to compare but..." I smirked. "There is that whole legal drinking age debacle."

Ruby Grace laughed. "Oh. Yeah. That old thing."

She swayed from foot to foot, grimacing a little as she eyed the barrels.

"Are you okay?"

Her face twisted again as she shifted her body weight to her left foot. "Yes. Sorry, it's just these stupid shoes. I told my mom I didn't need to wear heels to inspect whiskey barrels, but she was *not* having it with me wearing boots."

For a split second, I pictured her in said boots. I wondered if the brown leather would cap off under her knee, if her thighs would have been even more exposed in the shorts she would have paired with those boots. Or would she have worn jeans, covering her legs altogether?

*Stop thinking about her legs, Becker.*

"Take them off."

Her brows shot up, eyes widening as they found mine.

"What?" She asked, laughing. "I can't just *take my shoes off*." She threw her arms up, gesturing to our surroundings. "We're in an old, dirty warehouse."

"You act like you weren't born and raised in an old, dirty town."

"Yeah, well," she said, crossing her arms. "I wasn't exactly working in the distillery or out raising cows on the outskirts, now was I? A little bit of a different setting when you're the Mayor's daughter."

She tried to smile, but a soft curse left her lips when she shifted her weight again.

Without hesitation, I reached back for the collar of my t-shirt and ripped it up over my head, laying it down on the ground at her feet.

"Here," I said, holding out my hand. "You can stand on that. It might not be a freshly polished marble floor, but your precious feet should survive."

Ruby Grace was gaping, her jaw completely unhinged as her eyes crawled over my abdomen and chest. "I..."

"Shoes. Off." I pointed at her feet. "You do that, and I'll let you taste a few barrels. Just don't tell anyone, least of all your parents."

She chuckled, but finally stepped out of her heels. They fell on their sides as a relieved sigh slipped through her lips, and I watched her polished toes curl on my t-shirt.

"*God*, that feels so much better."

I shook my head, reaching back behind the first row of barrels for the tasting glasses we housed there. "Are you always so stubborn?"

"I wasn't being stubborn."

"I guess that's my answer," I said, pouring a tiny splash from one of the barrels before holding the glass toward her. "Here. Take a sip."

"Oh, no," she said quickly, shaking her head. "It's okay. Like you said, I'm underage."

"So you've never had a sip of alcohol in your life?" I challenged.

She bit her lip. "I mean... I *have*, but not whiskey. That's a man's drink."

At that, I full on belly-laughed. "What the hell kind of talk is that? Whiskey is a *man's drink*?" I shook my head. "It's whiskey. It's *expensive* whiskey, at that. And I assure you, it's delicious — whether you have tits or not."

Ruby Grace blushed, biting her lip against a smile. "God, sorry. I sound like my mother. More and more every day now, actually," she mused, glancing down at her toes before her eyes found the glass in my hand again.

I pushed it toward her. "Just a sip. You're not even going to get *close* to feeling a buzz. But this way, you can taste the difference between a few barrels that were aged in different ways." I swallowed. "You can pick out the perfect one for your future husband."

She hesitated, but her hand reached forward, taking the other side of the glass. Our fingertips brushed just slightly, just enough to make me jerk my own hand away.

"And, hey, bonus," I continued, shaking off the awkward tension. "You can be as 'unladylike' as you want here. I won't judge. You can even burp, if you're really feeling frisky."

Ruby Grace laughed, eyeing the whiskey like she still wasn't sure before she shrugged and tilted the glass in my direction. "Oh, what the hell. Bottoms up."

She took a sip, and then promptly grimaced and stuck her tongue out as soon as she'd swallowed.

"*God,* that's awful." She shook her head, shoving the glass back in my direction. "Definitely not doing that again."

I laughed, rinsing the glass with a splash of water from the bottles we kept nearby before filling it with the same whiskey.

"Okay, that was my bad. Maybe I should have told you how to taste it first." I handed it to her again, though she eyed it like it was poison. "Smell it first."

She did as I said, uncertainty shading her face as she looked my way again. "I'm not sure I'm doing it right."

"You're not sure you're smelling right?"

She narrowed her eyes. "You know what I mean. I don't... I don't know anything about this stuff."

"It's okay, that's why I'm here." I stepped closer to her, taking the glass from her hand, and when I inhaled to demonstrate, it was her I smelled instead of the whiskey.

She smelled like lavender, like an open field in the heat of summer.

"Watch," I said, taking another breath, this time focusing on the whiskey. "You smell it first, and ask yourself what you smell. Oak? Vanilla? Honey? Maple? Every whiskey is different, depending on how it's aged, how the barrels are charred and toasted. See what notes you can detect first. And then," I continued, taking my first sip. I let it linger in my mouth, swirling it a round before swallowing gently. "Taste it. I mean, *really* taste it. Does it give you different flavors on the tip of your tongue than it does on the back? Does it burn going down, or is it just warm? And what's the aftertaste?"

Ruby Grace watched me, fascinated, her lips parted softly, eyes falling to my bare chest where a small drop of whiskey had landed. I thumbed it away, handing her the glass again.

"Now, you try."

She took a deep breath, like she needed to focus to really do it right, and then she repeated my steps. And this time, when she finished swallowing, she smiled.

"Wow," she said. "It's different when you don't just throw it back like a shot."

I chuckled. "Well, this isn't shooting whiskey. It's Tennessee Sippin' Whiskey," I said, tilting my imaginary hat. I tucked my hands in my pockets, nodding toward the next barrel. "Take a little from that one."

"I can pour it myself?"

I nodded. "Just twist that spout a little, not too much. You don't need a lot to taste it."

She was hesitant as she poured a sip into her glass, and her eyes lit up, a little squeal of joy popping from her mouth. "I did it!"

And for the next ten minutes, I watched Ruby Grace be a girl.

She was so far from the snotty woman who had offered me her hand like a prize when we first met. She was just a teenager, a soon-to-be sophomore in college, drinking whiskey, learning something new and having fun.

I wondered when the last time was that she had fun.

I wondered if she'd ever had fun at all.

The way she looked when she laughed, I hoped she had. I hoped it wasn't the first time that laugh had been genuine, the first time that sound had made its way into the airwaves. She laughed the way the wind blew — softly, and then all at once, without an ounce of shame for how that sound might permanently shift the atmosphere around it.

When she'd decided on the barrel she wanted, Ruby Grace regretfully slipped back into her heels, and I tugged my t-shirt on before leading us out of the warehouse and toward the welcome center.

"So," I said, walking slow so she didn't kill her feet in the process of getting back to her car. "What are Anthony's plans when you go back to school in the fall?"

"What do you mean?"

"I mean, are you guys moving in together and he's getting a job there? Or are you guys doing long distance for a while or what?"

She laughed, her hair falling over her face a little as she watched our feet. "I'm not going back to school."

"Oh..." I paused. "You don't want to?"

"I mean, I guess I do... but, there's no point. You know? I'm getting married. I'll be his wife now, and I'll have so much to do. He's already getting into the political arena, and he'll need me to be by his side, campaigning and networking and all that." She shrugged. "I don't really need a degree to do that."

"Is that what you want to do?"

"It doesn't matter if it's what I want to do," she said quickly. "It's what I was bred to do."

"*Bred*?" I frowned. "You're not a horse. You're a human."

Ruby Grace stopped with an abrupt click of her heels once we reached the welcome center entrance, and she crossed her arms defiantly as her eyes found mine. She didn't even have to say another word for me to know I'd pushed the wrong button, and I was about to get the same woman I met in this very spot an hour before.

"Look, you don't know anything about me, okay? Or my family, or what I want or what I *don't* want, so just stop trying to presume whatever it is you're presuming."

"Oh, look at you," I chided, stepping into her space. "Using big words again."

She scoffed. "They say nothing changes when you leave this town and come back, I guess you just proved them right."

"Well, that's my job," I fired back. "Proving the ominous *they* right. Glad I've still got it."

Our chests were close again, the stains on my off-white t-shirt highlighting the crisp cleanness of her dress.

"Lucy will take your money inside," I said, nodding to the doors behind her. "Congratulations on your engagement."

I turned just as her mouth popped open, but I didn't look back.

"Thanks for the *tasting*," she said, making sure her voice was loud and clear.

"Go ahead and say it louder, princess," I threw behind me. "You'd be in just as much shit as I would."

She didn't respond to that, and when I chanced a glance back in her direction, there was steam rolling off that cute face of hers as she ripped the door to the welcome center open.

And I couldn't help it — I chuckled.

I didn't mean to ruffle her feathers, but damn if I didn't like getting under that pretty bird's skin.

# Chapter Three

## RUBY GRACE

"**E**rgh!"

I gripped the steering wheel on my convertible tighter, not even attempting to tame my hair as it blew around in the wind. Mama would be upset that I'd messed it up after she fixed it that morning, but I didn't care.

I needed the wind to blow away my anger.

*"Look at you, using big words again,"* I mocked in my best Noah Becker voice.

I turned the wheel, making another tour through town. I wasn't ready to go home yet, wasn't ready for Mama to hit me with a thousand questions on what kind of flowers I wanted and whether I wanted ribbon or twine around the edges of the ceremony chairs. I hadn't even been home from college for two full days and she was already driving me mad.

My stomach sank at the thought of the University of North Carolina, of the university I'd wanted to attend ever since I took a road trip with my best friend there when we were sixteen. I'd gotten in, and my first year there had been everything I'd hoped it would be.

But I wouldn't be going back.

*"Oh, you don't want to?"*

Noah's voice hit me again, like it was the ping pong ball and I was the paddle beating it against the wall.

I sighed, another grunt of frustration rolling through me as I let my left hand hang over the edge of my door. I slowed the car down as I hit the Main Street drag, not wanting to give any of the small town cops a reason to give me a ticket.

Lord knows they were bored enough that it didn't take much.

I wasn't even sure *why* I was so annoyed and frustrated with Noah. He was just making conversation, just asking questions — but they were questions no one else had asked. And, to make it worse, they were questions I didn't have answers to — at least, not *reasonable* answers.

I had the ones I'd been told, the ones I'd rehearsed, the ones I'd repeated to myself night after night until they stuck, until I believed them, too.

But it wasn't just his questions that had thrown me, it was the man, himself.

I think I recognized him even before he told me his name. Maybe that was why I'd been so insistent that he tell me. It was hard to forget the boy I crushed on as a young girl, and continued to fantasize about up until the very day I left Stratford.

The first time I'd laid eyes on him, I was only nine years old, and he was the cute boy who sat in the pew in front of me in church.

The last time I'd seen him, he was a drunken mess, yelling at his older brother at a farm house party about who was man of the house now that their dad had passed away.

That was five years ago, when I was fourteen and sneaking into my first party. I remembered I didn't drink a drop that night because I was afraid I'd end up just like Noah Becker.

But five years had changed him.

He wasn't a mess anymore.

That pecan brown hair of his that used to curl around his ears was cut clean and short now, making his strong jaw stand out even more than it had when he was a boy. Those eyes that had tipped me off to who he was before he'd offered his last name were the same as they were the last time I'd seen him — cobalt blue, almost gray around the pupil — but now, they were a little less haunted, and a little more determined, like he had something to prove, just like I did. His arms and chest were fuller — a sight I got to inspect *quite* closely after he stripped his shirt off — and he was tan the way only a man who works outside can be.

He'd grown up, from a boy to a man, and everything about him was just *bigger*. His presence was larger than life.

More than anything, his confidence poured off him in waves, or maybe it was *cockiness*. Either way, he'd thrown me. I'd walked into that distillery with my head as high as my heels, and I was prepared to show this town that I was the *new* Ruby Grace Barnett — polished and poised just like my mother, ready to take on this town with my husband-to-be as the future State House Representative of North Carolina. I'd left that knobby-legged, freckle-faced little girl behind and come back as a well-to-do *woman*.

At least, that was the plan.

In reality, I'd stood barefoot on Noah's dirty old t-shirt and giggled as I poured whiskey from a barrel for the first time.

*Classy. Mama would be proud.*

And maybe *that* was the most frustrating part — that not only had I strayed from the plan, from the woman I wanted others to see me as, but that I'd also had fun in the process.

The truth was, I could have stayed in that old, grimy warehouse full of whiskey barrels with Noah Becker all day. He made me laugh, and for that one hour in time, I wasn't just Anthony Caldwell's future wife. I wasn't a smile and a handshake and a side kick.

I was just me.

But Noah's questions at the end of our tour had whipped me back into reality real fast, and here I was, finally making the turn toward home.

Back to the real world for Ruby Grace Barnett.

My phone rang as I pulled down our long driveway, the familiar white house stretching out before me. It was two stories, completely symmetrical, with a porch that wrapped all the way around. Like any southern belle's dream, there was a swing on the porch, and a garden Mama had cared for as her own pride and joy for my entire life. An American flag hung proudly from above our stairs, waving in the gentle, Tennessee breeze.

I kept my eyes on that flag until I dug my phone out of my bag, smiling at the picture on the screen. It was Anthony's smiling face, his arms around me in one of my favorite dresses, the picture one we snapped at his parents' lake house that spring.

"Hey, you," I answered.

"Hey, yourself. How's my beautiful fiancé today?"

"Tired," I answered on a sigh, putting the car in park. I held the button to bring the convertible top back up, the sun fading from my shoulders.

"More wedding planning?"

"*All* the wedding planning. But, the good news is, I have your wedding gift taken care of."

"Oh, is that so? What'dya get me?"

I smiled. "Well, I can't tell you, now can I? It wouldn't be a surprise, then."

Anthony laughed, and I let my head fall back against the head rest, picturing what he looked like then. I missed his laugh, his smile, his arms around me.

More than anything, I missed our conversations.

Before he proposed, we would talk for hours — about everything. We'd talk about our dreams, our plans for the future, our pasts, our families, our deepest fears. But after the proposal, all of our conversation shifted to the wedding, to me becoming his wife.

"Fair enough. I can't talk long, but I wanted to see how you were doing. Dad's got me working with this media crew covering my first run for State House Representative. It's been madness over here."

"I'm sure it has, but you've wanted this forever," I reminded him. "Your dreams are starting to come true."

"And you'll be there beside me when they do."

I smiled, but couldn't help but notice the way my stomach dropped at his words. I was happy for him, and a part of me couldn't wait to move back to North Carolina after the wedding. Of course, I wished I was going back to the university, but I wasn't really sure why.

This was what I'd always wanted. It was what I'd always hoped would happen.

I was marrying someone with the same political heart as my father, and his father, and his father's father. It was what my family had always wanted for me. If anything, Anthony was *more* — he didn't just want to be mayor, he wanted to be president.

And I would be his first lady.

My smile grew a little more genuine at that, at being in a position where I could make a difference. That's what had always appealed to me about living in the political circuit. I could help children, or battered women, or the homeless. I would have a platform, a goal, and a voice to raise.

And a husband who would stand beside me, just as I would him.

"I miss you," Anthony said on a sigh, bringing me back to the moment.

"I miss you, too. But I'll see you soon. Six weeks."

"Six weeks," he repeated. "And then you walk down the aisle to me."

My stomach dropped again, and I placed a hand over it just as my mother appeared on the front porch. She hung her hands on her hips, her eyes hard on me.

"Well, the wedding planner is waiting on me," I said. "Good luck with the media circus over there."

"Thanks, babe. Talk to you soon. Tell your mom I said hi."

I laughed. "If I can get a word in edgewise, I'll do that."

Mama was already down the porch and en route to my car by the time I pushed the driver side door open. She held the handle, eyes wide as she took in my appearance.

"I cannot believe you put that top down after I spent all that time on your hair this morning, Ruby Grace," she tsked, but she offered a hand out to take my bag, anyway.

"I got it," I said, stepping out and shutting the door behind me.

Mama looped her arm through mine, the other hand picking at my tangled strands.

"How'd it go?"

"Fine," I answered as we climbed the porch stairs. "I still think it's way too much to spend on a barrel of liquor."

"It is," she agreed. "But, it's good to support the community, and your father has built a great relationship with the distillery over the years. Anthony will enjoy it, I'm sure."

"I don't even think he drinks whiskey."

"He will once he's in this family," Mama said with a chuckle. "Your father will make sure of that."

It was true. Anyone who married into the Barnett family, or *any* family in Stratford, for that matter, had to be a whiskey lover. Our town was built around the Scooter Whiskey Distillery, and it was our main source of income. It brought us tourism, fame, notoriety. If you lived in Stratford, you either worked at the distillery or had family who did. It was our livelihood.

Scooter Whiskey was known all over the world. You were hard pressed to find a bar that *didn't* carry it, and more than the whiskey itself, Scooter was a brand. Women wore the logo stretched across their breasts in tight little tank tops. Men wore it on their motorcycle jackets and tattooed it on their arms. There were houses all over that were decorated with Scooter Whiskey barrels and neon lights, with glasses and barware, with posters and branded chairs.

It wasn't just a whiskey, it was a lifestyle — and Stratford was where it was born.

"Speaking of which, where is Dad?"

Mom waved me off. "Oh, you know him. He'll be working until at least seven, and then I'm sure he'll find somewhere to play cards or bet on horses."

I nodded. Tennessee didn't have a single casino, but drive to any state border and you could find a way to gamble. Dad had always been big into cards and horses, sometimes sporting events, and if he wasn't at the casino on the Georgia state line, he was at one of the council members' houses, where they'd make a casino of their own.

I hung my purse on one of the hooks in our mud room, kicking off my heels and wincing as my feet adjusted to being flat on the hardwood floor. My toes ached, the balls of both feet on fire, my ankles screaming.

Mama bent to retrieve the shoes as soon as they were abandoned, shaking her head at me.

"These are designer heels, Ruby Grace. You don't just kick them off. Go put them away in your room."

*If only she knew where I'd kicked them off less than an hour ago.*

"Yes, Mama."

She handed them to me, but before I could make my way upstairs, her hands were in my hair again, trying to fix the mess the wind had made. I studied the faint lines on her face as she did, seeing so much of her features in my own reflection now that I was nineteen that it somewhat scared me.

Her hair was the same burnt orange as mine, though hers was cut just above her shoulders, and our noses were identical, the tips of them rounding in a little button. Her eyes were mocha brown where mine mirrored the hazel of my father's, and her freckles were more pronounced, her skin as pale as Snow White's, where mine was easily bronzed in the summer sun. She was rail-thin and just barely over five feet, where my curves were slight but still present.

We were different in so many ways, and yet in so many others, exactly the same.

I wondered if I was looking at my future, at the woman I would become — a wife, a mother, a last name known all over town.

Or maybe all over the nation.

She sighed, giving up on my hair and hanging her hands on her hips again. "Well, why don't you go up and get changed. Your father will be home in an hour or so. Come help me with supper and we can talk about the photographers again. I talked Mr. Gentry down on his price. And we need to make a decision between ribbon or—"

"Ribbon or twine on the chairs," I finished for her, fighting back a sigh. "I know."

I made my way upstairs, my feet aching with every step, but Mama kept talking.

"Yes, and your sister said we can video call her after dinner to talk about the shades of pink for the flowers." Her voice grew louder when I hit the top stair, making my way down the hall toward my old room. "Can you bring that book down here? Oh, and—"

"The seating chart," I said at the same time as her. "I've got it, Mama. Be right down."

When my bedroom door closed behind me, I pressed my back against the wood, closing my eyes and reveling in the momentary silence.

If my older sister, Mary Anne, were here, she would be in heaven. She was older than me by four years, and as soon as she graduated college, she ran off to Europe, hell bent on chasing her dreams of being a fashion designer. So far, Dad had said about all she'd done was blow through his money and kiss foreign boys. I didn't know if that was true, but I did know three things for sure.

One, she would have loved this wedding stuff more than I do. And she would have known what decision to make, what colors to choose, where to sit who at what table.

Two, I envied her a bit, that she got away from this town, from her responsibility as a Barnett daughter.

And three, she wasn't here — and even if she was, she could never save me from the mile-long wedding to-do list I was faced with.

I sighed, letting my head fall back against my door. I was supposed to be excited about all of this, wasn't I? Shouldn't I *want* to plan the seating chart, and care about the color of the flowers, and get excited about the photographs and the cake cutting and the first dance? It was my wedding. It would only happen once, and it felt more like a chore to me than the big day I'd dreamed of since I was a little girl.

I loved the man I was marrying, and I loved the town we were getting married in.

I had the dress of my dreams, my best friend to stand by my side, and the honeymoon of a lifetime planned in the Bahamas.

Everything was perfect, and if you asked any of my friends, they'd say I was the luckiest girl in Tennessee.

So then why did it feel like I was drowning?

"Why, that can't *possibly* be *the* Miss Ruby Grace, can it?"

My best friend, Annie, flourished her thickest Tennessee accent from behind the front desk at Stratford's only nursing home, her gap-toothed smile wide and welcoming as I let the door shut behind me. When I unwrapped the mint spring scarf from around my neck, she gasped, pressing her hand to her chest.

"Why, it *is*. Oh, heavens. Someone give old Mr. Buchanon his blood pressure medicine before she walks through the halls."

I chuckled, hanging my purse and scarf behind the desk before I lifted a brow. "Haven't seen you since Christmas, and that's the welcome I get?"

"Well, I'd jump up and hug you, but it's a little more difficult these days," Annie said, gesturing to the watermelon of a belly she had blooming under her oversized scrubs.

"How about I assist?"

I reached down, and when Annie's hands were in mine, I pulled her up, both of us laughing as she leaned back to balance out the weight of her belly. It was hard to believe she was the same girl I'd road tripped to North Carolina with just two summers ago, the same blonde, giggly girl I'd stayed up too late with on countless nights, laughing and dreaming and making plans for our future husbands, our future families. I was so sure we'd room together at UNC, or chase our dreams of traveling the country and helping others in AmeriCorps. It didn't matter what we did — I just *knew* we'd do it together.

But when Annie fell in love with Travis, everything changed.

It wasn't out of place for a nineteen-year-old to be pregnant in Stratford. Half my graduating class was already married and popping out babies. But, seeing my best friend with a stomach the size of Texas was new for me. It was proof that we were older now, that life had changed, that all those dreams we'd had on the days we'd played house as kids were coming true.

She was a wife. Soon, she'd be a mother.

And I wasn't far behind her.

"Annie, you look..."

"Fat? Sweaty? Like I did our freshman year with all this acne?"

I laughed. "You look *beautiful.* You're glowing."

"Why does everyone say that?" she asked, hugging me as best she could with her belly between us. "There is positively no glow going on here. Unless the fluorescent light is hitting my sweat sheen in some magical way."

That sent both of us into a fit of laughter, and when it settled, Annie shook her head, eyes sweeping over me. They widened a little when they took in the kitten heels Mama had insisted I wear, even though I'd be on my feet all day. "*You* look incredible. I swear, I'm going to blink and have your mother as a best friend one day."

I grimaced. "Please don't say that."

She chuckled, waddling back into her chair. "I didn't think I'd see you here so soon. Didn't you just get into town Sunday night?"

"Yep," I said on a sigh, flopping down in the chair next to her. "It's been a hundred miles a minute on wedding planning since I got here. I just needed a break, to do something for myself."

Annie nodded in understanding, patting my hand just as a visitor approached the desk. While she checked them in, I let out a long exhale, taking in the familiar surroundings of the nursing home.

I'd first volunteered as a fourteen-year-old my freshman year of high school. My dad had been the one to suggest it — more as a way for me to give back to the community than anything else — but he never could have known the love it would spark inside my heart.

I still remembered that first day, losing hours with people seven times my age who had the best stories to tell. I remembered the scent of Mrs. Jeannie's perfume, the collage of photographs she hung on her wall from her time as a nurse in the Vietnam War. I remembered Ms. Barbara's lemon cake, the way it melted in our mouths that afternoon after she gave me the recipe to try to make it since she couldn't anymore.

She'd nearly cried when that first bite hit her tongue.

I remembered the soft velvet of Mrs. Hamilton's hands in mine as we gently danced in her room, and the euphoria I felt when I turned on an old record from the fifties and saw a room of faces light up, and the incomparable joy I experienced when I was the one who made grumpy Mr. Tavos laugh for the first time in years.

It was the first time I felt the high of my own personal drug — helping others. It was the spark that gave way to a flame that burned brightly in me ever since. I loved to volunteer, to give my time to people, organizations, causes that mattered to me.

I'd dragged Annie with me, and though she hadn't taken to it quite as quickly, she'd made it her home just as much as I had. And now, she was a full-time employee.

"Well, do you want me to give you the run down or do you just want to frolic on your own?" Annie asked when the young family she'd checked in made their way down the hall to their mother's room.

"I'll meander, make myself useful."

She leaned back in her chair, one hand soothing her stomach. "Okay. Well, when you're done meandering, you owe me a lunch and a thorough run down of all the wedding planning I know your mother has you doing."

I chuffed. "We'll need more than one lunch break for that."

"I can't believe it's so soon."

"Six weeks from Sunday," I murmured, rocking in my own chair.

Annie watched me. "That's not the best reaction to have when you're six weeks from getting hitched."

I sighed, shaking my head before I let it fall back against the head rest of the chair. "I really *am* excited — to be married, to start a family, to be by Anthony's side as he makes his dreams come true. I just..."

My words faded, because it felt selfish and ungrateful to follow them up with something as petty as *I just wish I could travel or get my degree before I get married*. This was what so many girls in this town dreamed of, it was what *I* had dreamed of — I'd just found it sooner than I imagined.

And I loved Anthony. I was lucky to have found him at all.

I sighed in lieu of finishing my sentence, and Annie just continued rubbing her stomach.

"I know," she said. "I'm sure wedding planning with a family like yours is a lot of pressure and a lot of stress."

I lifted my head again and nodded rather than telling her my true feelings on the subject. "Yeah. But, I'm lucky to have parents who are paying for such an extravagant wedding, and to have a fiancé like Anthony. I couldn't have dreamed up a better match for me, for my family."

"Mm-hmm," Annie agreed, but the way she watched me, I knew I'd let my façade slip. She saw it, what I was trying to hide — not just from her, but from myself. "Speaking of wedding planning, I heard you got Anthony the classic wedding gift."

I frowned. "How did you possibly hear about that? I was at the distillery for all of an hour."

Annie scoffed. "Come on, like you don't already know this town is filled with bored old women who have nothing better to do than gab." She paused, biting back a smirk before she waggled her brows at me. "I heard something else, too."

"What? That I tasted the whiskey? Like no one in Stratford has ever had a drink underage."

"Oh no, it wasn't the barrel tasting making the gossip rounds," she said. "It was the certain barrel *raiser* who hosted the tasting that everyone wanted to talk about."

My jaw dropped, foot stopping where it had been rocking me gently in the office chair. "*Noah*? What were they saying?"

"Oh, not much," Annie said, glancing at her cuticles before she peeked at me again. "Just that he was looking hot as sin when he walked you into that warehouse, and that you looked a little flustered when the two of you came out."

My cheeks burned, the memory of Monday afternoon with Noah making my skin crawl in a way I wasn't sure how to decipher.

Annie shot up, eyes widening. "Wait, is there a little *truth* behind this rumor?"

"There's no *truth* in this town, period." I stood abruptly, making myself a volunteer name tag and smacking it on my blouse. "People are ridiculous."

"What happened? Did he get all up in your space? Did he give you that sexy Becker smirk?" She gasped. "Oh, my God. If he kissed you I will *die*."

"He didn't kiss me, for Christ's sake. He showed me the barrel, and the most scandalous thing that happened was he let me taste a single drop of whiskey."

"Off his tongue?"

"I'm *engaged*, Annie!"

She threw her hands up. "You say that like a Becker brother would even pause at that fact before they planted a hot one on you."

I rolled my eyes. "And on that note, I'm going to make the rounds."

"Don't leave me hanging!" she hollered at my back as I made my way down the hallway. I flitted my hands above my head, waving her off as she groaned. "That's just *cruel*, Ruby Grace."

I chuckled, shaking my head as I dipped into the first room and introduced myself to a new resident who hadn't been there before I left for college. His name was Richard, and it wasn't long after our introductions that he was telling me stories about his days in the distillery and showing me pictures of his late wife.

And just like that, all my wedding planning stress was forgotten.

I lost myself within those walls, surrendering my thoughts and energy to others. I asked to hear about the decades I hadn't been alive to experience, administered medicine, played board games, fixed hair, applied makeup, told jokes, crocheted, danced — and before I knew it, an entire morning had passed.

It was just the release I'd needed.

"Hey," Annie said after lunch, eyes softening as she watched me pull a stack of magazines out of my leather Kate Spade bag. "Remember what I told you."

"I remember."

She frowned more. "I just don't want you to be disappointed. She might not even recognize you."

"I won't be disappointed, even if she doesn't," I promised, balancing the magazines in the crook of my elbow as I smiled. "But, I talked with Jesus this morning, and I think she will."

Annie smiled, too. "I'm not sure how this place survives without you."

"Easy," I said, tapping her nose with my index finger. "They have you."

I was still smiling and confident as I turned, making my way down to the last room in the left hallway. My eyes scanned the names and decorations on the closed doors, and I nodded to those who peeked out at me from where they watched the TVs in their room or read in their beds. When I reached the door at the very end, the one that had donned a red and white wreath since I was a freshman in high school, I let out a shaky breath, eyes washing over the familiar name in gold above the wreath.

*Betty Collins.*

A smile touched my lips, memories of the spunky old woman I'd first met years ago resurfacing. Betty was an eighty-nine-year-old woman with a loud, genuine laugh and a birthmark that sprawled across her forehead. She covered it with white, whispy bangs that she'd constantly run her freckled fingertips over as she told me stories about her favorite movie stars.

She was a forgetful old woman, and though half the staff thought she was showing signs of dementia, I knew better. Betty was more in her right mind than half the people my age were. She just had *selective* memory — and also approximately zero patience when it came to people she didn't care for.

Annie worried that with me being gone so long, she might not remember me.

Again, I knew better.

We'd kept in touch while I'd been gone, writing letters and having the occasional phone call. She'd remembered me just fine when I came back for Christmas break, and I had a feeling she'd never forget me — even if she ever *was* diagnosed with dementia.

And I also knew I'd never forget her.

Betty was the first one to ever open my eyes to a world outside of Stratford, to challenge me to take risks, to move passionately and unapologetically through life. *"Anyone can lead an ordinary life, child,"* she'd said to me one lazy afternoon. *"But the best adventures are reserved for the ones brave enough to be extraordinary."*

I inhaled a deep breath, knocking gently before I pushed through the door and into her room.

Betty sat in the same rocking chair she'd been in the last time I left her to go back to UNC. She faced the window, though the curtains were drawn, and she rocked gently, humming the melody of "Good Morning" from *Singing in the Rain*. I smiled at the sight of her long, white hair, her magazine collages hung on each and every wall, old movie posters filling any space left between them. When the door latched behind me, Betty stopped rocking, ears perking up.

"Who's there?"

"Why don't you turn around and find out, old lady," I sassed.

Betty's head snapped around, her eyebrows drawn in like she was offended, but when her eyes settled on me, everything softened as a smile slid into place. "Well, I'll be damned. Look what the wind blew in."

I returned her smile, rounding the bed until I could sit on the edge closest to her chair. I leaned forward, folding one hand over hers as her eyes glistened with unshed tears. "You need to stop frowning so much," I said, squeezing her wrist. "You're getting wrinkles."

"Ha!" she guffawed, squeezing my hand where it rested on her arm. "I smiled too much when I was younger. I'm just trying to reverse the damage."

I chuckled as her eyes fell to the magazines in my arm.

"Are those for me?"

"Hmm... that depends. When's the last time you stole someone's pudding?"

"Last week," she confessed, her gray eyes almost a silver as she leaned in conspiratorially. "But it was a vanilla one, so does it even count?"

I smirked, handing her the stack of magazines. She took them with a smile that doubled the one she'd greeted me with, already flipping through the pages as I settled back on her bed. It only took a few pages before she started telling me how Anne Hathaway was named after Shakespeare's wife, and I nodded and listened intently as she continued flipping, pausing on each page to tell me a new story about a different celebrity.

Betty was born and raised in Stratford, and she'd never been farther than two counties from the town that she called home. Though she'd never physically traveled, her imagination wandered all the time, and she loved to escape into movies and books, to live the lives of spies and queens and young college students. The collages that decorated her walls brought her favorite adventures to life, and in her mind, she'd seen the world.

She'd seen everything.

"I'm getting married," I told her after an hour had passed, and she paused where she was reading about Chris Pratt's hobbies, a strange shadow passing over her features.

"That so?"

I nodded.

"How did he propose?"

"We were at a party with all his friends and family," I said. "He'd just announced he was running for state representative."

"A political man," Betty mused. "Your father must love him."

"He very much does."

"And do you?"

I smiled, throat thickening in a way it never had when I was asked that question — not until it was asked by Noah Becker, anyway. "I do," I said through the unfamiliar discomfort.

"Well," she mused, nodding as her eyes lost focus somewhere on the page. "I'd like to meet him. Will you bring him by?"

"He's coming into town in six weeks for the wedding," I told her. "I'll try to sneak him away."

"And where will you sneak away to once the knot is tied?" She looked at me then, brows tugging inward.

I leaned forward, folding my hand over hers. "Not too far. I'll never be too far."

I knew she didn't understand how much time had passed since she'd last seen me, but I also knew she could sense that it had been a while. I squeezed her hand, falling quiet as she flipped through the pages of the second magazine before a yawn stretched between us. I reached for the magazines, and once I deposited them on her bedside table, I helped her under the covers.

"This man you'll marry," she said as I pulled the knit blanket up to her shoulders. "Does he make you feel the way Richard Gere made Julia Roberts feel in *Pretty Woman*?"

I smiled, tucking the blanket around her arms as I considered the question. Did Anthony make me feel like that — special, desired, beautiful in a way that he can't resist? Not necessarily. But did he make me feel safe, comfortable, cared for? Yes.

"I think so," I whispered, but then I raised both brows as my eyes found hers. "He's not quite as handsome, though."

"Well, no one is as handsome as Richard Gere, my dear," she said on an exaggerated sigh, as if that were obvious. "Don't be so hard on yourself."

I laughed, and Betty smiled before her eyes fluttered closed. Within minutes, her soft breathing turned to a light snore, and I found myself staring at her favorite scene from *Pretty Woman* that hung above her bedpost. I imagined the scene, wondering what Anthony would look like if he swept in to save me the way Richard Gere did — a white knight in a limo instead of on a horse.

I was sure he would act out a grand gesture if he ever needed to. I was sure he would take care of me, that I'd be comfortable as I stood by his side on his race to his political dreams. And I was sure he was just as handsome as Richard Gere, regardless of what I'd told Betty.

But as I stared at Julia Roberts's wide smile, the one thing I *didn't* know for sure was if I wanted to be the princess he saved.

In the back of my mind, I heard a voice I'd been trying to forget since Monday afternoon.

*"No one asked you if you were ready to get married?"*

And I wondered why it never occurred to me that I had a say in the matter.

# Chapter Four

## NOAH

On Friday night, I sat at the table my father built with my three brothers and the woman who raised us, drinking a cold Budweiser after another long week at the distillery. I'd had family dinner with my friends, with a few girlfriends in the past, and I'd always been disappointed. Because where most families were quiet and orderly and respectful at the dinner table, my family was the exact opposite.

In the Becker household, it was always madness at dinner time.

Complete and utter chaos.

"God, you're disgusting," Logan said, tossing a green bean at our youngest brother, Michael, who had just belched so loud even I was impressed.

Mom swatted Michael's arm to show her own disapproval, but couldn't hide her smirk. "Manners, Mikey."

"What? Better out than in, right?" Michael grinned at all of us before burping again.

"Feet off the table, Logan," Mom said next, as soon as she finished plating the last of his meatloaf. She set it in front of him where his feet had been, smacking his hand away when he tried to dig into the mashed potatoes. "Not until we pray."

"Yeah, Logan. Not until we pray," I said, sneaking my own bite. He narrowed his eyes at me, and Mom smacked my hand next.

"Gray hairs," she murmured, shaking her head. "Every single one of you are giving me gray hairs."

She took her seat, hands reaching out — one for mine, one for my older brother, Jordan's — and the rest of us linked hands and bowed our heads.

"Heavenly Father, thank you for this meal, and for these boys, though they drive me insane. Please bless this food and this day, and be with those who need you most. Amen."

"Amen," we all echoed, and it was the quietest that house would be all night as we each stuffed our faces with the first bite.

Even though we liked to rag on each other, my brothers and I were close. We were like a well-oiled machine, and Mom and Dad were the grease that kept us in working order. After Dad died, Mom took on that job as a solo party, and that was the only time I ever remember the machine breaking down.

Our dad was well known in the town, especially since *his* dad was best friends with the founder of Scooter Whiskey. They had built the brand together, essentially built the town together, and anyone who watched the Scooter Whiskey brand take over the world knew my grandfather was a pivotal member in the team that made it happen.

But when Robert J. Scooter passed away, he left no will behind, and his family inherited everything — leaving our family cut dry. It wasn't long after that that our grandmother passed away, our grandfather following quickly after. Dad always said it was from a broken heart, but he never clarified if it was Grandma who'd broken it or the Scooter family.

I always thought it was a little of both.

Dad had never given up on our family, though, and he'd already established himself as an integral part of the Scooter Whiskey Distillery before the founder passed away. He was young, ambitious, and the Scooter family was happy to keep him around. He worked his way up the ladder, eventually becoming part of the board, and that's where the trouble started.

Somewhere along the line, my dad pushed the wrong buttons.

He wanted to stay true to the Scooter brand, to the company his dad had helped build, but the ones who inherited the distillery had other plans. Where dad wanted to keep the tradition, the "old ways" of making whiskey, the Scooter family wanted to lean more toward innovation. The more Dad fought them on it, the more they did to silence him, and sooner or later, Dad learned to just comply to get by.

But his pay suffered, and so did his job duties.

He went from essentially running the company to pushing papers, taking care of remedial tasks that were better suited for a secretary. One of his last tasks was cleaning out Robert J. Scooter's old office, and though Mom was upset when they assigned it to him, Dad took it in stride. He was always so optimistic, and used to always say that, *"Every experience is an opportunity, no matter how trivial it may seem. Some of my best ideas and most memorable achievements began from a seemingly ordinary day."*

Little did we know that that "seemingly ordinary" day, that "seemingly ordinary" task, would be the literal death of him.

There had only been one fire in the Scooter Whiskey Distillery, and my father was the only one who perished in it.

To this day, no one in our family believed the story the Scooter family fed to us. The fire department claimed the fire was started by a cigarette, and our dad didn't smoke. I would never forget when Patrick Scooter, Robert's oldest son, tried arguing with my mother that he'd seen Dad smoke plenty of times.

*Maybe he just never told you,* Patrick had said, and I'd seen murder in my Mom's eyes when she stepped up to that fully grown man, chest to chest, mascara streaked down her face, and told him no one knew her husband like she did, and she dared him to try to tell her otherwise again.

We'd never been given the truth, not in all the years we'd looked for it.

And that one time in our life was the only time I ever remember the machine breaking down.

We fought. And cried. And asked for answers when we didn't even know what questions to ask. Mom drank for the first time in her life, and Jordan and I struggled to hold the family together, all the while fighting for who was the *man of the house.*

I wanted that title so badly, and Jordan tried to take it simply because he was the oldest. So, we fought one night — literally, punched and kicked until we were both bruised, bloody messes — and then, we came together.

Jordan was the one who made me realize that we were *all* the man of the house — and we were all in this battle together.

Ever since that day, the machine seemed to work even better together than it did when Dad was alive. We were in sync, tuned into each other's needs, and forever protecting each wheel and axle.

God help any man or woman who ever tried to break down a Becker.

"What are you boys getting into tonight?" Mom asked, taking advantage of all of our mouths being full.

It was Friday night, which was like a weekly holiday in Stratford. Other than the tour guides, the weekends were slower for most employees at the distillery, and that meant less time spent working and more time spent living. We always did family dinners on Friday night before dispersing to whatever weekend plans lay ahead.

Michael was the only one of us who still lived at home with Mom, and he had just turned seventeen. He was going into his senior year after the summer, and we were all just waiting for the day he said he was moving out of the house and into a place with his high school sweetheart. They'd dated for two years now, and he was the only one of us I could ever imagine actually settling down.

I worried about when he moved out, though — and part of me wondered if I should move back *in* at that point. The thought of Mom living alone in a house that once fit a family of six was hard to stomach.

"There's a party out at the Black Hole," Logan answered, grinning at Mom. "Wanna come?"

"And have to bear witness to whatever debauchery lands one of you in jail tonight?" She shook her head. "Just bail each other out and I'll see you for dinner next week."

Logan's smile mirrored Mom's, the resemblance uncanny. He and Michael favored her — hazel gold eyes, olive skin, lean and fit, a smile that stretched across their entire faces. I looked more like our dad — stout, tan skin with a reddish tone that he attributed to the Native American in our blood, striking blue eyes that almost took on a silver hue in the sunlight. Mom said sometimes when she looked at me, she saw Dad when *he* was a boy, when they first met.

I'd always worn that like a badge of honor.

Jordan, who was the quietest at the table, didn't look a thing like any of us. His skin was a light umber, his hair black and cut in a short fade. He was the tallest, the largest, the one who always stood out in family photographs.

And yet, he was our brother just the same.

"Bailey and I are heading up to Nashville for the weekend," Mikey announced, and judging by Mom's widened eyes, it was the first she'd heard of the plan.

"Oh?"

He nodded, stuffing his mouth with more mashed potatoes and speaking around them. "Her label is doing a showcase at one of the bars on Broadway. It'll be kind of like Nashville's first taste of her as part of their team."

"I thought she hadn't signed with anyone yet?" Jordan asked, speaking for the first time since we'd dived into our dinner.

"She hasn't."

"And when she does?" Mom asked, brows pulling together.

Mikey was quiet, pushing green beans around on his plate before stacking a few on his fork with a shrug. "I don't know. I guess we talk about it then — where we'll move, what our next steps will be."

An uneasy silence fell over all of us then. We knew the day would come that he would move out, but what worried all of us — though no one said it — was that he was so sure his future was with Bailey.

And we couldn't be sure she felt the same.

She *seemed* to love him, to care for him the way he cared for her, and we all knew he was like me in the sense that he wanted what Mom and Dad had. They had met in high school, and I knew Mikey felt like Bailey must be *it* for him because she was his high school sweetheart, too.

But anyone who knew her could see that music was her first love. And we weren't sure where that would leave Mikey.

"Well," Mom finally said, forcing a smile. "Be careful. And don't get into too much trouble."

All of us scoffed at that, because just *being* a Becker meant trouble was never too far off.

After dinner, Logan and I helped Mom clear the table — Logan's favorite job — while Jordan helped Mikey pack up his car. I walked out onto our old wooden porch just in time to see Mikey's taillights pull away, the sun setting over the hills in the distance. I sidled up next to Jordan, draping my arms over the railing and cracking open the two beers I'd brought while he stood with his arms crossed hard over his chest.

"Your worry is showing, big bro."

He humphed, taking the beer I offered him and popping the lid open. "Kid pretends to be so tough, but if that girl leaves him behind…"

"It'll break his heart," I finished for him. "I know. He'll be okay. He's a Becker."

Jordan nodded, shoulders relaxing a little, as if that one fact was all the reassurance he needed that everything would be alright.

"How's the team looking?" I asked after a moment, taking the first swig from my beer.

"Better than last year. The seniors are strong, and we have some good freshman blood rolling in, some sophomores who got tougher while on JV." He shook his head. "But, still too early to tell how they'll all work together. It'll be a long summer of conditioning."

"And the parents?"

He rolled his eyes. "Still assholes."

I chuckled, sipping from the can in my hand before letting it drape over the railing again. Jordan was the head coach of the Stratford High School football team and had been for four years now. He was the only man in the family who didn't work at the distillery, who never had, who never *wanted* to. Part of me wished he were there with us, carrying on Dad's legacy and helping solidify the Becker name in the Scooter Whiskey history book. But, I couldn't blame him for not wanting to work in a dirty warehouse all day — and I couldn't do anything but support him when I saw him on that field.

Football was his everything.

He'd played his entire life, and where my brothers and I took our aggression out on each other or enemies in the town or even strangers at a bar, he took his out on the field.

And now, he was teaching other boys to do the same.

He was one hell of a coach, and the parents knew it — whether they wanted to argue about who started and who rode the bench or not. And the single moms in Scooterton?

Well, let's just say they were more than happy with Jordan's *coaching*.

The married ones didn't seem to mind much, either.

"So, I heard you caused a bit of a scene at the distillery this week?"

I cocked a brow. "*You* heard?"

"Look, I try as hard as I can to ignore the football moms chattering behind me in the stands, but sometimes I swear they speak louder just so they can be sure I hear them."

"Like when they talk about how tight your ass looks?"

"Or when they talk about you pushing your luck giving whiskey to a minor."

It was my turn to roll my eyes. "They have no proof."

"Do they need any? You know as well as I do that the people who run this town can find evidence for anything they want."

We both fell silent at that, each of us taking a swig of our beer as memories of our father filled the space between us. Crickets chirped to life, the sky taking on a purple glow.

"It was the Barnett daughter," I said, breaking the silence.

"Mary Anne?"

"Ruby Grace."

He balked. "She's like sixteen, Noah."

"Nineteen," I corrected, swallowing down another gulp of beer. "And she's getting married. She was buying one of the single barrels as a wedding gift."

"Wonder who the lucky guy is."

"Some young buck in politics she met at UNC."

"Politics, huh?" Jordan's gaze drifted somewhere beyond the horizon. "Guess he'll fit right in, then."

I nodded, but my stomach tightened as I pictured Ruby Grace's eyes — wide and taken aback when I asked her if she was ready to get married. I still couldn't believe I was the first to ask her.

I still didn't believe she knew the answer herself.

It made no sense, that I harbored some kind of sympathy for a girl who had looked at me like I was the mud staining her designer shoes. She and her family had never wanted for anything, and yet I felt sorry for her, because I knew without being around her for more than even three minutes that she wasn't happy.

She didn't know who she was.

Then again, did *I* at nineteen?

A familiar tune sparked to life from inside the house, shaking me from my thoughts of Ruby Grace as a smile stretched on my face. I glanced at Jordan, who was smiling, too, and he looked back into the house as a long exhale left his chest.

"I used to think she'd remarry, find someone else eventually. But, after the first full year of her playing this song every night, I knew I was wrong."

I followed his gaze, throat tightening at the sight of Mom and Logan dancing around the living room to Eric Clapton's "Wonderful Tonight." It was the song she'd danced to the night she and Dad got married, and I'd watched them dance to it so many times in that living room that I'd lost count.

But it was her son who held her now, swaying and smiling and acting like that song didn't hurt a little for all of us. Logan exaggerated a dip with Mom in his arms before spinning her around the coffee table, and she laughed and laughed, her messy pony tail swinging with the motion.

"I don't think there ever could be anyone else," I mused.

Jordan nodded, each of us finishing off our beers, and I wondered what it felt like to love someone that much.

I wondered if I'd ever know for sure.

## Chapter Five

### RUBY GRACE

"You've got to be kidding me."

I crossed my arms, deadpan expression on my face as I glared at my best friend — though I was debating the title at the moment.

The bonfire the Jensen twins had started was high and warm behind her, dozens of Stratford's residents littering the space around it, as well as stretching into the barn and beyond. There were five kegs, an entire table dedicated to liquor bottles and mixers, and every single person held a red plastic cup that housed either beer or a mixed drink. Ages ranged from sixteen to fifty-five, though everyone seemed to have their own little sections of the Jensen property marked off for their clique. The last time I was here, I was with the high schoolers who liked to party in the barn next to the resident DJ. Now, I was somewhere in the in-between, not sure where to stand or where I fit in.

The Black Hole was the main party spot in town, especially on Friday nights, and Annie had begged me to come with her since it was my first week back in town.

And now, she was bailing.

Annie cringed, forcing a smile through it as she gestured to her belly. "I know, I'm sorry. I really did want to come, but little man is rolling around so much tonight. I just want to go lie on the couch."

"I think that sounds pretty perfect," her husband, Travis, said, wrapping his arm around her. He pulled her into him, kissing her temple as she melted into his side. When she looked up at him, they shared a longing look before he kissed her nose.

And as cute as they were together, they weren't cute enough to bail on me.

"I didn't even want to come here," I reminded her, an almost whine in my voice. "You *begged* me, Annie. And now we've been here for an hour and you want to leave?"

She apologized again, going on about how she'd make it up to me, she'd take me out for ice cream at my favorite little diner in town later this week, and she'd come over and help me and Mom with wedding planning, too. The longer she rambled, her little belly bouncing with her as she pleaded, the less I could hold my anger.

My best friend was too cute for her own good.

I sighed, running a hand back through my lightly curled hair — hair that had taken an hour to fix — before I conceded. "Fine. Let's go."

Annie blanched. "Wait, I meant *we* would like to leave," she said, gesturing between her and Travis. "As in, the two of us. You should stay. Have some drinks, catch up with people."

"Catch up with *who*, exactly?" I probed. "The girls I thought were my friends in high school before you and I both found out the hard way that they only hung out with us for our money? Or how about the boys who, even after graduating, are *still* boys, and are already tripping over themselves with the urge to ask me out… even though they *know* I'm engaged?"

I glanced over at a group of guys I recognized from high school — some of them graduated, some of them seniors now — and they all looked away simultaneously, sipping on their beers and pretending like they hadn't been staring.

Annie chuckled. "Okay. Fair point," she said, but then her eyes flicked somewhere behind me. "Well, would you look at that. It's your buddy from the distillery."

I turned, following her gaze over my shoulder, and immediately locked eyes with Noah Becker.

He was standing with his younger brother, Logan, as they filled their cups from the keg. He smirked when I saw him, saying something to Logan before he started toward me, and I whipped back around, eyes wide.

"He's walking over here," Annie whispered as Travis pulled to the side, saying goodbye to his buddies.

"I noticed. Come on, let's head out," I murmured through clenched teeth, but before I could take even one step, Noah Becker was standing in the space in front of us.

"Ruby Grace," he mused, holding one of the red cups in his hands toward me.

"Noah," I nearly seethed. I didn't take the cup he offered. "We were just leaving."

"*We* were just leaving," Annie corrected, gesturing to her and Travis, who was a few yards away with his buddies now. "But, Ruby Grace, you were thinking of staying, weren't you?"

"No, I wasn't."

Noah smirked, first at Annie, then at me. "I saw you were empty handed. Thought I'd be a gentleman and bring you another beer."

"That was so nice of you," Annie said, practically melting in a cartoonish swoon.

I glared at her.

"I don't drink beer," I told Noah, my glare still on Annie.

"Oh, I didn't realize. Is it a *man's drink*, too?"

I rolled my eyes. "Honestly, yes. And it's carby. I have a wedding dress to fit into."

Noah kept his gaze on me, but the corner of his mouth twitched a little at that comment. "Suit yourself," he said on a shrug. Then, he lifted the cup he'd been offering me to his lips and drained it in three clean swallows before he stacked the other full one inside the now empty one.

"Classy," I mumbled.

"Thanks. One of my many party tricks."

I waited for him to walk away, but he didn't. He just stood there, one hand wrapped around that cup as his free one dipped inside the pocket of his faded blue jeans. I hated that I noticed the way they fit him, the way they hung off his hips, the edge of his brown belt just barely visible under the navy blue t-shirt he wore. It had a logo on it that I wasn't familiar with, but combined with the low orange light of the fire, that shirt set off the cobalt in his blue-gray eyes in a mesmerizing way. His thick biceps strained against the fabric of the sleeves, and when I glanced at his face again, I realized he was checking me out, too.

His gaze was fixed on my legs.

I cleared my throat, crossing my arms over my chest as I shifted my weight. "Aren't you a little old to be here?"

"Aren't you a little young?" he countered, taking a sip of his beer as his eyes scanned the scene behind me like he was suddenly bored.

I scowled. "Look, if you came over here to berate me, feel free to leave."

At that, his eyes snapped back to me. He pinned me with that gaze, like I was a child or his next target — which one, I couldn't be sure.

"I came over here to bring you a beer," he reminded me. "I was trying to be a gentleman, and I was going to apologize for upsetting you earlier this week at the distillery. But now, I'm not sure why I bothered."

Noah shook his head, his shoulder brushing mine a bit as he walked past me with my mouth hanging open like a fish. I blinked several times, digesting what he'd said before my cheeks flushed with embarrassment.

Annie cringed. "I don't think he's being a creep, Ruby Grace," she said as Noah walked away. "It seemed like he was trying to apologize. Maybe you should let him."

I closed my eyes, letting out a long exhale before I turned, jogging after him. "Wait!"

He paused where he was, turning as I caught up to him. I swallowed when our eyes met again.

"I'm sorry," I said, running my hands back through my hair before I let them hit my exposed thighs with a slap. "I didn't mean to be so rude. It's just..." My voice faded, and I had a laundry list of excuses I wanted to spew — about the stress of the wedding, the fact that my best friend had toted me to a party I didn't even want to go to and then wanted to leave an hour in — but, I knew Noah Becker didn't want to hear my problems, so I stopped there. "It's just been a hell of a week."

Noah nodded, waiting.

"Anyway," I continued. "Thank you for the beer, even though I didn't take it. And for apologizing for the distillery." I paused again. "I guess I should probably apologize for that day, too."

Noah tilted his head a little, his eyes curious. "So, are you going to?"

I rolled my eyes. "Can't you just *not* be a brat?"

He chuckled at that, sipping from his cup. "I don't think anyone has ever called me a brat, outside of my mom."

"Mom's always right."

"Touché," he said, tapping his cup with one of the fingers that held it before he nodded over his shoulder. "Come on. Let's ditch this place for a while."

My eyes widened. "What?"

"You don't want to be here," he reminded me. "And honestly, I'm bored out of my mind. There are some stables down by the creek. Let's go for a midnight ride."

"We can't just ride someone else's horses."

"One of them is mine."

That shut me up.

I shifted, tucking my hair behind my ears as I looked around us. People were already watching, whispering, wondering what in the world Ruby Grace Barnett was doing talking to a Becker boy.

"We can't leave together," I said, lowering my voice as I folded my arms back over my chest. "People will see."

Noah furrowed his brows like he didn't understand it, but when he followed my gaze, noticing the group of girls around my age with their eyes on us, he nodded in understanding.

"Ah," he said, sliding his free hand back into his pocket as he took another drink of his beer. "I see. You still give a fuck what other people think of you."

"No," I said quickly, too quickly, blowing my faint attempt at nonchalance.

*Yeah. Clearly he'll believe that.*

The truth was I *did* care — more than I wanted to admit. Our town loved to talk, and the last thing I wanted was to be the subject of anyone's gossip.

"No, that's not it," I said again, voice more steady, though it was still a lie.

"Mm-hmm."

"It's not," I argued again, like a child. "I don't care what anyone in this town thinks of me."

"Okay. Prove it, then," he said, draining what was left of his beer before he tossed the cups in one of the trash cans nearby. He didn't look over his shoulder to see if I was following him, just started off in the direction of the stables in the distance.

I bit my lip, looking back where Annie and Travis were — *were* being the big key word. They were gone, and when my phone pinged, I looked down to a text from her.

*We're heading out. Seriously, stay and have fun. Don't let the old married couple drag down your night. Call me if you need a ride later. Love you!*

I groaned, sliding my phone back in my pocket as I glanced back at Noah. He was already on the other side of the bonfire.

"*Prove it*," I mocked, crossing my arms. "Whatever. I'm not a kid, I don't need to prove anything to him."

But even as the words rolled off my tongue, I knew they didn't reflect what I actually felt. I *wanted* to prove him wrong, to prove to him and everyone watching and maybe even to myself that I could do whatever I wanted and it didn't matter what anyone had to say about it.

Plus... I hadn't gone riding since before I left for college. I used to love riding. That would be way more fun than sitting around drinking with a bunch of people I didn't really care about... right?

I told myself *that* was the reason I went jogging after Noah, telling him to wait up. It wasn't because I was being stubborn, or defiant, or because I wanted desperately to put my money where my mouth was and prove to Noah that he didn't know everything about me like he thought he did. And it wasn't because it was him, or because I wanted to be near him.

It was because I wanted an excuse to ditch that party and ride horses.

Noah chuckled when I caught up to him, my breath labored. He didn't say a thing as we walked, and when the voices and music from the party were out of range, the familiar sound of the creek and the crickets chirping came to life, instead. I sighed, my breath steadying, tension seeping out of me like water through a leaky faucet.

"Better?" he asked when the sound from the party was completely muted by the sounds of Tennessee, instead.

I smiled, shoving him in lieu of admitting he was right. I blushed a little when my hand wrapped around his bicep before I pushed him away, because even that brief contact reminded me how stout he was, years of raising barrels building him into a specimen unlike any other.

He smirked, bouncing back from my shove easily before his eyes trailed down my legs. "Now, let's see if you can ride in those boots."

## NOAH

I didn't know what made me do it.

I didn't know what made me fill a second cup up with beer after my own was full and walk it across the Black Hole to Ruby Grace Barnett. Part of me really did want to apologize for whatever I'd said that had upset her after the tasting at the distillery, but part of me also just wanted to talk to her — period. I didn't have a reason, so I'd brought that beer, thinking it'd be an ice breaker.

For a less stubborn woman, it might have been.

But, whatever the reason, I was glad I'd gone over to talk to her, because regardless of her being feisty and acting like she didn't want to give me more than two minutes of her time, she'd let that same part of her slip that she had at the distillery — the young girl inside. She'd let her guard down, confessed her anxiety over being back home, over being at the Black Hole. I didn't know the complete reason why, but she'd needed someone in that moment.

And I was that someone.

I smiled as Ruby Grace ran her hands over the smooth, white and black tobiano pattern of Tank's neck, her polished fingernails scratching a little as she did. Tank leaned into the touch, neighing softly, tail swishing back and forth in his stall.

"I never knew you rode horses," she said after a long moment, wide eyes glancing at me before she focused on the horse again. "No offense, but it's not exactly something I pictured a Becker doing."

I scoffed. "What, you think we just drink and fight all day, every day?"

She didn't respond, but her apologetic glance told me she actually *did* think that.

I chuckled, kicking off where I'd been leaning against the stable watching her. "My mom taught me how to ride when I was a kid. My other brothers never really got into it, but it's always been a release for me. Dad bought me Tank when I turned fourteen. He was just a year old, then." My heart ached a little at the mention of my father, just like it always did. "We keep him out here at the Jensen's because they have everything they need to take care of him. I pay them a monthly fee, and I can come out here and ride him whenever I want."

"And do you often?"

"At least once a week, sometimes more."

Ruby Grace smiled, both of us falling silent again as she ran her fingers through Tank's mane. He was an American Paint Horse, strong and muscular, his spotted coat and multi-colored mane the most eye-catching elements about him. Tank was fifteen years old now, and though he didn't show signs of becoming a senior horse anytime soon, I still went easier on him now than I had when I was younger. We used to jump logs and round barrels, dredge through the creek, gallop as fast as I could get him going. Now, I usually took him for long, easy rides, letting him stretch his legs as I got lost in my thoughts for an evening. Sometimes we'd go out to the old tree house Dad built for me and my brothers, other times we'd just walk the trails, along the river, or wherever Tank's hooves wanted to take us.

Watching Ruby Grace pet him made my pulse quicken. She wasn't the first girl I'd used that line on. I'd used it plenty of times, bringing whatever girl was into me that night down to the stable to watch them pet Tank and fuss over how cute he was before I laid them down in the straw bales and fucked them until the sun came up. But Ruby Grace was the first one I brought here because I knew she needed to get away, she needed to escape.

And this is where I came to do just that.

I knew I wasn't going to fuck Ruby Grace. For one thing, she was nineteen. For another, she was engaged. She was also the most infuriating girl I'd met, stubborn and judgmental, and nowhere near my type. I liked my women wild, little spitfires who could give me a run for my money in the sack. But none of that changed the fact that she was very, *very* nice to look at.

I'd wondered that day at the distillery what she would look like in boots instead of heels, and I'd gotten my wish. Her brown and turquoise buckaroo boots covered her calves, spanning up to just below her knees where her smooth, tan skin was exposed. That skin was mesmerizing, her toned thighs seeming somehow longer in those boots and the tiny, ripped-up white shorts she'd paired them with. The outfit was nothing like what I'd seen her in that first day, no fancy dress or belt or designer heels. She was just a girl in a tank top and shorts and boots.

A country girl.

And I hated what seeing her that way did to me.

I swallowed, shoving those thoughts aside and tearing my eyes from her legs as I crossed the space between us. I reached up to pet Tank right under where she did, debating if I was really ready to offer my next statement, because I never had before.

"Wanna ride him?"

Ruby Grace lit up, smile as wide as her face as she turned to me. "Really? You'd let me?"

My chest tightened again, because I'd never let *anyone* ride Tank — save for the Jensen family who cared for him. But, this was the most relaxed I'd seen Ruby Grace since she barreled back into town, and for some reason, I wanted to keep her like that.

"Yes, really," I said on a chuckle. "Hang on, let me get her suited up."

Ruby Grace looked around the barn as I brushed Tank, strapping him up with his riding pad, saddle, girth and bridle next. I checked everything twice, including each and every hoof. I'd been out earlier that week to trim his hooves, but I wanted to be sure they were in good shape to ride. Once I was satisfied with my inspection, I guided Tank out of the barn and into the warm summer night.

"Alright," I said, patting the saddle before I turned to Ruby Grace, reins still in my hands. "Hop on up."

I expected her to whine, or scoff, or ask *how in the world to you expect me to do that in these shorts*? But to my surprise, little miss Ruby Grace didn't say a single word. She put the toe of her boot in the stirrup, reached one hand up to grab the horn, and heaved her opposite leg up and over, shifting her weight a bit until she was comfortably seated.

She smirked when she saw my face, tossing her long red locks behind her shoulder as she shrugged. "What? Did you think I was too prissy to know how to ride a horse, Noah Becker?"

I put my hands up in a surrendering gesture. "I didn't say a word."

"You didn't have to. That trout mouth of yours said it all," she said.

"Alright, watch your foot for a second," I said, ignoring her last remark. She frowned as I handed her the reins, confusion rolling over her as I put my own foot in the stirrup and heaved myself up to sit behind her. When I edged forward, the zipper of my jeans hitting the back pockets of hers, I inhaled a steep breath, looking up to the moon like it would somehow save me from getting a boner once we started riding and that sweet ass was rubbing up against me.

"Oh," she said, and even from where I sat behind her, I could see her cheeks flushing in the moonlight. "I... I didn't realize you would be up here, too."

"You think I was just going to walk alongside while you rode, princess?"

She frowned. "Don't call me that."

"Whatever you say, ma'am."

She growled a little at that, elbowing me in the ribs as I laughed. Then, I grabbed hold of the reins, and away we went.

The moon was full and bright that night, reflecting off the creek as we rode along its edges. For a while, we were both quiet, soaking in the dampness of the night's humidity, the sounds of the water and insects around us, the smell of the country. I closed my eyes and inhaled a deep breath, finding that peace and comfort I always did on Tank's back, mixed with a little of something unfamiliar with Ruby Grace being there, too. I wondered what she was thinking, if she was happy to be there, if she was still anxious about what people would say tomorrow.

And they *would* have something to say.

I couldn't remember how old I was when I realized that would never change, but that I changed *my* perspective on it, not giving people the power they wanted with their gossip. I knew I was older than Ruby Grace when it happened, and I knew it was after my father had passed. At first, I'd been so triggered by the rumors, by the way that whole town talked about my father like they knew him when they didn't. But after a while, I started to care less, and less, until I didn't give a single fuck about anyone but my family.

We trotted along my favorite trail, ducking our heads when the branches of the trees dipped a little too low. I was right about Ruby Grace's ass rubbing against me, and when she edged back, adjusting her weight for what I assumed was comfort, the fabric of her jean shorts rubbed over the length of my cock in a way that made me bite my lip to keep from groaning out loud.

"So," I said, trying to spark up conversation that would get my mind off her body touching mine. "What's got you so stressed out that you're biting off a nice guy's head when he offers you a beer?"

I expected her to pop off back at me, but she just chuckled, letting out a sigh on a shrug before she spoke. "I don't know. Being back home, I guess. UNC felt like my new home, and now I'm back in this place where I'm not sure where I fit in. And my mom is all over me about the wedding, which I know we still have a lot to do with it being only six weeks away. But... I don't know. It's summer, it's supposed to be fun, and I just feel..."

"Smothered," I finished for her.

She turned a little over her shoulder, and though our eyes couldn't meet, I knew I'd struck a nerve. "Yes," she agreed, turning back forward. "Exactly that."

I nodded. "I'm sure it's a lot of pressure, being the Mayor's daughter. And now, getting married." I debated my next words carefully before speaking them out loud. "Don't take this the wrong way, because I don't mean anything by it, but... you're young. I was surprised when my boss told me I was showing a barrel to an engaged nineteen-year-old."

"Plenty of people get married at nineteen," she spouted back. "Especially in Stratford."

"I know," I said, soothingly, calming my voice so she could see I wasn't picking a fight. "I guess it's just that when *I* was that age, I didn't even know who I was, let alone who the person was who I wanted to spend the rest of my life with."

Ruby Grace fell quiet at that, and for a while, it was just the sounds of the night around us. I thought I'd overstepped again, and I waited for her to push me off the horse or demand that I take her back, but instead, after a long pause, she just sighed.

"I think they just expect me to be like my sister," she murmured. "Mary Anne loves this kind of stuff — picking colors of flowers, choosing between ribbon or twine, finding the perfect dress."

I remembered her older sister, especially because she was only a couple years younger than Logan. They'd run in similar crowds, been in similar parties. But, after college, Mary Anne had made her way over to Europe to study fashion design. The town hadn't seen much of her since.

I wondered if that was part of Ruby Grace's sense of obligation — the fact that her older sister was gone, and she was here, waiting to fulfill her family's legacy.

"And I guess a part of me always thought *she'd* be the one to get married first," Ruby Grace continued. "That she'd be the one to find a husband like our father and make the grandkids I know my parents want."

I was nodding, realizing my instinct had been true until she mentioned the word *grandkids*.

I stiffened. "Are you already thinking about kids?"

"I mean... not *immediately*, but, Anthony wants to have them sooner rather than later."

My blood boiled a bit at her statement. "And do *you* want to have them sooner rather than later? Or at all?"

"Of course, I want children," she defended. "But, I admit, I thought I'd be much older when I had them. I thought... well, it doesn't matter."

Tank neighed, as if he spoke my thoughts before I got the chance. "It does matter, Ruby Grace. What did you think?"

She fiddled with the reins that I'd let her take over. "I don't know... I just always thought I'd graduate, maybe do a year or two in AmeriCorps before I settled down."

"AmeriCorps?"

"Yeah, it's like the Peace Corp, but specifically here in the states. You can be a teacher or camp counselor or even work in wetland restoration." She shrugged. "I've always loved to help others, to volunteer my time, and I thought it'd be a great way to do that before I got married and had kids of my own."

I gritted my teeth against the urge to tell her she still *could* do those things — married or not. Just because she was committing to this man as his wife didn't mean she had to lose her identity, surrender what she wanted for all that *he* wanted, but I knew it wasn't my place to say any of that.

Then again, it probably wasn't my place to have her ass rubbing against me, but I wasn't doing anything to change that at the moment.

"But," she said after a long, awkward pause. "That's what's so great about marrying Anthony. He's a politician, and as his wife, I'll have so many opportunities to help the communities we serve in. And when he's president, I'll be the first lady. I'll be able to create and manage whatever charities and organizations I want. I'll be able to make a difference."

I nodded, but I still didn't agree with it. "Well, that's good, then."

"Yeah," she said, and for a moment, she seemed lost in her own thoughts before she came back to the moment with me just as I grabbed the reins from her, turning Tank around to head back toward the stables. "What about you?" she asked.

"What about me?"

"Do you want a wife, kids?"

"I do," I answered.

She waited, and when I said nothing more, a soft laugh escaped her lips. "Well, please don't tell me too much. After all, I didn't share anything personal with you."

I smirked, shrugging. "There's nothing more to really say, is there? I do want to get married and have kids one day."

"You're twenty-eight," she pointed out. "What are you waiting for?"

"The right woman."

The answer rolled off my tongue so easily, but it shocked both of us. I stiffened behind her, aware of the space of vulnerability I'd put myself in, and Ruby Grace glanced over her shoulder, like she wished she could see my eyes after saying that.

"Oh," she said after a while. "Well, that's nice, Noah. That's really nice. And I'm sure you'll find her."

I cleared my throat, ready to change the subject, but she beat me to it.

"What else?" she asked. "What else do you want in life?"

I shifted. "Honestly, not much. I just want to make whiskey barrels. I'm a pretty simple guy."

"Why do I feel like that's the first time you've lied to me?"

Her question surprised me, and I swallowed down the discomfort building more and more rapidly the more the conversation was focused on me.

"It's not a lie. I'm a family man, I want to be here for my brothers, my mom, and, someday, my future family, too."

I paused, and she waited, wanting me to keep going even when I didn't know what else to say.

"I guess I kind of feel like a dad already, in a way," I confessed. "Jordan and I really stepped up after my father died, and we've been taking care of Mom and the house and our younger brothers ever since. And now, Mikey is going into his senior year. He's going to move out of the house soon after he graduates, and then Mom will be on her own, and I'm not sure what she'll do then. If we sell it, put her in a smaller place, it'd probably be better for her. But then again, I can't imagine us not having that house to go home to."

Ruby Grace pulled Tank to a stop, turning enough so she could look at me. "So, it seems that where I feel smothered, you feel a little lost, huh, Noah Becker?"

I smirked. "I guess so, Ruby Grace."

"Well, I've heard some of the best adventures come from finding yourself a little lost," she offered.

"Oh, who told you that?"

"The wise Betty Collins, of course." She smiled, shrugging. "This older woman I care for down at the nursing home. We've become good friends over the years."

Looking at Ruby Grace in that moment, I didn't see a girl. Her fair, young skin and wide, innocent eyes glowing in the moonlight told me she was still a girl, but her heart that volunteered her time to the elderly told me she was more of a woman than most I'd slept with.

"Well, if she's got more wisdom like that, you'll have to introduce me to her sometime."

Ruby Grace smiled at that. "I just might."

We were quiet the rest of the way back to the stable, and when we both hopped down and I took all the riding equipment off Tank, I gave him a treat, patting his butt affectionately before Ruby Grace and I made our way back toward the party.

"Thank you," she said, tucking her hands in the back pockets of her shorts. "For tonight. I haven't felt that kind of peace in a long time."

"No problem," I said, coming to a stop. She turned, brows furrowed. "Figured I'd let you walk up first, go find your friends. I'll come up in a bit, that way no one thinks we were together."

She rose one brow. "I'm pretty sure they already know."

"Well, then, let's fuck with them," I said. "Give them something to make them doubt it all when they're gossiping in the morning."

Ruby Grace smiled even wider at that, and before I knew what she was doing, she crossed the space between us and threw her arms around my neck. I opened my own just in time to catch her, to feel her tight little body pressed against me as she gave me a hug.

"Stay out of trouble, Noah Becker."

"Never."

She chuckled, letting me go and waving at me over her shoulder as she strutted back up the hill toward the bonfire.

# Chapter Six

## RUBY GRACE

My first thought was that my skirt was too short.

It was Sunday afternoon, and church had let out on a beautiful day where Dad had some time blocked off for his daughter being back in town. He'd insisted we go golfing — much to his delight and my disdain — and so here we were at the Stratford Country Club golf course.

The Stratford Country Club golf course only existed because Dad had insisted the town needed a proper country club back when he was running for his first term as mayor. He'd worked with the wealthiest families in the town to bring it to life, and then they'd made the requirements to get in so specific and the spots available so limited that it was pretty much just a place for him and his friends to hang out and play golf.

Daddy was lining up his shot on the fourth hole, his pot belly stretching the light pink fabric of his polo as he tightened his grip on the club. He'd picked that shirt so he could match me — a daddy-daughter-duo. Dad was a big man, standing six-foot-three and close to two-hundred-

and-fifty pounds. He had a smile that took up his entire face — one that Mama called his "mega-watt" smile. She swore it was how he won elections.

I favored my mother, but I did have my dad's hazel eyes.

It was a gorgeous day, mid-seventies with big, puffy white clouds rolling over us, giving us a brief reprieve from the sun before it'd beat down on us again. For all intents and purposes, it was the perfect day to be on the course.

But, I hated golf.

I respected it for the tradition it had in the sports world, and I figured that, had I been raised differently, I might have found joy in watching it or playing from time to time. But, as it was, Daddy had taught me as soon as I could *hold* a golf club that business deals were made on golf courses, and I needed a strong game to represent the family — especially once I was a politician's wife.

Or, a politician myself — which Daddy had said he'd have been just fine with, too.

So, golf for me had always been a chore. It started with the pressure of learning, then, the pressure to be *good*. And once I'd achieved that, once I could hold my own with Dad and his buddies on the course? Well, by that time I was just so tired of golf I didn't want to be there at all.

I hated golf.

But, I loved my dad.

So, when he'd asked me to spend the afternoon with him, I was excited — even if it *was* to play golf. Daddy was always busy, running around the town of Stratford and making sure every wheel and axle was in place. Any time I could steal him for more than a twenty-minute conversation at dinner, I was thrilled.

"How come your ears are steaming over there when *I'm* the one lining up a shot?" Dad asked, glancing at me with a quirked brow before he took a practice swing, stopping the club right before it hit the ball.

I tugged on the hem of my skirt — which was *plenty* long enough, by the way — with my eyes on the group of four older women eyeing me and whispering from the seventh hole.

"Mrs. Landish and her gaggle of geese are looking at me like I'm not a member," I said. "Or like my skirt is so high my tush is showing."

Dad followed my gaze, smirking as he turned back toward the ball. "Well," he said, squaring up his feet and lining up the club with the ball. "You know they're always looking for something to talk about — and you skipping off with Noah Becker in the middle of the night is worthy gossip."

He swung, smacking the ball down the green. It flew high and arched, about two-hundred feet before it came back to Earth, and Daddy turned, a toothy grin of pride on his face.

My jaw was hanging — and not from his shot.

"What do you *mean* that I 'skipped off with Noah Becker'," I scoffed, neck heating.

"I don't know," Dad said on a shrug. "I just heard them saying something about you and Noah Becker at the Black Hole when we were checking in for our tee times earlier."

"We were at the same bonfire party, yeah. But, so was half the town."

I glanced at Mrs. Landish again, who shook her head with pursed lips, saying something to her passenger seat rider before cruising off in her golf cart of gossip.

I rolled my eyes. "Honestly. And Mrs. Landish wasn't even *there*."

"She doesn't have to be — not with the way news travels in this town."

"*News*," I spat, plucking my driver from my bag and stepping up to the tee. "Stratford needs a craft fair or something to keep them entertained."

Dad chuckled at that, putting his own driver away before he leaned an elbow on our golf cart, watching me line up my shot. "Don't worry about them. Someone else will do something equally as innocent and have them drawing other dramatic conclusions in no time."

I smirked.

"But, just to be clear... you *didn't* skip off with Noah Becker in the middle of the night... right?"

I stopped where I was lining up my shot, leaning one hand on the butt of my driver as I leveled my face at my father. "Dad."

He put his hands up. "I was just checking. You know the reputation those boys have. Gotta make sure my little girl is safe."

I smiled, shaking my head as I got back to my shot.

My pulse ticked up a bit at the lie I'd told my father as I took a practice swing. Daddy was right — the Becker boys *did* have quite the reputation. But, if I was judging only by the Noah I was with Friday night, I would never understand why.

He was kind. And patient. And funny.

My smile widened remembering how focused he looked as he brushed his horse down and got him ready to ride. But, as soon as he'd popped into my mind, I shoved him back out.

*Smack.*

My own ball went flying down the green, landing about twenty-five yards shy of where Dad's had. He cheered, clapping me on the shoulder as we watched the ball roll a bit.

"That's my girl! Come on, you drive."

The rest of the afternoon slid by easily, but I didn't miss how Daddy was checking the time on his watch often. If I knew him, he'd likely scheduled out the *precise* amount of time it would take to get in a round of golf before he had somewhere else to run.

I was his daughter on *his* time, but it didn't bother me. I knew I wasn't the only one who needed him. When you're the mayor of a small town in Tennessee, you're pulled a million different directions. And, if I was being honest, he inspired me. He was the reason I'd gotten involved with volunteering, the reason I hadn't stopped at just showing up there, but took it into my own hands to make our nursing home the nicest in the county.

Dad was a doer, and he'd raised me to be one, too.

"So, how is my little girl?" he asked when we were riding out to the ninth hole later that day. "Ah, I don't even know if I can call you that anymore, now that you're an engaged *woman*."

I smiled, taking my sunglasses off to wipe the lenses as he drove. "I'm alright, Daddy. And I'm still your little girl — even after you walk me down the aisle."

"Wow," he breathed, and if he wasn't wearing his own sunglasses, I'd have bet those hazel eyes of his were glossy. "It sounds so real when you say it like that."

"It's pretty real," I mused, putting my glasses back on. "I bet you're tickled pink that your baby girl is marrying a politician, just like you always wanted."

Something in Dad's demeanor changed then, and he cleared his throat, switching hands on the steering wheel. "Yes. Anthony is a good man. He'll do right by you."

I nodded. "Yes."

We both fell silent again, and I watched him carefully, wondering why the sudden shift in his mood. But, as soon as he parked the cart, he was out and lining up his last shot. He glanced at his watch as soon as he'd hit the ball, turning back to me with a smile that told me he was cutting it close.

"Daddy, it's okay," I said, plucking my driver out of my bag again. "We're almost done here, anyway. If you need to go, go."

His brows folded together. "Are you sure?"

"Of course." I smiled, leaning my club against the cart before walking over to give him a hug. "I'll see you at dinner sometime this week."

He sighed when I was in his arms, wrapping me in a bear hug with a gentle kiss pressed to my hair. "You're the best kid ever."

"I love you, too, Daddy."

I insisted Dad take the cart so he could get back faster, assuring him I wanted the walk. We weren't far from the club house the way the course was lined up, anyway. And once he was gone, I swung my driver a few times behind where the tee was set up, preparing for the last long shot of the day.

As I lined it up, my thoughts drifted first to Dad, to his reaction when I'd brought up Anthony. He *loved* Anthony — he and Mama had both made that very clear just after one dinner with him. And, provided that he'd just asked me to marry him a month ago and we were six weeks out from the big day, it was safe to say they both approved.

So, then, why the odd response?

I shook it off, cracking my neck and focusing on the ball. But as I squared my shoulders, my thoughts drifted again, this time back to Mrs. Landish and her cackling crew.

Which then led my thoughts to Friday night.

To Noah.

I wondered if he saw it that night at the bonfire — the stress I swore I was wearing like a choker. Annie didn't seem to, nor did anyone else. But Noah... it was like he saw right through me.

I swallowed, let out a long breath as I cleared my mind once more, and hammered the ball down the green.

## NOAH

Everyone knew not to talk to me that Wednesday.

I showed up to work an hour early, desperate to get my hands dirty, my muscles fired up, my mind on anything other than the anniversary of my father's death. That day marked nine years of him being gone, and I thought with time, that sting would fade. I thought I'd become immune to the pain, to the anger, to the aching emptiness I felt that no justice had ever been served in his honor.

But I'd been wrong.

Most of the week, I'd been fine. It was a normal weekend, a little partying and a little relaxing with the family. Church happened on Sunday, just like always. Once Monday arrived, I was back in work gear. And through all of that, my thoughts had been occupied by the Mayor's daughter.

I didn't like that Ruby Grace was on my mind, that when I was playing cards with my brothers on Saturday evening, I thought about the way her hair smelled as she sat on that saddle in front of me. I didn't like that when I saw her at church, prim and proper in her lavender dress, I thought about how much I liked her better in the jean shorts and tank top she'd worn. And I definitely didn't like that when I woke up on Monday morning, I had a hard-on the size of a sledge hammer after having a dream about her.

I wanted her off my mind. She was someone else's fiancé. She was also nearly ten years younger than I was.

But now that my mind was taken over by thoughts of my father's untimely death, I wished it was just her in my head again. I wished I could think about anything other than how badly this day would always hurt, for the rest of my life.

Marty, Eli, and PJ worked alongside me without saying a word that day. They didn't even joke around with each other, sensing the mood I was in, the somberness that settled over the entire distillery.

The Scooter family and the board always glorified this day. The morning announcements asked for a moment of silence for the only employee to ever perish at Scooter Whiskey. They praised the safety plans they'd had in place, attributing the fact that there weren't *more* deaths because of that plan they'd had in place. They praised the firemen, too, that they arrived so "quickly." Then, they would read off my father's accomplishments like a grocery list, have that one minute of silence, and then everything was back to normal.

Even though Logan was across the distillery preparing for his first tour when that morning announcement came, and even though Mikey was in the welcome center, getting the gift shop ready to open, I still felt them in that moment those announcements were read. I felt their hearts squeezing in pain the same way mine did, felt their anger, their hostility toward the company that paid their bills, that our grandfather had helped build, that we both loved and cherished but were also bound to in some sick, sadistic way.

I thought of them, of our family, all day long as I kept my head down, focusing on the task at hand. I built more barrels than my daily quota called for, but I didn't care. As long as I was busy, I was okay. I just needed to get through the day.

I just needed to survive.

It was well after lunch when Patrick Scooter swung through the doors that led to the barrel raising warehouse. I hadn't even noticed, hadn't stopped working until I felt a number of eyes on me. I looked up at Marty first, who warned me with a stern brow fold, like he was worried I'd do something irrational. PJ and Eli watched me, too — their eyes flicking back and forth between the door and me. When I followed their gaze and saw Patrick talking to Gus, a clipboard in his hand, dressed like he was in an office in New York City rather than a distillery in Stratford, Tennessee, I clenched my jaw.

Patrick Scooter was a few years older than my father would have been if he were still alive. They grew up around the distillery together, almost like brothers until Patrick's dad passed away, leaving the distillery to him.

Everything changed then.

I didn't have any certified or blatant reason not to like Patrick, other than the fact that something in my gut told me he was a shit guy. Something in my gut told me he didn't like my family.

Something in my gut told me he had something to do with my father's death.

I didn't know why, and it wasn't ever something I'd speak out loud, but it was there, deep in my belly like an ache I'd never be rid of. And I'd learned as a young country boy that you trust that gut feeling.

Patrick signed something on Gus's clipboard before his eyes scanned the warehouse, finding mine after one sweep. He gave a grim smile, saying something to Gus before making his way toward me.

I ground my teeth, lowering my head to the barrel I was raising in an effort to school my breaths and the rage I felt boiling inside me. If he knew what was best for him, he'd stay away from me today. But of course, he didn't care. Part of me thought he actually reveled in the fact that he still had my father's kids working for him, like somehow that meant he'd won.

But we weren't here for him. We were here for my father, for the legacy *he* built — that my grandfather built. Patrick and his family may have wanted to erase us from their history books, but my brothers and I would make sure that never happened.

I had just shoved the last stave of wood into the barrel I was working on when I felt a clammy hand clap me on the shoulder, squeezing and staying there until I was forced to lift my head and take the orange sponges out of my ears. Patrick met me with sympathetic eyes, a sorrowful smile, like he knew my pain, spread on his face.

"Hey, Noah. How ya hanging in today?"

*Do not punch him. Do not give him a reaction at all.*

Patrick stood there in his suit, eyes surveying his surroundings like he was well above the men working for him. And I knew he thought that to be true. He was so much like my father — tall, stout, tan — but his hair was gray, where my father never had the chance to get there, and his eyes were smaller, beady and evil, his face too long, nose too big. He looked almost like a live action Frankenstein.

I wished I could put the bolts through his head to bring the whole look together.

"I'm well, thanks for asking," I responded as politely as I could. "How are you, Patrick?"

"Oh, you know me. Just rocking and rolling through every new day," he said, his smile showing his too-white teeth now. It slipped again in the next instant. "Although, this particular day is always a rough one on all of us."

I swallowed down my pride, forcing the best smile I could muster. "Indeed."

"He would have been proud of you, you know," Patrick said, squeezing my shoulder where he held it. "Your father was such a close friend of mine, and my heart aches every day that he's gone. But his boys are serving him well here at Scooter Whiskey." His lip twitched a little. "We're so lucky to have you."

*Liar.*

It was all lies, all bullshit — and we both knew it. But this was the game we played. The Scooter family kept us around as to not stir up more trouble or gossip than they already had with the fire, and we stayed to avenge our father's death, to ensure the Scooter family didn't get what they wanted by erasing the Becker name from their history.

I simply nodded, lips in a flat line. I reached out my hand for his, shaking it once before I put my ear plugs back in and got back to work on the barrel. Patrick stood awkwardly at my side for a moment longer before he made his rounds to the other men, then he waved goodbye to Gus through the window of his office, and he was gone.

I tried to keep my head down, tried to breathe through the rage, tried to forget he was even there, but once he left the room, everything I'd been fighting down all day rose to the surface. I reared back, kicking the barrel I'd just built and splintering the wood everywhere. I hadn't tied it down with the metal rings yet, and the time I'd spent putting it together went to waste with one heavy heave of my boot.

No one tried to stop me as I continued kicking, hitting wood, equipment, whatever was near. The only thing that stopped me was when Marty placed a gentle hand on my shoulder, and when I looked at him, he nodded toward the tour group that had just walked in.

I locked eyes with Logan, his brows bent together in an understanding sympathy, and I felt shame wash over me.

I was his *older* brother, and I was acting like a child. I'd let Patrick get under my skin, and I hated it.

The tour group was still watching me, murmuring as Logan pulled their attention back to him, listing off his usual spiel. Gus came over to join Marty and me, excusing Marty before he pulled me to the side.

"I think you should take the rest of the day off, Noah."

I just nodded, yanking off my work gloves and powering toward the door that led to our little locker room. My blood was still red hot as I grabbed my shit, and then I slammed my locker closed and barreled through the back warehouse door with only one destination in mind.

Eric Church blared from the jukebox, and I bobbed my head, singing along a little between sips of my whiskey. I'd had way too many for it to be only eight o'clock, but it was numbing my body, and my mind, which was exactly what I needed it to do.

"Noah, I love you, kid. But I'm cutting you off after this one," Buck said. He was the bartender at my favorite watering hole in town — namely because it was the *only* watering hole in town — the neon sign outside flashing his name in a simple manner. He was also a longtime friend, and he'd saved me from my own drunk ass too many nights for me to count.

"Alright," I said on a nod, not willing to argue. I was getting tired anyway, and was ready for the godforsaken day to be over already. I had half a glass of whiskey left and then I'd roll my ass home, crawl into bed, and wake up to a new day tomorrow.

A day that wouldn't be the anniversary of Dad's death.

I pulled out my wallet to pay Buck, and once my cash was on the bar, my thumb hovered over the corner of the only photo I carried with me. I pulled it out slowly, eyes scanning the younger faces of my brothers, of Mom, and of Dad. It was the year before Dad had died, when we'd taken a fishing trip to the lake, and we were all grouped together in front of one of our tents, sunburnt and smiling. Mikey was missing a front tooth, his adult one yet to replace the one that had fallen out. Logan and Jordan had their arms slung around each other, Mom standing behind Logan with her hands on his head.

And then there was me and Dad.

I had jumped on his back for the photo, giving him a noogie as the picture was shot. He was full-on laughing, looking up at me, and when I looked at that picture, all I felt was happiness. All I felt was indescribable joy for a family that didn't know what hardship lay ahead, that had everything they ever wanted or needed.

If I could go back in time, I'd go back to that exact moment and live there forever.

"Two beers, Buck. Whatever you got that's cold and wet," someone said from beside me, knocking their knuckles on the bar. I was fine to ignore them, just like I'd ignored everyone else that night, but then I felt eyes on me, and I turned, meeting the gaze of Patrick's youngest son.

Malcolm was a scrawny kid, just a few years older than Mikey. His older sister was Logan's age, and she was about the only Scooter that I didn't hate — maybe because she was sort of the black sheep in their family, acting out in every way possible, down to getting her septum pierced her senior year of high school.

I liked a girl who ruffled feathers.

Malcolm, on the other hand, was long-faced just like his dad, with skin that somehow always looked dirty. He was scrawny, liked to wear his ball caps a little to the left like it was still the 90s, and had a knack for getting under my skin, too.

"Well, if it isn't the oldest Becker boy," he spat — literally, *spat*, the words coming out of his mouth just as a thick wad of chewing tobacco did. He spit it into an empty Mountain Dew bottle, grinning at me with pieces still in his gums, and already, he was trying to push my buttons by calling me the oldest.

It was Malcolm's way of saying that he didn't recognize Jordan as a proper part of our family, because his skin wasn't the same color as ours and some bullshit paperwork said he wasn't blood.

My pulse kicked up a notch.

"Rough day at the office?" Malcolm asked when he didn't get a rise out of me.

I blinked. "Fuck off, Malcolm."

"Ohhh," he said, raising both hands in a mock surrender as he elbowed his buddy next to him. I didn't know his name, but recognized him from around town. "Someone's on their rag."

His eyes dropped to the photo still in my hand as he rested his elbows back on the bar.

"Ah," he mused. "I see. You're crying into your whiskey over your daddy, huh?" He framed his chin with his thumb and forefinger. "Was it today's date that that fire happened?" He shrugged, smiling at his buddy. "Guess I forgot."

Buck slid Malcom the beers he asked for, eyeing me with a warning and a slight shake of his head. "Here are your drinks. Now go play pool or sit at a table far away from here, understand?"

"Aw, come on, Buck," Malcolm said. "We're just kidding around. Noah and I go way back. We're buds." He clapped me on the shoulder, and every nerve came to life at his touch. "Ain't that right, Becker?"

"Get your hand off me."

"Or what?" he seethed.

And I should have let it go. I should have slammed back my whiskey and walked out that damn door. But instead, I slammed my hand into his chest, gripping his shirt and yanking hard until his back hit the bar. He yelped a little as I stood, lowering my nose to his, steam rolling off me as I poked a finger in his face.

"I told you to fuck off, Malcolm. You should have listened to me."

I reared back, ready to plow my fist into his smug smile, when Buck intervened, jumping over the bar and grabbing me from behind. He yanked me away, my fist still twisted in Malcolm's shirt until his buddy tore it away from me, ushering Malcolm to the other side of the bar.

He was laughing.

I charged after him again, which only made him laugh harder as Buck caught me around the chest, spinning me around to face him.

"Hey!" he said, voice loud and firm.

I had no idea if he'd said anything to me before that moment. I couldn't hear anything but that asshole's laughter.

"Listen to me," he warned. "You know that pussy will call the cops and have charges pressed against you. You don't need to spend any more nights in jail. Okay? So finish your whiskey and get the hell out of here."

I tried twisting out of his grip, but he held me more firmly, and my breath singed my nose with every exhale. Finally, I growled, shaking him off and reaching for my whiskey. I tilted the glass back, finishing what was left, and then plowed through the bar door just as I had the one leaving the warehouse earlier that day.

My vision was half red, half black as I barreled through town, walking the short distance to my house that was a few blocks behind the main drug store. I stayed on Main Street until I hit that street, and as soon as I turned, I nearly ran over Ruby Grace Barnett.

"*Oof.*" She gasped as I plowed over her, both of us spinning and her nearly toppling over before I caught her by the upper arms, righting her again. The paper bag she'd been carrying out of the drug store fell in the process, toilet paper and toothpaste and other miscellaneous girly shit that I didn't recognize spilling out onto the concrete.

"Shit," I murmured, bending to help her retrieve it all.

Ruby Grace bent down as much as she could in her skirt, and once everything was back in the paper bag, we both stood, an awkward, heavy silence passing between us.

"Sorry about that," I murmured, scratching the back of my head. Then, I turned, ready to close the distance between me and my house that was just a couple of blocks away now.

"Wait," she called, and I paused, forcing a breath before I turned to face her. "Are you okay?"

"I'm fine."

"You almost ran me over," she said, smiling a little. "And you look like you're ready to kill the next person who looks at you."

"Not far from the truth."

She crossed her arms over the bag, balancing it on her hip as she cocked a brow. "Want to talk about it?"

"No," I answered definitively. I made to turn again, but she spoke before I could.

"Someone's particularly moody tonight."

My nose flared, head aching with how tightly I gritted my teeth. I needed to get home. *Now.* "And someone else is particularly nosey."

Her face fell at that. "Noah..."

"Look, why don't you stop prying into my life and get back to your own? I'm sure you've got cake to taste or ribbons to tie or something."

Ruby Grace's mouth popped open. "Why are you being so mean to me? I was just making sure you're okay."

"Oh, is that right?" I asked, seething as I stepped into her space. Our chests were an inch apart, my breath hot on her nose as I looked down on her shocked expression. "You want to go back to the Black Hole, sit on my horse and rub your ass on me while we ride? Pretend like you don't have a fiancé who would mind while I tell you all my fucking problems?"

Her brows folded together, eyes narrowing into slits. "Fuck you, Noah Becker."

"I'm sure you'd like to, sweetheart. But, not tonight." I somehow managed a smirk before I turned on my boot, shoving my hands in my pockets and picking up my pace to get back to my house.

It was out of line. It was nowhere near what I felt about Ruby Grace, but she'd been in the wrong place at the wrong time, and my fury needed a friend to call home.

She was the lucky winner.

I heard a cross between a huff and a growl behind me, but I didn't turn around to see the face of the girl I'd just insulted. I couldn't bear to see her anger, just as I couldn't be bothered to apologize for my own. I didn't owe Ruby Grace anything, anyway. What did it matter if I upset her?

I shoved it out of my head as I walked, hell bent on getting home, into a hot shower, and then into my bed.

I'd had enough bullshit for one day.

# Chapter Seven

## RUBY GRACE

That Sunday at church, I was everything I was supposed to be.

I was dressed prim and proper, thanks to Mama picking out a gorgeous, sunshine yellow dress that hugged my waist and flared at the hips, cutting off just below my knees. It was covered with lace, and she'd paired it with a large white hat with a yellow ribbon that matched the dress, as well as white designer heels — the same ones I'd worn to the barrel tasting my first week back in town. My hair was curled and smoothed to perfection, makeup classy and well done.

I was on time, in the third-row pew where Mama always liked to sit, and sitting like the young lady I was.

I was smiling, shaking hands with the congregation as they chatted before taking their own seats.

I was proudly and properly representing the Barnett name, the town of Stratford, the mayor everyone knew and loved.

And I was happy.

*I am happy*, I told myself, over and over and over.

This is me. This is my family. This is everything I'm supposed to do and know and *be* on a Sunday morning.

But right in the center of my chest there was an ache. A tight, unfamiliar pressure, like I was in a glass box sinking deeper and deeper into unmarked waters, sipping air as casually as I could and ignoring the feeling that there would soon be none left to sip.

I felt marginally better when the congregation was fully seated, our pastor taking to the podium on stage to open service with a prayer. Soon, we'd sing and praise the Lord, witness a few baptisms, hear the message of God through our pastor, and then I'd be set free for the afternoon.

At least for the next hour, the attention would be off me.

I hadn't realized what I'd been feeling until Noah Becker pinpointed it with the perfect word.

*Smothered.*

And ever since he'd said it, I couldn't shake it.

When Mama wanted to plan, to spend hours and hours every single day working on the tiniest details of the wedding, I wanted to crawl out of my skin. I felt the collar to any dress or shirt I wore growing tighter as the days grew longer, summer in full swing. The only bit of relief I got was when Anthony would call and talk to me at night, calming my breaths and easing my mind by assuring me he would be there soon, that he'd help, that no matter what, it would all be okay.

No matter what, we would be married in five weeks. And that was what mattered.

Those conversations with him that drifted into late night laughter were the only things that saved me.

That, and the night with Noah.

But that had been tarnished.

I found him one section over in the front row, sitting with all his brothers and his mom. Last Sunday, I'd watched him with a curious smile, thinking about our night at the Black Hole together.

Today, I wanted to shoot laser beams through the back of his head with my eyeballs.

I frowned, narrowing my eyes as I stared at his perfectly styled hair, the collar of his olive green button up, the tan skin of his neck. I'd been naïve to think Noah Becker could be anything less than an asshole. I thought he'd shown me a softer side of him that night at the Black Hole — he listened to me, saw that I was anxious before I did, and even opened up to me a little. All week, I'd caught myself thinking about that night, about the way it felt to ride Tank in the moonlight, to have the heat of a man behind me, the ear of the last person on Earth I expected bent to listen to every word I had to say.

But it was just an act, or a drunken game, or some way for him to mess with me.

He'd shown his true colors again when I'd run into him Wednesday night.

First, he'd nearly run me over. And as if that wasn't enough, he'd *yelled* at me — speaking to me like I was just another nosey, gossiping bitty in town. Add in the fact that he'd practically accused me of wanting to cheat on my fiancé, and I knew one thing for sure.

I was *done* with Noah Becker, and I never wanted to talk to him again.

But I still wanted to knock him upside the head.

I was still staring at that head of his when I heard my name flow from the pastor's mouth.

I blinked, turning my gaze to the stage as the congregation applauded. My heart rate ticked up a notch as I tried to dig through the haze to see if I'd heard anything that had just been said.

"Stand *up*," Mama said under her breath, keeping her smile as she clapped.

I did as she said, tucking a strand of hair behind my ear as I offered the warmest smile I could to the pastor.

"There she is," he said, hands outstretched.

Pastor Morris had been the pastor for Stratford's Baptist Church since before I was born. He was a jolly man, average height with a belly built on all the church baking fundraisers. He was pale as snow, with hair that he dyed the black it was in his youth — though the gray peppered it now.

"Ruby Grace," he said, shaking his head as the applause died down. "I remember when you were just a young girl, singing for us up here during Vacation Bible School. Hasn't she grown into a lovely young lady?"

The congregation applauded again, Mama dabbing at the corner of her eyes with her handkerchief as my cheeks burned.

"Ruby Grace has been such a woman of God, giving her time to those in need by volunteering all over our town, namely at our nursing home, and she's continued to help spread the word during her time attending the University of North Carolina. And five weeks from today, right here in this church, our lovely Ruby Grace Barnett will become Mrs. Anthony Caldwell."

The applause was deafening at that, whistles ringing out as I fought the urge to curl into a ball under the nearest pew.

"There will be an open reception at our house after!" Mama called out, standing long enough to say her peace before curtsying and sitting back down. Everyone laughed at that, a few hollers about free champagne echoing before it was silent again.

"Now, for those of you who don't know Anthony, he is a good Christian man. I had the pleasure of meeting him when I sat them down for their pre-marriage interview, and he absolutely blew me away," Pastor Morris said. "And, much to Ruby Grace's father's delight, I'm sure — Anthony is running for State Representative of North Carolina!"

A mixture of *ooh's* and *ahh's* touched my burning ears, and I smiled as widely as I could, waiting to be dismissed, to sit back down, to blend in again.

"Ruby Grace, we are all so very proud of you," Pastor Morris said, his eyes shining as he placed a hand over his heart. "And we honor your choice to forego your education and follow your mother and father's footsteps. Lord knows they have done so much for us in this town, and we know you and Anthony will do the same for North Carolina, and someday, the United States of America as a whole."

Daddy's chest swelled at that, pride rolling off him in waves as he beamed up at me from where he sat next to Mama. I wasn't very close with my father, but in that moment, he looked at me like I was the only thing that mattered in the world.

"Congratulations, Ruby Grace," Pastor Morris finished. "May God bless you and your union."

*Amens* rang out in unison across the congregation, and I finally sat with the applause fading as Pastor Morris continued with service. Mama squeezed my hand, still smiling, and I smiled back as much as I could before turning my attention to the program in my hand.

Once the attention was firmly off me, I looked up again, watching Pastor for a while before I scanned the stage absent-mindedly, my thoughts drifting. I was ready to send more laser beams into the back of Noah's head, but this time, when I looked at him, he was staring back at me.

I blinked, surveying the bend in his brows, the sympathetic line of his lips pressed together in understanding. He was the only one I'd opened up to about the pressure I felt, about the wedding, in general.

And now, it was like he was the only one in the world who truly saw me.

I tore my eyes away.

After the service, Mama insisted that I stand with her near the door to shake hands with everyone as they passed. It felt like we were practicing for the receiving line at my wedding, and all I could think about was how badly my feet hurt, and how much I couldn't wait to get away from that church.

I was in a daze, smiling and repeating the same sentiment with each hand I shook, until Noah Becker stepped into view.

I paused, my smile slipping into a frown as I met his hand with mine. "Have a blessed day," I said flatly, ignoring the warmth I felt from his calloused hand.

He chuckled, cocking one brow. "That sounded more like a curse than a blessing."

"Take whatever you want from it," I said, pulling my hand away to shake his mother's and the rest of his brothers'.

He still stood there, waiting.

They were the last ones out of the church, and though Mama was caught up talking to the pastor, I excused myself, making my way to our car. Daddy had already left, saying he had business to attend to, and I was more than ready to join him in that escape.

"Hey," Noah said, jogging to catch up to me even though I'd made it clear I had nothing more to say to him.

"Mm?" I asked nonchalantly, not stopping. In fact, I took my phone out of my pocket, instead, proving my disinterest as I typed out a reply text to one I'd missed from Anthony.

"Giving me the cold shoulder now?"

"You're lucky that's *all* I'm giving you," I mouthed back, still looking at my phone.

His rough hand caught the crook of my elbow, pulling me to a stop when I was just a few feet from Mama's car.

"I deserve that," he said as I finally lifted my eyes to his. They were strikingly blue against the dark hue of his shirt, the clear sky behind him highlighting them even more. "And I wanted to apologize."

"Wanted to? Or are you actually *going* to?"

He smirked. "I'm going to. I am, if you'll let me speak."

I narrowed my eyes, tucking my phone in my purse and crossing my arms before leaning on one hip to wait.

Noah bit his lip against a bigger smile, glancing at our shoes before he met my gaze again. "I'm sorry for nearly knocking you over, and for taking out my anger on you. I shouldn't have said those things I said."

"You're damn straight, you shouldn't have."

"I know. It was uncalled for. I also know it doesn't make up for anything, to feed you an excuse, but..." He sniffed, glancing around us as if to make sure no one was close enough to hear before he spoke again. "It was the anniversary of my dad's death, and that's always a really tough day for me. Even nine years later."

My cocky glare slipped from my face, heart aching in my chest as Noah softened like butter in the warm summer sun.

*There he is again,* I thought. *There's the man from last Friday night.*

"Anyway, I want to make it up to you," he said, grabbing the back of his neck with one hand. "Just tell me how."

I chewed my lip, watching him as if I was looking for anything other than sincerity in his steel gaze. When I found nothing, I smirked, standing straight as I uncrossed my arms. "Fine. You can make it up to me by meeting me somewhere in a couple hours. Bring your swim trunks."

He cocked a brow. "Swim trunks? Where exactly am I meeting you?"

I smiled wider. "I'll text you the address. Be there at two, sharp."

Noah checked his watch, nodding with an amused smile before he tucked his hands into his pockets. "Alright, then."

"Alright," I repeated.

We watched each other for a long moment, until someone clearing their throat brought our attention to my left.

"Ruby Grace," Mama said, smiling at Noah before she eyed me cautiously. "Why don't you hop in, now. We better get going."

"Yes, Mama," I said before turning back to Noah. "See you around."

"See you," he said, catching on to the fact that I didn't say *see you in a couple of hours.*

Some things Mama didn't need to know.

She smiled politely at Noah, wishing him a blessed day, but her smile faded when he turned to walk back toward the church. She eyed him until he was around the corner of the building before sliding into the driver seat next to me.

"What were you talking to Noah Becker about?" she probed.

I shrugged, pulling out my phone to text Anthony. "Nothing. Just the barrel for Anthony. He wanted to know which one I'd decided on."

"Oh," Mama said, a mix of doubt and relief in her voice.

I thought she'd say more, but she just put the car into reverse, backing out of the parking spot as I let my gaze float out the window.

# Chapter Eight

**RUBY GRACE**

"No, no, no," Betty said, shaking her head — which was quite comical, considering her long, silver hair was wrapped up in a hot pink swim cap. "You've got to really get your hips into it. Channel Mr. Swayze, son."

I covered my smile with one hand, and Noah cocked a brow at me as if to say *are you enjoying yourself* before he grinned at Betty. That grin was deadly on any occasion, but when he was shirtless and slick, the pool cutting him off right at the hem of his board shorts, it was absolutely lethal. His arms were a little more tan than his abdomen, but the way his skin was already bronzing, I knew it wouldn't take much time outside for him to even the lines.

My eyes slipped to the ridges of abs that lined his stomach, smaller at the top and growing larger toward the bottom.

I wondered what those ridges felt like.

"Yes, ma'am," Noah said, hanging his hands on his hips as he caught his breath. "I'm sorry, it's just that you're so much better at this than I am."

She waved him off. "Years of practice. Don't worry, you'll catch on. Now, let's get through this. Lord knows we're going to need more time to work on the lift."

Betty winked at Noah then, and I couldn't help the chuckle that escaped me. He eyed me again, fighting against a smile of his own as Betty sidled up beside him once more. Noah took her hands in his, listening carefully as she walked him through the dance at the end of *Dirty Dancing* for about the seventh time.

It was a hot afternoon — a warning that summer was here to stay. I relished it, leaning back on my hands and angling my face toward the sun as I swung my feet in the pool. Summer was Betty's favorite time of year for this exact reason — pool days. The other residents generally skipped out, or if they did come outside, they'd stay under the umbrellas and watch the pool rather than get in it.

But not Betty.

She moved best when she was in the pool, like she hadn't had a hip replacement a few years before, and like her body wasn't failing her just as quickly as her mind. In the pool, she was free to move, to dance, to laugh.

And she did all three that afternoon.

She was having a good day — a day when she remembered everything, when she wasn't too tired to leave the bed, when she was the same, sassy old woman I'd met when I was fourteen. I'd been spoiled by her good days, lately, and I was thankful. Annie said it was the most she'd had in a row since Christmas.

She also said it was because I was back in town.

I couldn't know that for sure, but I took whatever time I could to be there with her — just in case.

I watched from the sidelines as Betty schooled Noah on the final dance scene from the classic movie — and one of her favorites. Noah, bless his heart, took it in stride. He held her hands, spun her gently, even went under water completely to give Betty some sort of "lift" that made her feel like Jennifer Grey.

That was when her smile was the largest — her eyes closed, face cast upward, arms out in the same iconic flight stance that the actress had done.

If I wasn't laughing so hard, I might have cried at the sentiment.

After a dozen more run throughs, Betty called for a break, and the two of them swam up to the side of the pool where I sat. Betty took the lemonade I offered her, sipping and hollering across the pool at Mr. Buchanan — who was seated under the umbrellas. Noah rested his arms on the concrete edge, crossing them and resting his head on his forearm before he peered up at me through lashes still dripping with water.

His eyes were an endless blue, the light from the pool reflecting off them like a tropical dream.

"Enjoying your entertainment this afternoon, Miss. Barnett?"

I bit my lip against a smile. "Very much so, Mr. Becker. I never knew you were such a great dancer."

"Oh, you should see me on the actual dance floor. I can two step and waltz and cha cha with the best of them. And don't even get me started on what happens when 'Watermelon Crawl' comes on."

"I'm sure it's quite entertaining," I mused, still dangling my feet in the cool water.

"When do I get to see your dance moves?"

I barked out a laugh at that. "Um, that would be approximately... never."

"Never?" he asked, popping his head up off his arms with a look of injustice. "But you've seen all my moves, now. I show you mine, you show me yours. Isn't that the deal?"

"I never agreed to that."

He narrowed his eyes, running his forefinger and thumb over the stubble on his chin before he nodded. "I see..." Then, a wicked gleam came over those blue steel eyes, and before I could so much as scream, his hand wrapped around my wrist, tugging forward until I was off the ledge and under water.

I popped up instantly, not even able to open my eyes against the chlorine yet before I was swinging at him. "Noah!"

He laughed, catching my advances easily and pulling me into him. I blinked several times, shaking the drops from my eyes before I glared up at him.

"You jerk. Mama's going to kill me for ruining my hair."

"Mama will live," he said, and then one arm wrapped around my waist, the other taking my hand in a leading position. "Now, let's dance, little lady."

With one pull of my hand and push of my hip, I spun away from him, reeling back in like a yo-yo and falling in line with his steps before I realized what was happening. Surprise ripped through me, brows shooting up to my hairline as he somehow managed to smoothly twirl me around that metaphorical dance floor even with water hitting us waist deep. My feet felt sluggish, the moves slower than if we were in boots on a hardwood floor, but somehow, that made it even more fun.

I laughed and laughed as he danced me around — until he had the bright idea to flip me like a swing dancer. I emerged from the water beating on his chest again, which just made him laugh harder. And when we were breathless, Noah tugged me to the side of the pool again.

"Thank you for the dance," he said, both of us still breathing heavily as he wrapped his strong, rugged hands around my waist. For a moment, he just held them there, the rough pad of his thumbs smoothing over my exposed hip bones. My smile fell, chest still heaving as my eyes slipped to his lips.

I didn't know why I looked at them.

I didn't know why I couldn't look away.

Noah swallowed, tightening his grip on my hips before he lowered in the water a little and helped push me back up onto the edge of the pool where I'd been seated before. Once I was steady, he released his hold on me, backing away with a distant look in his eyes that I couldn't decipher before he tore them from me and looked at Betty, instead.

"Now, how come you don't move with *me* like that?" Betty teased, hanging her hands on her hips.

"I did!" he defended. "You just out-dance me. Hard to realize how great I am when you're out there showing me up."

Betty smirked, taking a sip of her lemonade before she leaned against the edge. "I knew your father, you know?"

Those words sucked the air out of my lungs, and judging by the way Noah's smile slipped off his face, they did the same to him. He glanced up at me, a question in his eyes, but I just shook my head slightly.

I hadn't told her anything about him, not before we got here. And all I'd said was, "*Betty, this is Noah.*"

I shrugged, an apology in my eyes as Noah cleared his throat, turning to Betty once more. "*My* father?"

"Oh, yes," she said, nodding with a knowing smile. "You're Noah Becker. I'd know those eyes and that mischievous grin anywhere."

At that, my mouth popped open, and Noah stilled completely.

"Your father took a liking to my Leroy," she explained, her eyes growing misty as she watched the water from the pool lap the sides. "And my Leroy sure did appreciate having a friend, especially there toward the end."

I swallowed. "Leroy was Betty's husband," I explained. "He passed away about twenty years ago."

"I'm sorry to hear that," Noah said in a hushed voice, and the confusion in his eyes shifted to sympathy as he put a hand on Betty's shoulder.

"It was a hard time," she said. "But, honestly, it's him I feel sorry for. Poor bastard has been waiting at Heaven's gates for me all this time. He had to know I'd take a while, but I'm sure if he could, he'd holler down at me just like he used to holler up the stairs." She chuckled, brows folding together as she did her best impression. "*Woman, get your cute behind down here. Ain't no makeup or hair curlers gonna make you look any more beautiful than you already are.*"

My heart swelled, and Noah smirked up at me before he dropped his hand from Betty's shoulder. "He sounds like quite the guy."

"He was," she agreed. "But, then again, so was your father. It seems we lose all the best ones too young."

Noah sobered at that, nodding just once. "Yes, ma'am."

"Your father would come see us every Good Friday," Betty explained, which was the nickname the distillery had given to the last Friday of every month, when they would give each of their employees a free bottle of whiskey with their paycheck. "Every single one for about four years, right up until the time the good Lord took my Leroy. They had met down at Buck's one night, and I don't know what transpired there, but boy, did those two take a liking to each other." She smiled. "So, every Good Friday, your father would come by with his bottle of Scooter Whiskey and a bag full of fried chicken. We'd all sit out on the porch and eat and drink and laugh until it was way too late for two old folks to be up. Sometimes your mom would join, sometimes not. But John? Well... Johnny was always there."

Noah swallowed, looking down at the water for a long moment before he met her gaze once more. "Sounds like a wonderful friendship."

"It was," she agreed. "And your father, he was a good man. When I met you today, I almost swore a ghost had come back to life. You look just like him, you know?" She beamed. "Same eyes, same hair, same Becker Trouble Grin."

She pinched his cheek at that, and Noah smirked.

"You've got his spirit," she said, her voice softer now as she watched Noah. "You're a good man, too, Noah Becker. And I'm glad I got to spend the afternoon with you."

I watched what I would have sworn was Noah's bottom lip trembling, but as soon as I thought I'd seen it shake, it was steady again. He smiled through whatever he was feeling — and I knew he was feeling *something* — as he reached forward to pull Betty in for a soft hug.

"Me, too, Miss Betty. Even if you did show me up on the dance floor."

She chuckled, her little shoulders shaking in his broad arms.

When he pulled back, he cleared his throat. "If you'll excuse me, I'm going to go get a shower and dry off. I've got this thing I've got to get to."

"What thing?" I probed.

He grabbed the back of his neck. "Oh, it's nothing, really. Me and my brothers try to get together every weekend to play cards. I usually host, and they'll be heading over in about an hour." He shrugged, giving me a soft smile, though he still seemed caught up in his thoughts. "Someone's gotta order the pizza."

I nodded, but my stomach sank at the realization that the day was nearly over. Noah would go hang out with his brothers, and I'd go home...

To wedding planning.

And Mama.

And all the stress I'd forgotten about over the last few hours.

I chewed my lip, eyes bouncing back and forth between Noah's before I swallowed. "I like cards..."

He blinked, the tiniest smirk climbing at the corner of his lips. "Yeah?"

I nodded. "I used to play blackjack and Texas hold 'em with my dad and his friends sometimes. Just for fun, but... yeah."

Noah smiled wider. "You want to come over? We could use some fresh blood at the table."

"Are you sure?" I asked, a little too quickly. "I don't want to impose."

*Please say yes.*

He shook his head. "We'd love to have you. I'm just going to go change and we can head out, grab the pizza and beer on our way. Meet you out front?"

"I'll be right behind you."

Noah placed his palms flat on the edge next to me, lifting his body out easily and saying one last goodbye to Betty before he made his way inside. Betty and I both watched him go, the water spilling down his back like water falling over the strongest side of a mountain, carved carefully over thousands of years.

When he disappeared through the doors, I turned back to Betty, and she was smirking at me.

"What?" I asked.

Betty's smile climbed higher. "You sly devil. You didn't tell me you were engaged to a *Becker*."

The color drained from my face.

"You lied about him not being as handsome as Richard Gere, my dear," she said, wagging her finger at me. "But, hell, I suppose I would have done the same. If that boy was mine, I wouldn't want a single other woman coming onto him."

"Betty..."

"I like him," she said, not letting me interrupt. "He's a good man, from a good family. He'll treat you right, Ruby Grace." She smiled wider, squeezing my knee where it hung off the edge. "You did good, my girl."

My cheeks burned, because somewhere under my haste to tell her she had the wrong guy, I felt something else, something stronger.

*Longing*, I realized distantly.

And then I stamped it down in the same breath.

"Noah's not my fiancé," I explained with a gentle smile. "We're just friends."

Betty frowned. "*Friends*?"

I nodded, but Betty's eyes drifted over my shoulder. When I followed her gaze, I saw Noah through the pool fence waiting for me in the parking lot, his hands shoved in his pockets, back leaned against his old, beat-up truck. I felt Betty watching me, but I couldn't hide the blush on my cheeks, the bob of my throat as I swallowed.

A few feet from the pool, my phone vibrated on my towel, screen lighting up with Anthony's name — with the picture of us that I loved so much.

Betty eyed it with me, and when I turned back to her, she just lifted one silver eyebrow. "Are you sure about that?"

## NOAH

Dad was still on my mind as I watched Ruby Grace hustle my brothers in poker that night.

We were all gathered around my folding table in the middle of my modest home, Sturgill Simpson on the stereo, two half-eaten boxes of pizza propped open on the kitchen counter behind us. My house was the one most "in town" between me and my brothers, just a few blocks off the Main Street drag on the south side. Jordan's house was ten minutes out of town, to the west, and Logan's was northeast, a little farther out than Mom's.

I still couldn't be sure if we'd meant to surround Mom's house the way we did, flanking her on all sides, or if we'd done it subconsciously. Either way, none of us were more than twenty minutes from each other, and we were all less than ten from Mom's.

My house was the closest to beer and pizza, however, which meant it was the prime choice for poker night.

It was pretty standard for my brothers and me to get together sometime during the weekend to play cards.

Ruby Grace, however, was a new addition.

"That's bullshit!" Logan yelled, thrusting his cards forward. They fluttered over the massive pot he and Ruby

Grace had built up during the hand, and he sulked further when she reached forward with a grin to rake it all in.

"Don't hate the player, Logan."

"I hate the *cheater*," he said, folding his arms over his chest.

"I don't even have sleeves to hide cards," she pointed out, gesturing to her toned, tanned arms. "Come on, now. Beckers aren't sore losers, are they?"

"Don't let his little boy actions speak for all of us," Jordan chimed in. He was being a good sport with our new guest at the table, but I didn't miss the questioning glances he shot me over his cards the whole night.

Logan stuck his tongue out, but then smirked, shaking his head and gathering the cards for his turn to deal. "You didn't warn us that you were bringing a shark to the table tonight, Noah."

I shrugged. "Ruby Grace is full of surprises."

Her eyes caught mine, then, my brothers picking up the conversation around us as we stared. Her smile was soft and sweet, the blush on her cheeks just barely visible now that her tan from the day was setting in. She held my gaze for a long while before tucking a strand of red hair behind her ear and picking up her cards for the next hand.

I kicked back in my chair, checking out my own cards as the day floated through my mind. I couldn't believe Betty knew my father, and the way she'd talked about him made my chest tighten. She was right — he was a good man. He was the *best* man, and it was a knife to my gut every time I realized that he wasn't here anymore, that he didn't get to see us boys grow into men, that he wouldn't be there to stand next to Mikey when Bailey walked down the aisle to him.

Or next to me, if I ever found a woman who would do the same.

The next dozen rounds of poker flew by, and after Ruby Grace knocked all the guys out once again in a bigger hand, Mikey groaned, tossing his cards in and standing. "I need a root beer float. Anyone else?"

Logan scoffed. "Uh, no thanks, Mikey. We're all old enough to drink *actual* beer. But thank you."

"She's not," he pointed out, gesturing to Ruby Grace.

That fact soured my gut a little.

"And besides, you're telling me that just because you're old enough to drink beer, you don't want a delicious root beer topped off with creamy vanilla ice cream right now?"

Logan's mouth pulled to the side, his eyes glancing around the table, to his cards from the last game, and back up again.

"Alright, I give. That does sound fucking delicious."

Mikey smirked triumphantly. "That's what I thought. One round of root beer floats coming up."

"You better not spill it down the sides," Logan called after him. "I swear, if my glass is sticky, I'll thwomp you!"

"Extra sticky glass, you got it, big bro!"

Logan humphed, pushing back in his chair before trotting after Mikey into the kitchen.

"I better help," Jordan said, standing. "If Logan goes into an OCD attack, no one is safe."

Ruby Grace chuckled lightly as Jordan tipped his imaginary hat at us, leaving us alone at the table. She leaned back in her chair, then, gathering her hair in one fist before letting it fall behind her. It exposed the delicate lines of her collar bone, the lean muscles of her neck, and I hated that I wanted to taste her so bad I had to physically hold onto the edge of the table to keep me from getting up and doing just that.

Seeing her with Betty and the rest of the residents at the nursing home today hit me in a way I didn't expect. She wasn't anything like the girl in church. No, at the nursing home, she was boisterous, playful, entertaining. She was everyone's highlight of the day, and she shone as bright as the sun did at that pool.

They loved her, it was easy to see.

And it was also easy to see *why*.

When she came back to my place for dinner and to play cards, I'd sat on the opposite side of the table from her. I needed to put space between us — especially after being skin to skin in the pool, her toned stomach pressed against mine, her surprisingly ample breasts exposed in her little bikini top.

But getting away from her didn't prove to be helpful.

If anything, it only gave me a better view of her hazel eyes, the freckles dotting her cheeks, her smooth, plump lips. I was thankful I couldn't see her legs under the table, because I already knew what those did to me.

And watching her with my brothers, handing out shit just as well as she was taking it from them, it made me feel something I never had before. I couldn't even put my finger on it, what that warmth in my chest was, that sinking in my gut.

As her phone lit up yet again with her fiancé's name on my folding table, I realized it was a longing, a sense of loss.

Because no matter how I tried to deny it, I wanted her to be mine.

It was silly to even think it when we hadn't so much as held hands, but I felt it — some sort of deep possessiveness over a girl I'd never have. She was going to marry another man, entertain *his* brothers, or family or friends. She would cook for him, hold him when shit got rough, be his rock when he needed to lean. She would wrap those pretty little legs around *him* at night, and I'd never get to touch them.

Jealousy ripped through me, and I knew it was the wrong move, I *knew* I shouldn't have, but I couldn't stop myself. When she reached for her phone like she was finally going to answer him, I called out her name.

"Ruby Grace."

She paused, frowning at the phone before she looked up at me.

"Want to get some fresh air with me on the porch while Mikey makes those floats?"

I expected her to hesitate, to say, *"Yes, but let me answer this call first."* Or to just flat out deny me. But, she smiled almost instantly, her cheeks high and rosy as she nodded, tucking her phone away in the purse she had hanging on her chair. "Sure."

Jordan eyed me suspiciously from the kitchen as I rose from my chair, meeting Ruby Grace on the other side of the table. I didn't meet his gaze for long, though — maybe because I knew what facts he wanted to point out.

I knew them very well.

The night was pleasantly cool, considering how hot the day had been. That was what I loved about June in Tennessee. The days were long and hot, but the nights were cool — perfect for a bonfire or to get close to someone for a little warmth.

"It's beautiful out," Ruby Grace commented, leaning her arms on the wooden railing of my porch. It had been old and rotted when I moved in, but it was my first project — fixing up the exterior. Now, the porch was maybe the best part of the entire house, rebuilt and painted white with a couple of rocking chairs Mom had gifted me when the project was done.

I considered asking Ruby Grace to sit, but she looked so comfortable against the railing, her eyes scanning the yard and the houses across the street, that I just slid up next to her, instead.

"It is. It was a nice day at the pool, too."

She smiled. "Thanks for coming with me today."

I shrugged. "Hey, there are much worse ways you could have made me pay for being such an asshole to you."

"Betty adored you."

"Oh, we're totally getting married," I joked.

"Funny. She said the same thing."

I chuckled, letting the sounds of the crickets settle between us before I spoke again. "You were really in your element there."

Another smile bloomed on her lips, but this one fell a little too quickly. "Yeah."

"I liked you like that today."

She frowned, turning to me, then. "Like what?"

"I don't know," I started with a shrug. "Carefree. Young. Unrestrained. You're always so put together." I paused. "I like it better when you're just a girl being a girl."

I could see the warmth in her eyes under the porch light as I spoke, but when I finished, she stood taller, shoulders back. "I'm a *woman*, thank you very much."

"Oh, trust me," I said, eyes trailing down her legs. "I know that, too."

When I met her gaze again, she was biting her lip against a smile, and she turned back toward the yard, draping her arms over the railing once more. "I really do love it there," she said after a while. "It was my favorite thing to do when I was in high school, spend a day volunteering at the home. My best friend, Annie, works there full time now."

"Did you think you would, too?"

She considered that. "No, I don't think so. I always pictured Annie and I going to UNC together, and then..." Her voice faded, and she glanced down at her hands hanging over the railing.

At her ring, maybe?

"And then?" I prompted her.

"Oh, it's silly. Anyway, I suppose nothing turns out how we imagined, right?"

I frowned, turning toward her. I chanced touching the soft skin of the inside of her elbow, getting her to face me, too. "Hey, don't do that."

"Do what?"

"Don't act like what you want doesn't matter."

She swallowed, looking at the porch beneath us. "It's just like I told you that night we went riding. Annie and I always had dreams of joining AmeriCorps. We wanted to give back, to travel and help others for a while after we graduated." She smiled. "I just thought it'd be so fun, you know? I'd be with my best friend, we'd see new places, meet new people. I'd get to do what makes my heart happy."

"I remember you talking about that," I said, also remembering how frustrated I'd been that she didn't see that as an option anymore. That night, I had left it alone. But tonight, I wanted to probe. "What happened?"

She sighed, finally pulling away from where I held her and leaning her hip against the railing. "Well, Annie found Trav. They got married, she's pregnant now. She never did go to UNC. And I... well..." She held up her left hand, pointing to the rock on the third finger.

I nodded. "Yeah. I mean, I know it'd be a little different without Annie, but you could still go. Right?"

She scoffed. "Of course not. I'm getting married."

"I guess I just don't understand what that has to do with anything."

"It has *everything* to do with all of it," she said, flustered. "I'll be a wife. A *politician's* wife. I have new duties now, new things expected of me."

"And would your new husband not understand if you wanted to chase your own dreams for a while?" I countered. "It wouldn't be forever. Why can't you have what you want while giving him what he wants, too?"

She shook her head. "You don't understand."

"Oh, I think I understand just fine."

I stepped into her space, and before I could think better of it, my hand touched her arm, sliding up to her neck, her jaw, until I slipped my fingers in the soft strands of her hair and framed her face, tilting her gaze toward me again.

"You deserve to have the things you've dreamed about, Ruby Grace," I said. "And when you marry someone, you become a *team*. It's not all about him and his dreams and his achievements. You are not just a sidekick."

I paused, licking my bottom lip as I considered my next words. Ruby Grace's eyes were soft, wide, almost a little scared as she watched me.

"You are the heroine just as much as he is the hero," I reminded her. "And if he loves you, he will support you and your dreams just as you've supported his and will continue to in the future."

She leaned into my touch, eyes fluttering shut before they opened slowly again. "You make it all sound so easy," she whispered. "So simple."

"With the right person, it is," I told her. I swallowed, glancing at her lips before I found her gaze again. "If you were mine, Ruby Grace, your dreams wouldn't come second to anything."

It was an overstep I didn't mean to make.

The words came out before I even realized what I was saying, and now, it was too late to go back. There was a line between us, one we never had to draw because that ring on her finger had drawn it for us the first day she came back into town. But there on my porch, in the soft, cool, Tennessee summer night, those rules didn't seem to apply.

We were in another universe altogether, and in this one, that ring on her finger didn't exist.

I hadn't even realized her hands were on me, not until they fisted in my t-shirt at my abdomen, pulling me closer. My hand in her hair gripped a little harder, her eyes on my lips, mine on hers until we were so close I couldn't even see them anymore. Our breaths met in the space between, hot and heavy with words we wouldn't say.

Her lips parted.

Mine grazed hers, eliciting the sweetest gasp.

But before I could connect the kiss, before I could pull her in, feel her melt into my arms, the front door swung open.

Ruby Grace jumped back, folding her arms over the railing and looking out over the yard like she had been before. I looked up at the awning over my porch, suppressing a groan as Mikey bounded out, completely oblivious.

"Two root beer floats," he announced proudly, handing me two Mason jars filled to the top with the frothy vanilla ice cream and soda mixture. "And Ruby Grace, we demand a double-or-nothing rematch."

She finally turned toward us, her smile weak.

She wouldn't look at me at all.

"Thank you, Mikey, but I actually have to run. I didn't realize how late it was. Would you mind grabbing my purse?"

He shrugged — again, completely oblivious. "Sure! Be right back."

When Mikey dipped inside, I sat the floats down on the table by the rocking chairs before turning back to her. "You're leaving?"

She still wouldn't look at me.

"I think we both know it's for the best."

Her words twisted like a knife in my chest, but I didn't have any words to say to make her stay.

She was right.

I hated it, but it didn't change the fact that she was right.

Mikey came out moments later with her purse, and the guys met her at the door, giving her a hug and a little more shit for taking their money. She was all gracious smiles and warm thank you's until the door shut, my brothers back inside, leaving us alone on the porch again.

I opened my arms. "Thank you for today. For tonight."

But she just stared at me, her eyes filling with tears that wouldn't shed. "Why did you have to do this?"

I frowned, letting my arms fall. "I—"

"No," she said, shaking her head, hands clinging to the strap of her purse like a lifeline. "Everything was fine. I was *fine* until I met you. You've messed everything up."

My brows furrowed more. "What, by reminding you that you have a choice? That you don't have to marry someone who makes you feel this way?"

"I *love* him," she spat.

"Fine. But does he love you?"

She scoffed. "Of course he does. How dare you even insinuate otherwise."

I smirked at the word *insinuate*, sensing the well-to-do woman she was raised to be slipping back into place just like she always did.

Shaking my head, I put my arms up in a mock surrender. "You're right. I'm sorry. Just forget about AmeriCorps, about school, about anything that doesn't revolve around Anthony and *his* career. Clearly, you're very happy and I was mistaken by saying anything at all. I sincerely apologize."

I was being an asshole. I knew it, but just like I'd overstepped earlier, I couldn't stop myself from doing so now.

I wanted her to wake up, to see what I saw.

Even if it hurt.

Ruby Grace's bottom lip trembled a bit as she pressed it to the top, adjusting her purse on her shoulder before she growled and stormed off my porch.

"See you around?" I called after her.

My only response was one middle finger thrown my way over her shoulder.

## RUBY GRACE

Once again, I found myself speeding through town with the top down on my convertible, cursing Noah Becker's name.

"Oh, the *nerve* of that man!" I growled, punching the gas again once I made the turn down the old road that led to my parents' house. The warm night air whipped through my hair, little tendrils of fire red invading my vision as I drove. The radio was silent, the only noise the revving of my engine and the revving of my temper.

Noah had crossed a line. He shouldn't have held me the way he did in the pool, with his hands on my hips, his chest so close to mine. And then on his porch, he'd stepped into my space like he owned it, like I was *his* and not Anthony's.

And he'd even said it.

*"If you were mine, Ruby Grace, your dreams wouldn't come second to anything."*

My cheeks heated, a rush of blood flowing through me at the memory of my hands in his shirt, his in my hair, our lips touching just long enough to send a zip of desire through me.

I'd nearly cheated on my fiancé.

I shook my head, letting out another frustrated growl as I took the turn into my driveway.

"It wasn't even a kiss," I reminded myself out loud. "We got a little too close, but that was it. It was a mistake. We were just caught up in the moment."

It would never happen again.

And I promised myself I'd stay far away from Noah Becker to ensure it.

By the time I put my car in park, punching the buttons on the consul to put the convertible top back in place, I'd made my decision. Noah was nothing more than the guy who showed me the barrel I purchased for *Anthony*. He wasn't my friend, and he wasn't someone I should lean on the way I had been.

It didn't matter how I felt around him, or how I found myself already caring about him and his family.

He was a lightning storm, fun to watch from afar but dangerous to dance with.

I wasn't going to toy with that line of danger.

I dragged myself out of the car, exhausted and ready for a hot shower and my bed, but the sight of a familiar car next to my dad's truck in the driveway made me pause.

Before I could even register what that car meant, the voice that belonged to it spoke in the darkness.

"There she is."

Anthony trotted down the steps of the front porch, his wide and brilliantly white smile visible even in the dim light of the night. He held his arms open, but my feet remained glued to the spot I stood.

"Come here, beautiful," he said, taking my hesitance for shock as he chuckled and pulled me into his chest. He wrapped his arms around me, swaying me in a hug before he pulled back and framed my face with his hands. "*God, I've missed you.*"

His lips were on me in the next second, kissing me with the longing of the last few weeks we'd been apart. I didn't come to until halfway through it, and when I did, I wrapped my arms around his waist, kissing him in return as my mind reeled.

And I couldn't figure out why when his lips were on me, I was still thinking about Noah.

When Anthony pulled back, he wrapped me in his arms again, threading his hands on the small of my back as he smiled down at me. He was tall, body built like a brick wall from playing lacrosse his entire life. His bicep muscles were the size of my thighs, and with them encompassing me like that, I felt an equal measure of warmth and confinement.

"Shocked?" he asked with an amused smile when I still didn't say anything. His blond hair was styled in a neat wave, his hazel eyes matching the hue of mine. He reminded me a little of a Ken doll, or Superman, or a combination of the two with his cleft chin and strong jaw line, his face freshly shaved and smooth, his skin a perfect shade of bronze.

I nodded, forcing a smile.

He chuckled. "I thought you'd be. Where have you been? I've been waiting all night to see this look on your face."

Panic zipped through me, but I swallowed it down, running my hands over his chest. "Oh, just at the nursing home. I didn't know I had such a surprise waiting for me."

Warmth touched his eyes. "My girl, always the giving heart." He shook his head, leaning down to peck my lips before he pulled back again. "One of the things I love most about you."

My smile was genuine this time, and I mentally slapped the guilt I felt away. I hadn't done anything wrong with Noah. We hadn't actually kissed. It was a mistake, a weak moment where I was too close to him, too close to my feelings of anxiety surrounding the wedding.

It could happen to anyone.

But it wouldn't happen again.

I pulled Anthony in for another kiss to seal that promise to myself, and when I pulled back, he threaded his hand in mine, tugging me toward the house.

"What are you doing here, anyway?" I asked. "And how long are you here?"

"Well..." he said, and before he could answer, he swung the door open and Mama bounded toward me, wrapping me in her arms in an excited hug.

"Oh, Ruby Grace! You're home!" She squeezed me tight before pulling back and framing my arms in her hands. "Can you believe it? Anthony surprised us all this afternoon. And he's staying until the wedding! I'm just so thrilled!"

My brows shot up. "You are?" I asked Anthony.

"I am," he said, a soft grin on his perfect lips. "We've been getting a lot of media attention with me running for state representative, and it seems that marrying you is everyone's favorite topic. Can't say that I blame them," he said, chucking my chin. "Anyway, Dad thought it would be good to capitalize on all the attention. He sent me out here with a small film crew. They're going to film us preparing for the wedding, capture our love story for the media outlets and possibly some campaign commercials. Don't worry," he said when he saw the worry in my eyes. "They won't be with us all the time. And we'll have a say in what they can use."

I nodded through my discomfort, especially since I couldn't quite place its origin. Was it the thought of cameras following me that made my stomach lurch like that, or the fact that Anthony was in my hometown to stay for the next five weeks?

And if that was the case, *why* did it make me uncomfortable?

"Oh, I just can't believe it!" Mama said, clapping her hands together. "I'll have to plan a dinner this week for the crew. We can all get to know each other and I'll make my famous lemon bar cookies. We're just so thrilled to have you, Anthony!"

She wrapped him up in her arms before scurrying off, calling down the hallway for Dad to come join us in the living room for a night cap.

I stood in the foyer in a daze, blinking repeatedly, sensing the disarray of my hair as if it were the only sense I could focus on in that moment. I smoothed my hands over the frizzy curls, over and over, staring at the family photo that greeted all our guests who entered the house.

"Hey," Anthony said, taking my face in his hands. He leveled his gaze with mine. "I know this is a lot, and surprises aren't really your thing. Why don't you run up and take a shower, get changed, take some time for yourself. I'll handle entertaining your parents until you feel ready to come down and join us. Okay?"

My heart squeezed painfully in my chest. He was so aware of my needs, of who I was, and I'd just been in the arms of another man. I wanted to cry, to throw myself into his arms and beg for forgiveness, but I didn't even know what to apologize for.

Or, maybe part of that came from the fact that I wasn't sorry, not the way I should have been.

"Okay," I said, eyes watering a little as I nodded.

Anthony kissed my forehead in understanding, and once he let me go, I dragged myself up the stairs and to my room. Anthony's stuff was in the guest room down the hall, and I passed it, eyeing the luggage before I swept into my own room and locked the door behind me.

I ran the shower water as hot as I could stand, hoping it would scald away my guilt, my confusion, my warring thoughts.

My fiancé was in town. He would be here to help with planning, with all the decisions. We'd be able to spend time together, celebrate this time leading up to our wedding like a normal couple.

The man I loved was here, and I wanted to find relief in that, to wrap myself up in the comfort of his arms.

I just had to fight through the feeling of suffocation, first.

# Chapter Nine

## NOAH

Against my strongest urges, I left Ruby Grace alone after that night at my house.

I told myself it was because I was respecting her claim that she loved Anthony, and that he loved her, but the truth was probably somewhere more along the lines that I knew I'd see her later that week. I fought the urge to text or call her Monday through Wednesday because I knew on Thursday, I'd get to see her in person.

And I always did my best work in person.

I needed to apologize, that much I knew fairly clearly. I didn't necessarily *want* to, because the bigger part of me wasn't sorry for pulling her close on my porch, for nearly kissing her, for calling her out on the bullshit rules of the marriage she was about to enter into. I didn't want her to give up *her* dreams for his.

There should have been balance, and room for both.

I didn't know why I felt so passionately about it, why it irked me so much that she was so willing to push everything she wanted aside for him. More sane people might have seen it as an honorable sacrifice. But me? I thought of my parents, of how Mom supported Dad in all his aspirations at the brewery while he supported her dreams when it came to building our family. They respected each other, and not one part of the team was more important than the other.

I wanted that for me.

And for some unbeknownst reason, I wanted it for Ruby Grace, too.

So, on Thursday, the night of the annual Scooter Whiskey Single Barrel Soirée, I went over everything I'd say to her while my hands worked on autopilot getting the event ready.

"Can you even imagine what it would be like," PJ spoke through grunts as he unloaded another barrel from the truck. "To have enough money to just blow fifteen grand on a barrel of whiskey?"

I smirked, reading the name inscribed on the golden plate of the barrel he'd just pulled off the truck. I scribbled a check next to the one on my sheet, nodding to Marty, who loaded it onto a dolly and took it on down the line to the buyer's VIP tent.

"Trust me, if I had money like that, I wouldn't be blowing it on alcohol," he continued.

"Oh, yeah? What *would* you spend it on, PJ?" Eli teased, leaning one elbow on a barrel. "Let me guess. Hookers."

The guys snickered while PJ turned a bright red. "*No*," he answered quickly. "I get plenty of sex. For *free*."

"Right," Eli said. "And Noah is celibate."

"Hey, don't drag the innocent bystander into this," I said, chuckling as I checked off another barrel before sending it down the line.

"I don't, nor would I ever, pay for sex," PJ insisted again. When no one answered with more than a lifted brow, he threw his hands up in the air before letting them hit his thighs with a slap and a groan. "You guys suck."

We all laughed at that, me ruffling his hair before telling him we were just teasing. He was the youngest, just like a little brother to us, and we couldn't help it. He didn't seem appeased, but he got back to work, each of us falling into the groove as Eli rambled on about what *he* would buy if he had stupid money.

They didn't ask me what I would do, and I was glad for it. I probably would have lost a few of my man points if I told them the truth. All I'd want is a modest house, big enough for my family and my horse. I'd want to spend our time traveling or farming or building memories together, never working another day in my life and making it so my wife wouldn't have to, either. Not unless she *wanted* to.

That thought was still in my mind when Ruby Grace's barrel stopped at my feet.

I stared at the cursive loops of her name on the gold plate, tracing them a little longer than necessary before I checked the box next to her name and sent the barrel on. My eyes followed it halfway to the buyer's tent, pulse picking up speed at the thought of talking to her tonight.

It made no sense. I didn't know what I expected to get out of any of it. She was getting married — in less than five weeks, no less. I had nothing to offer her that she didn't already have and she couldn't give me a single thing more than what she already had.

And yet, there was some part of me that desired her, that needed her in whatever way I could get her.

I didn't really give a fuck if it was right or wrong.

I was still analyzing it all, trying to pinpoint what it was about that girl that got under my skin, when the rest of the guys and I retreated to the staff tent to freshen up before the opening speech from Patrick Scooter. In less than an hour, the entire Scooter estate would be littered with people from Stratford and the surrounding area. It was the biggest party of the year, a time when no matter where you lived or how much money you made, you got to come together with the rich and the fabulous and drink the same whiskey as them. For one night, our town was united — though everyone would likely still stay in their little circles.

The band was already playing when I emerged from the staff tent, dressed in my good blue jeans and white, button-up shirt. I left the top button unfastened, rolled the sleeves up to just under my elbows, and topped the whole look off with my best cowboy boots and my favorite cowboy hat. It was a Stetson, made of premium wool that matched the dark mocha brown of my boots, and before it was mine, it had been my father's.

Gus had me running around, greeting the barrel buyers I'd worked with throughout the season, making sure they knew where their barrel was to take home after the event and getting them set up in the VIP area with whatever they needed. I'd take pictures of them with their barrels, introduce them to the rest of the barrel raising team as well as the scientists behind the creation of their unique whiskey, and answer any questions they had before moving on to the next.

*This* was my element.

I knew whiskey. I knew Scooter Whiskey. I knew the barrel raising process, the science behind our whiskey, what we could and what we *couldn't* tell the buyers about the product they'd paid top dollar for. I knew how to charm a crowd, how to impress someone and make them feel good about blowing all that money, and how to represent our company the same way my father had.

What I *didn't* know was what to do when Ruby Grace walked into the VIP tent hanging on her fiancé's arm.

I knew he was Anthony without needing an introduction. He just *looked* like a politician — all navy suit, complete with tie and pocket square, dress shoes shined to perfection, hair styled in an immaculate wave like one you'd see on the red carpet at a Hollywood award show. He carried himself with a mixture of arrogance and confidence, a balance not many men could pull off. He was both welcoming and threatening all at once, and I found myself hating him before I even had reason to.

Maybe it was because of the girl he held by the waist.

A small crew of cameras and microphones followed them around, staying back just enough to give them space while capturing every interaction they had. I assumed it was something he was doing while running for office, some sort of propaganda. Anthony seemed to shine with those cameras on him.

Ruby Grace seemed to want to disappear.

She didn't even notice me, not with Anthony toting her around from group to group, a politician's smile on his face while she wore a more subdued smile of her own. I watched her for a long while, and I noticed she did nothing more than shake the hand of whomever they were talking to before Anthony would take over, commanding all the attention, leading the conversation.

She was a sidekick, a wallflower, and it made absolutely no sense to me.

If he would let her speak, she'd steal the show. It would be *her* everyone wanted to know. It would be Ruby Grace who would light up the room with her smile, knock men on their asses with the modest yet somehow classically sexy emerald dress she wore. The collar was high, the sleeves covering her shoulders and upper arms, but the hem of the skirt cut just above her knees, showing her deadliest weapons — those killer legs.

But it wasn't just the way she dressed, or her body, or her smile or her fire-red hair. It was her passionate and giving heart, her quick and witty banter, her *intelligence* that made her stand out.

No one would know that, though. Not if he never let her speak.

I tore my eyes away from her long enough to toast a glass of whiskey with two buyers I'd met in the winter. They had traveled all the way from California to pick up their barrel and spend a week in Tennessee. The barrel they'd selected had high notes of vanilla and nutmeg, giving it a holiday feel that captured their hearts since they had visited during Christmas break when they bought it. The whiskey warmed its way down my throat, settling in my stomach along with the dozen other ounces of whiskey I'd tried when welcoming our guests.

It was a perk of the job, and right now, it was also the liquid courage I needed.

"Enjoy the rest of your evening, Mr. and Mrs. Wheeland. I'll be around if you need anything at all." I shook their hands, offering a tip of my hat before I excused myself.

And then I made a beeline for Ruby Grace.

Her eyes were distant, a little glossed as she listened to the woman Anthony had engaged in conversation with. She stood with her husband, too, both of their gazes fixed on Anthony while Ruby Grace stood there like his shadow.

Those hazel eyes popped to life when they saw me.

At first, she didn't register me. But on a double take, her eyes widened, brows rising just marginally as I made my way toward her. I was confident in my walk, slow and purposeful, letting her drink me in as I crossed the space between us. She'd never seen me dressed up like this, and the flush of her cheeks told me she was affected. I wondered if she was thinking about us standing together on my porch, of my hands in her hair, my lips grazing hers before my brother forced us to tear apart.

The way her ruby lips parted, I would have bet money that she was.

It shouldn't have brought me satisfaction, not with my intention of apologizing to her and setting everything straight between us. I knew I needed to fall into the friend zone, that that was all we could be.

But damnit if seeing her there with him didn't light the *other* fire inside of me, the one that said a feverous *mine*, over and over and over again.

Her eyes shifted from something between desire and shock to warning and anger the closer I got. She didn't want me there. She was likely still pissed about what had transpired between us Sunday night, and she likely didn't want me bringing it up in front of her fiancé.

And I wouldn't. I was a gentleman, after all.

But I was still going to talk to her.

I slid my hands into the pockets of my jeans, sidling up next to Ruby Grace with my eyes on her fiancé as I waited for him to finish his conversation with the couple. I could feel Ruby Grace staring holes into the side of my face, but I just kept my smile, waiting patiently.

Anthony glanced at me quickly before turning his attention back to the couple, acknowledging my presence with a hint of annoyance. When the conversation was wrapped up between him and the couple, he shook their hands — and then they shook Ruby Grace's, of course — before finally turning to me.

"I'm so sorry to interrupt, Mr. Caldwell," I said, the most southern and welcoming smile on my face as I stretched a hand toward him. "I'm Noah Becker, one of the barrel raisers here at Scooter Whiskey. I helped your fiancé pick out her barrel, and I'm at your service tonight."

Understanding shaded the annoyance, and Anthony returned my smile in the most genuine way I imagined he could before taking my hand and shaking it firmly. "Ah, yes. Of course. How do you do, Noah?"

"Oh, I'm fantastic. It's our Academy Awards, after all, and I'm akin to the host of the show." I grinned wider, squeezing his hand a little too hard before I dropped it and offered my calloused palm to the girl he still held possessively by the waist. "Ruby Grace, always a pleasure to see you. And might I say you look beautiful this evening."

Her eyes narrowed into slits as she let me take her hand, and I lowered my lips to the back of it, pressing an appropriate kiss to the soft skin before turning back to Anthony.

"I thought I might show you to your barrel, let you taste it, since you weren't there for the original purchase?"

Anthony eyed me, his gaze flicking to his blushing bride-to-be — who pretended not to be affected by our embrace — before it pinned me again. "Of course."

"Wonderful," I said. "Right this way."

I gestured to the rows of barrels lining the far side of the tent, falling into step beside Ruby Grace as we made our way. Her jaw was clenched tight, skin pale as she watched me from the corner of her eyes. She seemed to be warning me, begging me for something, but I kept my attention on the man who demanded it so much.

"Ruby Grace surprised us all with her very generous wedding gift to you, Mr. Caldwell," I said, stopping when we reached their barrel. "She surprised me even further with her impeccable knowledge of our whiskey. It's such a rare sight to behold, a woman who knows how to detect the special flavors and notes, to pick out a fine whiskey. Your fiancé has great taste," I said, watching his expression the entire time.

Anthony sized Ruby Grace up, like he was seeing her for the first time, and his brows lowered as he found me again. "I wasn't aware there was a tasting involved."

"Oh, only a small one. No more than an ounce or two," I assured him. I leaned in closer, whispering conspiratorially. "Of course, that's between us three. Wouldn't want anyone getting wind of an underage tasting. But, hey, when the mayor's daughter is getting married to such a prestigious, up-and-coming politician?" I shrugged. "The rules can be bent."

I saw the war in his eyes, the struggle between wanting to feel threatened battling with the base level of my words that were flattering him. He cleared his throat, adjusting the lapels of his suit jacket before he gestured to the barrel. "Well, let's have a taste, then, shall we?"

I poured each of us a one-ounce pour, handing them their glasses first before I lifted mine in a toast. "To a beautiful and happy marriage," I said, smiling at Anthony. My gaze fell to Ruby Grace, then, eyes pinning hers. "And to the *team* you two will become. May you always love and *respect* the other."

Anthony mumbled some sort of acknowledgement before throwing his whiskey back like a shot.

Ruby Grace, on the other hand, watched me with murder in her eyes.

I just smiled, tilting my glass toward her before I took a sip, tasting it in the same way I'd shown Ruby Grace. She followed suit, and she couldn't hide the smile on her face when she tasted it the right way, indulging on all the notes of the fine alcohol while her husband-to-be grimaced against the shot he'd taken.

"Wow," he said, face still twisted up. His eyes watered a bit as he handed his empty glass back to me. "She really does have great taste." He sniffed, putting his arm around her and tugging her close. "Such a thoughtful wedding gift. I'm glad I got to be here to taste it at the unveiling. Thank you, sweetheart."

She smiled, but before she could answer with a *you're welcome*, Anthony dipped her back, kissing her possessively.

Ruby Grace was stiff as a board in his arms, and when he slipped his tongue inside her mouth, she pressed against his chest, breaking the kiss with a glare of disapproval masked by a forced smile.

"My parents are right over there," she whispered, not bothering to look at exactly *where* her parents were to make her point clear. She cleared her throat, instead, turning to me with the same tight smile. "Thank you for the tasting, Noah. Now, if you'll excuse us, we have to get back to the party." She rested her hand on Anthony's chest — the hand that shone with the diamond he'd given her. "So many people to introduce Anthony to. You understand."

I swallowed past the thick knot in my throat, forcing a smile that was just as tight as hers. "Of course," I said, waving my hand toward the rest of the crowd. "Enjoy your evening, and let me know if I can be of service to either of you."

Ruby Grace rolled her eyes, though Anthony didn't see, and I smirked a little at that.

"Will do," Anthony said, shaking my hand. He held it in his vise grip a little too long, letting Ruby Grace walk a few steps away before he lowered his voice. "You enjoy your evening, too. Somewhere far away from my fiancé, preferably."

I tilted my head to the side, smile not wavering. "I'm sure I don't understand what you're implying, Mr. Caldwell."

"And I'm sure I don't need to repeat myself to make my point clear."

He dropped my hand, wiping his palm on his jacket like I'd given him some sort of disease before he turned, offering his arm to Ruby Grace and toting her off to the next victim.

I tucked my hands back in my pockets, watching them go with a sense of jealousy settling over my chest like a hot, wet, suffocating blanket.

And I knew I wouldn't find relief until I kicked my way out from under it.

## RUBY GRACE

The Scooter Whiskey Single Barrel Soirée had always been a grand event in Stratford. I remembered attending as a child with my parents, hanging out in the kiddie area where there were endless games and blow-up slides to crawl all over. As I got older, I'd come with my friends in high school to dance and sneak illegal sips of whiskey — of course, *I* never drank the whiskey, because I had always been told by Mama that it was a man's drink.

I hadn't tasted it at all until the day Noah Becker showed me the barrel I'd purchased for my fiancé.

He was still on my mind as Patrick Scooter gave his welcoming speech, relaying a short history of the distillery and his family's legacy before he launched into the details that made all the barrels in our presence tonight so special. While those of us who purchased barrels were the only ones who could taste those specific ones, there were three barrels of single-barrel whiskey that were cracked open for the town to indulge in. Considering how poor most of Stratford's residents were, this was a special occasion. Everyone was dressed up, smiling, and celebrating.

And somehow, on our town's most joyous night, with my fiancé's hand on the small of my back, I felt more numb than I had in my entire life.

"You okay over there, sweetheart?" Daddy asked in between one of his conversations.

I smiled, assuring him with a squeeze on his upper arm. I knew it wouldn't be long before someone else would pull him aside and need his ear, whether to pitch an idea for the town or to lobby for his support on an issue. "I'm fine, Daddy. Just a little tired."

His eyes softened. "I know this can be a lot. I've got my truck keys, if you want to escape for a while."

Even though my father and I didn't talk much, he understood me in a way Mama didn't. She was an extrovert, outgoing and social in every way. Daddy was more like me — he preferred to be with his close circle of friends. We both struggled in big settings like this, and I had a feeling it was *him* who was thinking about escaping in that truck.

"Thank you, but I think we're both stuck here for a few hours. Might as well make the most of it." I held up my glass, which held a tonic and lime, and cheersed it with his whiskey tumbler just as the Parkers approached him.

It was always like that for Dad — just a constant revolving door of people.

I leaned in closer. "And, hey, if you really need to escape, give me the signal and I'll fake an extreme illness."

Dad chuckled at that, squeezing my shoulder with eyes that said, *Okay, here we go*, before turning to the Parkers and greeting them.

The night passed in a sort of daze after that, a blur of names and *how do ya do's* and dances with strangers. I ate the little hors d'oeuvres as they passed by on the silver trays, sipped on the tonic and lime I'd ordered to not be the only one without a drink in my hand, laughed at the jokes Anthony told — the same ones over and over to new people — and when asked, I danced with whoever wanted to dance. That was what was expected, after all. Whether it was my father's business partners or someone Anthony had just introduced me to, my job was to entertain, to charm and dazzle and impress.

And while I sparkled on the outside, I felt dead on the inside.

"Ruby Grace, could I trouble you for a spin on the dance floor?"

I blinked out of the daydream I'd been in, plastering on my best smile to turn and accept the invitation from whoever had asked. But when I spun on my heel and found Noah Becker's cobalt steel eyes, I frowned.

"No, thanks," I spat.

Noah tilted his head. "Come on, now. That's no way to speak to a gentleman."

"I see no gentleman here."

He chuckled, stepping into my space with his hands sliding easily into the pockets of his dark blue jeans. They were so tight they might as well have been painted on, and

I hated that I noticed. I hated that every girl ogled him as he walked around, eyeing his ass through the fabric — me included. He was every country girl's dream tonight — crisp, white button-up, dark, lethal jeans, smooth, tan skin, boots and a hat that matched and topped off the look.

My grandmother would say he looked "sharp," if she were here. And I agreed.

He was a blade, and I knew I needed to stay away or I'd end up shredded.

"Hey," he said when he was closer, lowering his voice. "Look, I'd really like the chance to properly apologize to you. And I *know* you'd love a break from all of... *this*." He looked around us for a moment before he found my gaze again. "So, please, Ruby Grace — dance with me."

Noah pulled one hand from his pocket, extending it to me with a gentle smile. Something in my chest loosened at the sight, at someone seeing me without me saying a word. To everyone else, I was the charming, entertaining Ruby Grace tonight. But Noah saw what no one else did.

It seemed he had since that first day at the distillery.

A long sigh left my chest as I nodded, slipping my hand into his and letting him lead the way. Anthony had disappeared to go to the restroom about twenty minutes prior — the cameras from his media crew disappearing with him — and I imagined he'd been wrangled into conversation with someone else on his way back. And besides, I had danced with countless men that night. Noah was just one more, and it wasn't frowned upon for the barrel buyers to dance with the raisers.

Logic and explanation aside, I *wanted* to dance with Noah.

And maybe that was all that mattered to me in that moment.

I stared at my hand in his as he guided me to the dance floor in front of the band. His hand was so large, hard and calloused, his wrist thick and forearms lined with muscles and veins. My hand disappeared inside his grasp, my dainty wrist sparkling with the tennis bracelet I wore. He was all down-home country, and I was refined country royalty.

Still, I marveled at how well my hand fit in his.

When we made it to the dance floor, he stopped, pulling me into him until his hand was on my waist, the other still holding my hand. For a long, stretched moment in time, he just watched me, his eyes dancing between mine. A small smile found his lips, and he nodded once before taking the first step, leading the way and guiding me along with his movements.

And then, we were dancing.

The song was a familiar one in Tennessee, "I Cross My Heart" by George Strait. The lead singer of the band crooned out the lyrics as everyone on the floor gently swayed or two-stepped.

But Noah?

Noah guided me in a beautiful waltz.

"How do you know this?" I asked, smile breaking on my face despite my urge to be angry with him after Sunday night.

"What? Waltz?"

I nodded.

Noah smiled, stepping with me into a soft turn before pulling me back into his arms. "My mom. She and Dad used to dance after dinner every single night — in the living room, the kitchen, wherever. And after Dad passed, the tradition didn't stop. My brothers and I take turns dancing with her. And bless her, she taught us all with patience."

My heart squeezed. "I bet that means so much to her."

"Yeah," he said, and I waited for him to continue, but he just swallowed, forcing a bit of a smile before he changed the subject. "I'm sorry about what I said Sunday night, Ruby Grace. I was out of line."

He twirled me again, and I was thankful for the break in eye contact before we spun back together. Of course, that break in eye contact was long enough for me to realize how many *other* pairs of eyes were locked on us at the moment.

"Thank you," I said, glaring right back at one of Mama's friends until she tore her gaze away before I looked back at Noah. "Seems like half our conversations are apologies."

"Well, I'm an asshole," he offered honestly. "And you're stubborn."

I narrowed my eyes. "Am not."

Noah just smirked, falling back into step as the song's chorus flowed around us. His smile leveled out the longer he watched me. "So, why didn't you tell me Anthony was coming into town?"

"I didn't know he was," I shot, and I couldn't stop the defensiveness from breaking through. "And even if I did, I don't see why I would owe it to you to tell you."

Noah lifted his brows. "I was just trying to make conversation."

"Mm-hmm."

"Why are you so defensive?"

"I'm not," I said quickly. "I just know how you feel about him, and I don't want to play into it anymore."

"I don't even know him," he responded. "I don't feel anything toward him."

"Sure," I said, twirling out twice before I slipped into his arms again. "I totally got that vibe with the barrel tasting earlier. And with everything you said to me on Sunday."

"I told you I was sorry for that."

"Yeah, but did you mean it?"

His jaw clenched at that, and he watched me for a long moment before his eyes cast up to the top of the tent and back down. "You're infuriating, you know that?"

"Well, then, it's a good thing you're not the one marrying me, isn't it?"

Noah slowed, his hand on my waist squeezing a little tighter. He opened his mouth to say something, but then his eyes skirted behind me, and he cleared his throat, forcing a smile as Anthony slid up beside us.

"Mind if I cut in?" Anthony asked. His threatening tone wasn't lost on me.

Noah swallowed, his Adam's apple bobbing hard in his throat before he released me, offering my hand to Anthony like I was some sort of prize. "Of course not. She is your bride-to-be, after all." He looked at me with those words, and I felt those eyes like the hot blade of a knife. "Thank you for the dance, Ruby Grace."

Without another word, he dropped my hand, tipped his hat at Anthony, and walked calmly off the dance floor.

A flurry of girls chased after him — ones who'd been watching us dance from the sidelines — and when he granted one of them her wish of completing the dance with him, my stomach twisted.

Daphne McCormick.

No one could keep a secret in this town — and it was *far* from a secret that Daphne and Noah had hooked up a few times, that she had had him in her bed more consecutive nights than any other woman in town could say. And the way her long fingers curled around his bicep possessively as she dragged him back to the dance floor, she knew it.

His smile was tight as he took her in his arms, but then she said something to make him laugh — *really* laugh — and seconds later, he was spinning her around the same way he had me.

I tore my eyes away, ignoring the sinking in my stomach and smiling at Anthony as he wrapped me in his arms. I started to waltz, but Anthony's face screwed up in confusion before he slowed us into a gentle sway like the rest of the patrons.

Except for Noah and Daphne.

"What's up with that Noah guy, anyway?" Anthony asked, noticing that my gaze had shifted again.

I snapped my attention to him, frowning in confusion. "What do you mean?"

"Did you two used to date or something?" He was eyeing Noah menacingly, like he could somehow squash him like a bug with that look.

"Of course not," I assured him, shaking my head. "We're just friends."

"Friends," Anthony murmured, watching Noah a long moment before he turned his gaze to me. "Before, he was just the guy who showed you the barrel. Now you're best buds."

"Don't be like that," I said, voice low. "I'm *yours*, okay?" I held up my hand with the Harry Winston diamond on it to prove my point. "Yours. No one else's."

Anthony let out a long breath, nodding as a smile bloomed on his face. "I'm sorry. I guess you just bring out the possessive side in me."

I smiled at that. "Guess that means you like me, huh?"

Anthony kissed me long and slow, stopping our dance altogether so he could frame my face.

And somewhere across the room, I felt another pair of eyes on me.

Later that night, when we were back at my parents' house, Anthony strengthened a kiss between us, turning that sweet and romantic one from the dance floor into one heated with passion. He peppered my neck with hot, sucking kisses, his hands roaming, breath picking up speed in the hallway outside my bedroom.

"Anthony…" I sighed, pressing my hands into his chest to stop his advances. "I think we should wait."

"Wait?" he asked, one brow cocking. "I took your virginity a month after we met, Ruby Grace. I think we're past waiting."

He moved in again, and though I chuckled, I felt a shade of embarrassment leak into my gut at his words. "I mean that we're sleeping in my parents' house, and we get married in five weeks." I shrugged, running my finger over his chest. "I don't know, it might be kind of fun to pretend. Go the traditional route. Wait until our wedding night."

Anthony's face screwed up like he thought that was the most ridiculous thing he'd ever heard, but as his eyes searched mine, he blew out a long sigh, dropping his forehead to my shoulder with a groan. "Fine."

I chuckled, patting his head like he was a child.

"I'd do anything for you," he said, lifting his head. He ran the pad of his thumb over my chin, pulling me in for a long, sweet kiss. "And you're worth the wait."

I swallowed, smiling through the unfamiliar discomfort I felt. He was my fiancé, I used to squirm under his touch, anticipating more.

Now, I wanted to crawl out of my skin.

"Thank you," I whispered, kissing him again, this time with my hands in his hair and pulling him closer. I wanted to erase the discomfort, convince myself it was just pre-wedding jitters, or the overstimulation of the day.

*I love him*, I told myself as we kissed. And I knew it was true.

I just couldn't place the *other* emotion that I felt.

"Okay, okay," he said, breaking our kiss and smacking my butt playfully. "Stop kissing me like that if you're not going to put out, little lady."

I giggled, pecking his cheek once more before I let him go. "I'm going to take a shower and get some sleep. See you at breakfast in the morning?"

"See you then. And, hey," he said, sweeping my hair from my face. "You were wonderful tonight. I'm so lucky to have a woman like you standing behind me."

My throat tightened again at the phrasing he used. I knew what he meant, that I was by his side, his partner in crime — but the thought of me only standing *behind* him made my stomach turn.

And Noah's words popped into my mind.

I smiled, running my hand over his arm until I held his hand in mind. I squeezed it once, excusing myself in the next breath and escaping to my bedroom.

As I showered and got ready for bed, I tried to decompress from the night. I ran through everything I loved about it, and chose to acknowledge the things I didn't love so much without judging them. I let those thoughts pass almost like clouds in the sky, touching each of them before I let them pass without another thought.

I had a tendency to overthink, and I knew in my heart that was what was happening now. I still loved Anthony. I still wanted to marry him. I still wanted to be the woman next to him when he was sworn into office as State Representative, and one day, as the President of the United States.

This was the life I wanted. This was the life I was always meant to live.

I crawled into bed with a renewed sense of ease and excitement for the weekend. I had wedding planning to do, and Anthony would be there with me. I wasn't alone anymore, and I took comfort in that as my eyelids grew heavy, the gentle breeze outside lulling me into a peaceful sleep.

Until around three in the morning, when I woke from a dream with a sheen of sweat on my forehead and Noah Becker's name on my lips.

# Chapter Ten

## NOAH

The next night, my brothers and I sat on Mom's porch, drinking beer and decompressing from work while Mom made her famous pork chops inside. She had Fleetwood Mac's *Rumors* album blasting as she sang and danced along, moving around the kitchen, occasionally popping outside to see if any of us needed another beer. Family dinner night was always the happiest I saw Mom. It was when she had all her boys home, a meal to cook, a purpose.

I kicked back in one of the rocking chairs on the porch, one boot propped on the porch railing as I cracked open a new beer. I was still dirty from raising barrels all day, my muscles aching from the additional lifting I'd done loading up the single barrels the night before into buyer vehicles after the Soirée.

The sun was beginning its slow descent over our sleepy Tennessee town, casting Mom's small garden in an evening glow as I took in the sight of my brothers. Jordan was still in his coaching gear, fresh off a day of summer training with Stratford High's football team hopefuls. Logan wore his Scooter Whiskey tour guide polo and faded denim jeans, his face as worn as mine from working the night before at the Soirée and then an entire Friday shift, too. And though Mikey didn't have to work the Soirée, he had still been there all night, dancing with Bailey before having to report for an all-day shift at the Scooter Whiskey gift shop.

It'd been a long Friday for all of us, and the normally rowdy Becker brothers were almost completely silent as we watched the sun set, sipping on our beers, rocking in our chairs, just existing together. We'd talk for a little bit before falling silent again, until someone else felt enough energy to pipe up.

"The boys looked good out on the field today when I drove by," Logan commented to Jordan.

My older brother nodded. "Glad that's what you saw. It was a mess from where I was standing."

I chuckled. "You say that every year, and then you make it to state or damn near."

He humphed. "Sometimes we get lucky. Sometimes we don't."

"Luck has nothing to do with it," Logan said. "A hard-working team and the best coach in Tennessee does, though."

"We lost half of that hard-working team when this year's seniors graduated," Jordan pointed out.

"I wish Dad was here."

The words came from Mikey, who had been silent up until that point, and they sliced through the quiet evening like the screeching tires of a car seconds away from slamming into a tree. Every single one of us paused where we were rocking in our chairs or taking a sip of our beers, a heavy silence falling over the entire family like a weighted fog.

Jordan cleared his throat first, clamping a hand on Mikey's shoulder with an understanding, soft smile. "We all do, buddy."

Mikey nodded, working the tab on his root beer back and forth before it broke off and he dropped it inside the can. "I think it's different for me, though."

"Why do you think that?" Logan asked.

Mikey shrugged. "Because I was only eight when he died. You guys were all older, teenagers, at least. You had all this time with him." His voice faded, eyes still on his can. "He won't be at my graduation."

Logan and I exchanged a glance, then, realizing why the topic had been brought up. Mikey was seventeen, heading into his senior year — and Jordan had just mentioned graduation. I remembered that time of my life so well — the excitement of being at the top of the school, of finally finishing, mixed with the worry of what would happen next, where life would take me.

I had so many questions when I was that age — a teenager, becoming a new adult.

And I had Dad to answer them.

So did Jordan.

So did Logan, though Dad died just weeks after his graduation.

We'd all had him there, and once again, Mikey was left out of that equation.

"We'll be there," I finally said to Mikey, breaking the silence. "Mom, too. And Dad *will* be there, even if you can't see him."

Mikey sighed. "It's not the same."

"It's not," Jordan agreed. "And it's okay to be sad that he's not here anymore. We all have days. We will for the rest of our lives. He was our father."

He paused at that, swallowing hard, and I could see it in his eyes, that sad truth like a ghost in his pupils. He *was* Jordan's father — no matter what anyone in the town had to say about it. But, I still knew he wondered who his *biological* one was.

I wondered if any of us would ever know.

"It happens to me more in the small moments than the big ones," Logan chimed in, finger tapping on the koozie wrapped around his beer can. "Like, I didn't really think about him when I got the tour guide job at such a young age. But, when I'm fishing out at the lake, or when I catch a whiff of cologne that smells like the one he used to wear... that's when it hits me. That's when I have that *I wish he was here* moment."

My stomach twisted. "For me, it's always when I dance with Mom."

We all glanced over our shoulders and inside the house, watching Mom bop around the kitchen with a soft smile on her face.

"I can take your turn tonight," Logan offered. "If you want."

I shook my head. "Nah, I don't mind missing him, or thinking about him." I shrugged. "Like Jordan said, it's just become a permanent part of my life now."

We were all silent for a long moment, facing the garden again, sipping from our drinks.

"I think it's the unresolved part of it all that gets to me most," Mikey said after a while. "Do you think Mom will ever stop looking for answers?"

None of us responded. None of us had to. We all knew she'd never stop asking, stop looking for holes in the reports, for foul play at the distillery. No matter how many years passed, she would never believe that fire was started by a cigarette.

"Hey, how was Nashville with Bailey?" Logan asked, effectively changing the subject.

Mikey seemed a little hesitant to let the topic of Dad go, but after a moment, a grin spread across his face, his eyes sparking with the kind of love-sick look only Bailey brought out in him. "It was so crazy. Seeing her on stage, the crowds going wild for her?" Mikey shook his head. "I'll never forget it. She told the label she wants to finish high school, but that she'll sign the contract as soon as we walk across the stage. Can you believe that?" He just kept shaking his head. "She's going to do it. She's going to be the next country music star. A hometown girl from Stratford, Tennessee."

"And are you ready for all that comes with that?" I asked.

"As long as I'm with her, I'm ready for anything."

I opened my mouth to point out every flaw I saw in this potential plan, starting with the fact that Bailey's entire life would change when she signed that contract, but Jordan locked eyes with me, shaking his head almost imperceptibly to warn me off the subject. It didn't matter right now, and just because I was a pessimist didn't mean I had to drag my little brother down with me.

He had hope. And love. And a bright-eyed view of what the world could be for him.

I just hoped he could keep all of it.

"The Soirée was fun last night," Logan said, changing the subject yet again. One thick eyebrow ticked up as he appraised me. "Seemed like you found yourself in some drama, big bro."

Jordan narrowed his eyes. "What drama?"

"My thoughts exactly," I said to Jordan before giving Logan an incredulous look. "I showed up and did my job just like I do every year."

"You also ticked off the future State Representative of North Carolina," Logan shot.

I scoffed, draining the last of my beer before slamming the empty can on the table between us. "That guy's a douche. And I was nothing but polite to him, even though he didn't deserve it. I treated him just like all the other buyer's."

"Did you dance with all the other buyer's *fiancé's*, too?"

Logan waggled his brows, and I glared at him before thumping his arm.

"Ah," Mikey said, a shit-eating grin spreading on his face. "Ruby Grace's fiancé is in town, huh? Does he know about that close call you two had on your front porch after poker last weekend?"

"Shut it, Mikey," I warned, at the same time Jordan asked, "What close call?"

"Did you kiss her?" Logan asked immediately after, a grin sliding over his face. "You sly dog. You kissed her, didn't you?"

"I didn't kiss her," I growled, letting my feet drop off the porch railing and onto the wood below my chair.

"But you *wanted* to," Mikey said. "I saw you two. If I hadn't shown up with that root beer float, there would have been some lip lock action and you know it."

Logan and Mikey chuckled. Jordan just watched me, waiting. I leaned forward, elbows balanced on my knees as I tried to school my breaths, tried to think of anything I could say to get them off my back, but I knew it was useless.

I could deny it all day long, but these were my brothers. They'd see right through me.

I shook my head, letting it hang between my shoulders a moment before I lifted it again, eyes scanning the fading sun over Mom's yard. "Yeah, okay. Maybe I did want to kiss her."

"I knew it," Mikey chimed.

"But I didn't," I pointed out again, glaring at my youngest brother before I acknowledged the other two. "And it doesn't matter anyway, because she's getting married in less than five weeks."

"If she's so set on marrying that guy, why has she been spending so much time with you?" Mikey asked.

I shrugged, eyes falling to the porch. "I don't think she actually *does* want to marry him, to be honest. She's young, under pressure from her family. From what I know about her, this isn't the life she wants at all. But I think she feels... stuck."

Logan frowned. "That's sad."

I nodded. "It is. You know, when I first met her, I thought she was just another prissy, privileged rich girl. But she's so much more than what her family portrays her as. She's smart, and caring, and funny. She volunteers down at the nursing home, did you know that?" I shook my head. "That whole place lights up when she's there. And she had dreams of finishing college, going into AmeriCorps. But she's dropping out of school to be Mr. Asshole's wife — all because that's what she's expected to do."

My brothers were quiet for a long moment before Mikey spoke again. "I've never seen you like this before. You usually have girls lined up who want your attention, and you can never be bothered."

"Not for more than a one-night stand, anyway,"

Logan chuffed.

Mikey grinned, but it slipped when he faced me again. "You really like her, don't you?"

My stomach clenched, and I wished I hadn't drained my beer. I needed something to do, something to hold or drink or *anything* to keep my hands from tightening into anxious fists.

I couldn't answer that question.

I guessed I didn't really have to.

"Of course, she's under pressure from her family. She's a Barnett," Jordan reminded me after a long pause, as if that was a fact I could ever forget. "And that's even more reason for you to stay away from her."

"I disagree."

We all looked at Logan, then, who was never one to speak out against Jordan.

"I'm just saying, if there's something between you two, maybe she needs more time to see what you already see — that she's making a mistake. If you were around her more, showing her what it could be like if she was with someone who really gave a shit about her, someone who cared what *her* dreams were..." Logan shrugged. "I don't know. Maybe you could save her from making a mistake."

"That's not his job to do," Jordan fired back.

"Isn't it?" Logan kicked back in his chair, leveling eyes with our oldest brother. "We're Beckers. We always stand up for what's right. And Ruby Grace being auctioned off like an eighteenth-century bride isn't right. Her marrying someone she doesn't want to isn't right. And if Noah can stop her, if he can show her something more?" Logan looked at me, then. "I say, why not?"

"Because it's wrong," Jordan chimed in again before I could answer. "She's engaged to someone else. Whether she made that decision the right way or not is not Noah's or anyone else's business. As long as she has that ring on her finger, she's off limits."

"They could just be friends."

It was Mikey who spoke, then, and we all turned to him as he shrank under our gazes.

"I mean, I'm just saying, you don't have to do anything inappropriate," he clarified. "Just be there for her. Give her someone to talk to, someone to work through what she's feeling with."

We were all silent at that, and I mulled it over, tossing the thought around in my mind like a poker chip between my fingers. Ruby Grace and I hadn't crossed any lines, we hadn't done anything that she needed to feel guilty about. I didn't want to leave her alone. I missed her. And I wanted to be around her — in whatever way I could be.

But could I *just* be her friend?

It seemed impossible, knowing the way I felt about her now, the way I couldn't stop thinking of her, the way my blood boiled when I imagined that douchebag going home to her at night, putting his hands on her, touching her, kissing her.

My fists tightened.

"You'll just get yourself hurt," Jordan said after a while. "If you're her friend, if you're *more* than that — regardless, she's marrying that guy this summer. And the closer you get to her, the more that is going to gut you in the end."

"He's probably right," Logan agreed.

My heart sank, realizing how futile it all was.

"But," Logan continued. "I'm just saying, I know I wouldn't want to give up on it without knowing I tried. I'd rather be fucked up in the end and know I tried to get the girl than to just let her go without ever showing her what her options are."

Mikey nodded. "Same. I know I couldn't walk away from Bailey, even if there was another guy in the picture. She's the kind of girl you fight for. And it seems like Ruby Grace is, too."

Jordan stood, throwing his hands up. "Do what you want, Noah. But just know I don't approve of this. She's nearly a decade younger than you, she's the Mayor's daughter, and she's engaged. If you won't hit the brakes with all those road blocks in your view, then don't be surprised when you crash at the end of it all."

He walked inside, the screen door slamming shut behind him as he joined Mom in the kitchen. When he was gone, Logan and Mikey watched me carefully, both chewing the inside of their cheeks.

"This is idiotic," I finally said.

"Completely," Logan agreed.

"Jordan's right. I'll probably just end up even more messed up than I am now."

Mikey nodded. "Most likely."

I sighed, head bobbing between my shoulders as I ran over all the reasons I should stay away from Ruby Grace, all the reasons I should walk away and wish her luck and forget she ever came back to town at all. I ticked off each warning sign like a mental checklist, but while my chest should have been tight with dread, it was floating on the smallest ounce of hope.

I knew Logan was right.

I couldn't walk away from her. Not without fighting for her first.

I let out another long breath, eyeing Mikey before my gaze landed on Logan. "Will you help me make a plan?"

# Chapter Eleven

## RUBY GRACE

The weekend passed in a blur of chiffon and cake frosting.

Mama packed every waking minute of my days with dress alterations, cake tasting, seating chart adjustments, wedding photography pose research, and more. By the time I made it to church Sunday morning, I was so thankful for an hour of sitting down with nothing to do but listen to the preacher, that I nearly started crying.

When I saw Noah walk through the door, that urge to cry doubled.

I'd been so busy over the weekend, I hadn't had much time to think about anything other than whatever wedding task was at hand. Still, when my mind *did* wander, it frustratingly wandered to those cobalt blue eyes.

Noah took his usual seat in the front row of the left pew section, alongside his mother and three brothers. I was still fixated on the back of his head when Anthony's hand reached over, squeezing my knee over the turquoise fabric of my dress.

"I'm so excited to spend the day with you," he whispered, leaning in close.

I frowned, turning toward him. "I'm volunteering at the nursing home today. Remember?"

"Oh," he said, confirming that he, in fact, did *not* remember. "Can't you just cancel?"

"Anthony, you know how important this is to me."

Disappointment sank into my every feature. I'd been telling Anthony all weekend that I had plans after church, just like I did every Sunday, and it was like he'd listened the way a child does to its mother.

"I know, babe. I know," he said quickly, squeezing where he held my knee. "I'm sorry. I just miss you. I've been here a week now and we've barely spent any time together."

My neck heated, because I was *very* aware of the fact I hadn't seen him much. Anthony conveniently had something to do with the media crew anytime Mama came running at me with a wedding task. He hadn't helped with a single thing since he'd been in town, and if anything, I felt *more* pressure with him here.

Pressure to make the wedding perfect. Pressure to be available to him when he needed me.

Pressure to be everywhere and everything to everyone.

"Why don't you help me register for our gifts on Thursday?" I asked. "We could spend the whole day together, pick out our future serving dishes and napkin holders." I leaned into him on a nudge. "You know, super thrilling stuff."

Anthony smiled, running the back of his knuckles over my cheek. "You know I wish I could, but we're going to shoot a little *around the town* short to air on our YouTube channel that day. I was actually hoping you'd be a part of it, if you have time?"

I sighed, fighting off the sinking of my heart. This was Anthony's life. This was how he'd always been, ever since I met him. He was dedicated to his dream, to his passion to hold office. It was something I loved about him, and I didn't know why I was suddenly annoyed by it just because he couldn't help with stupid wedding stuff.

In four weeks, we'd be married, and none of this stuff would matter, anyway.

"I understand. I have to get that registration done, but when it's over, I'll give you a call and see if I can come help out," I offered.

Anthony smiled wider, shaking his head before he leaned in and pressed his lips to my forehead. "I'm such a lucky man."

We were quiet as the service got started, and I reveled in the peaceful bliss of not needing to answer to anyone or be anywhere. If anything, the service didn't last long enough, and before I knew it, we were outside the church, Mama shaking hands and sending blessings with everyone as they left. Anthony joined in beside her and Dad, and I pulled up the end of the line, a numb smile on my face.

I was so fixated on counting down the minutes until I'd be away from everyone and in my safe place that I almost didn't notice when Noah Becker darted away from the receiving line, kissing his mother on the cheek before he climbed into his truck without so much of a look over his shoulder at me. Not that he owed me a look, or a handshake, or a Sunday greeting. But, we hadn't spoken a single word to each other since the Soirée, and part of me wondered if he'd ever speak to me again.

Part of me wondered why I cared if he did or not.

His truck peeled out of the church parking lot as Anthony put his arm around me, pressing a kiss into my hair.

"Are you *sure* I can't convince you to ditch on the nursing home?" he asked.

I tried my best to smile, turning in his arms to thread mine around his neck. "I'll see you for supper."

"It's my only free day," he pointed out again.

"I understand that. But *I'm* not free."

"But you *could* be."

My shoulders sagged. "Anthony..."

"I'm kidding, I'm kidding," he said, kissing my forehead again before steering us toward Daddy's truck. "I'll find something to do, maybe go check out the casino with your dad or something. He's been begging me to go."

I smiled as much as I could, aiming for lightness in my voice. "Well, that's not at all surprising. Hope you're ready to lose all of your Sunday in that dungeon of bells and flashing lights."

Anthony held the back door of Dad's truck open for me, closing it gently once I was inside.

In that moment of silence, I took my first real breath in days.

I couldn't wait to get home, get changed, and get away.

"You look like hell," Annie greeted, still somehow cheerful even with the insult flying from her lips.

"Happy Sunday to you, too," I replied on a chuckle. I flopped down into the chair next to her, sighing as the cushion gave into my weight in a familiar, soft *whoosh*. "Can I just... can I just nap right here?"

Annie snickered. "Mama Barnett pushing you that hard, huh?"

"You were there for the seating arrangement fiasco," I reminded her, referring to our Friday morning spent with my mom. "Now, just imagine that same frenzy... All. Weekend. Long."

She cringed, sliding her coffee toward me. "Here. You need this more than I do."

I took the hot mug gratefully, tilting it toward her in thanks before taking a sip. I hummed as the mocha-flavored magic made its way into my stomach, reaching forward to flip through the events calendar for the day. I'd only been inside the building for five minutes and I already felt my muscles relaxing, the tension leaving that spot between my eyebrows, my breaths coming easier. These walls and the people who lived within them were comfortable to me, safe, familiar. It was the one steady thing in my currently chaotic life.

"Everyone already at the pool?" I asked, noting that water aerobics had been added to the schedule for the day.

"Mm-hmm," Annie said, biting against a smile.

"Betty having a good day?"

"Oh, she's having the *best* day," Annie said, still with the weird smile.

I cocked a brow.

"She's out there with our newest volunteer — hell, the entire nursing home is out there. No one has been able to teach water aerobics since the summer started, so it was a welcome surprise for us to have some help."

"I could have done water aerobics," I offered.

"You still can," Annie said. "I'm sure the new guy would love the help. Those old ladies were practically ripping his swim trunks off when he made his way through the halls to the pool. I swear, in the five years I've worked here, I've never seen Mrs. Hollenbeck go swimming. Until today."

I frowned. "Interesting. We haven't had any new volunteers in a while, either — aside from those completing community service. Who is this guy?"

Annie's grin widened. "Oh, you know him."

My best friend had that look in her eyes, the one she used to get when she was about to ask me for a huge favor or to go to a party I didn't want to go to.

"Annie…" I warned. "Who is it?"

She just did a little shoulder dance, fishing one of the volunteer pool keys out of the desk and tossing it my way. "Why don't you go find out?"

I frowned deeper, clutching the key in hand as I stood. "You're a brat."

"You love me, anyway."

"Debatable."

She was still chuckling as I made my way down the hall to the bathroom, changing into the swim suit I'd brought with me. For some reason, my stomach was fluttery as I changed, mind swirling with the possibilities of who it could be. I wondered if it was Tanner, the guy I'd dated sophomore year. Or maybe Annie was joking about the guy being hot. Maybe it was someone weird, like the scrawny, perverted kid who delivered newspapers and always liked to stare a little too long into the windows of whichever girl didn't leave their curtains drawn enough.

My heart thumped even harder when I realized Anthony had left to go to the casino with Dad before I left for the nursing home. Dad hadn't even left yet, saying he had a few stops to make along the way and he'd meet him at the main bar.

*Maybe it's him. Maybe he's surprising me.*

I couldn't fight back my smile at the thought. It was a classic Anthony move, to surprise me and make a show of himself in the process. He loved to be the center of attention, and I knew him volunteering at a nursing home on a Sunday would be candy for the film crew.

With that thought in mind, I practically skipped to the pool, ditching my backpack at the front desk on my way out. Annie was still smiling like a loon, and I thought I finally understood why. She was in on the whole thing, the whole surprise.

But when I scanned my key card at the pool gate and flung it open, I stopped dead in my tracks, the smile sliding off my face like a limp noodle off a wall.

Noah Becker stood in the shallow end of the pool, leading a group of women and one brave man in a charade of water aerobics to an old 70's disco song.

His smile was blinding, hair wet and glistening in the sun as he pumped his arms and legs to the music. He shouted out instructions, laughing at all the women who were attempting to follow and giggling like a bunch of school girls in the process.

Betty was front row.

Noah threw his head back on one particularly loud laugh, elicited by something Betty had said that I couldn't hear, and when he was facing her again, his eyes flicked up to me.

Everything muted in that moment — the splash of the water, the bass of the music, the laughter of the women and the men lined up on the sides watching them. Noah watched me for what felt like an eternity — but was actually only a second — before he smiled.

That smile turned my knees to putty.

"Alright, take a break, ladies. Grab water, lather on some sunscreen, and meet me back here in fifteen."

Everyone let out various sounds of disappointment as Noah climbed out of the water, turning the music down on the pool stereo and swiping a towel off the back of one of the lounge chairs before he jogged over to me.

It was like a stupid scene out of a *Baywatch* episode, the way his pecs bounced as he ran, the water dripping slowly down every lean, toned, tanned muscle of his body. He shook the water out of his short hair right before he reached me, and when he did, his grin doubled.

"Hey there, Legs."

"Noah," I seethed, crossing my arms and ignoring his attempt at an adorable nickname. "*What* are you doing here?"

He just smiled wider, toweling his hair and a little of his abdomen before hanging the towel over his shoulders. He held it at each end, letting his arms hang in a way that accented his biceps.

Asshole.

"I volunteer here," he offered innocently.

I narrowed my eyes.

At that, Noah barked out a laugh, the hands holding his towel lifting as he shrugged. "Look, I came here to call a truce."

"I didn't realize we were at war."

"Oh, didn't you?" he countered, one thick eyebrow climbing.

I didn't respond, just shifted weight onto my other hip, keeping my arms crossed as I waited for him to continue.

"I know I crossed some lines, and I know I said some things that upset you."

"You already apologized for that."

"And clearly, all is forgiven," he shot back, still eyeing me with a cocked brow. "Would you just let me talk, Miss Stubborn?"

I pursed my lips. "I liked *Legs* better."

Noah chuckled, taking a step toward me, and the way his smile was shadowed with sincerity as he spoke his next words softened my heart. "I like having you as a friend, Ruby Grace."

I swallowed, eyes searching his as the sun above danced in the ocean blue waters of his pupils.

"I have to admit, my life was pretty boring before you showed up. It was work and family dinner and cards with my brothers and some random girl in my bed Saturday night. Wash, rinse, repeat."

I tried not to be affected by the mention of a woman in his bed. I had no right to be, but it still made my neck hot at the thought. I wondered if he'd taken Daphne home after the Soirée, and as soon as I thought it, my chest tightened painfully.

"I have fun with you," he said on a shrug. "And I think you have fun with me, too. I know you're not in town much longer, so what if we just... put all the bickering and bullshit behind us and be friends?"

"Friends," I deadpanned.

The corner of Noah's mouth lifted. "Yes. Friends. As in, let's volunteer together, and maybe hang out when you're free." He shrugged. "I can help you with wedding shit, take some of the pressure off. I'll even put up with your crazy mother and whatever task she needs handled."

A breath of a laugh escaped me at that, and I watched Noah carefully, looking for some sign of crossed fingers or a trick that I wasn't seeing. "You'd do that?"

"I'd do just about anything for you, it seems."

I smirked, chest fluttering at the mixture of excitement and warning blending in my gut. Part of me knew it was better to stay away from Noah Becker — especially with how much he'd been on my mind. I knew I had a crush on him, some sort of feelings that were beyond the friend zone he was proposing.

But the bigger part of me? She didn't care.

The bigger part of me felt the same way Noah did. I had fun with him. I liked being around him.

I missed him.

So, against every nerve in my body that warned me not to, I sighed, extending one hand toward him.

"Fine. Friends."

Noah glanced at my hand, a wicked smile on his face as he took it in his and gave it a firm, mock handshake with a serious business look on his face. "Friends."

"On one condition."

"And that is?"

I cringed. "We can't let my mom find out."

Noah full-on belly laughed at that. "What, Princess Barnett can't be seen with a Becker ruffian?"

"Not when the whole town has been whispering about us and it's been making its way back to my dad... and therefore, my mom."

Noah nodded. "Fair enough. An on-the-low friendship, it is."

He was still staring at me like he'd won some sort of prize when I rolled my eyes and shoved him back toward the pool. "Stop looking at me all goofy and get back in that water before these women lose their damn minds."

Noah laughed, wrapping his hands around my wrists where I was pushing against his chest. "Fine. But you're coming with me."

I blanched. "Noah... don't you dare."

In the next second, I was tossed over his shoulder like a bag of sugar, and he ran, jumping into the deep end with a splash that earned us applause from the entire nursing home once we emerged.

I swatted at him, splashing water in his face as he laughed at me catching my breath. As much as I wanted to, I couldn't even pretend to be annoyed. I laughed, too, tossing my head back and letting the sun warm my face.

And for the first time all weekend, I was happy.

# Chapter Twelve

**NOAH**

I didn't know if my plan was working, or if I was just setting myself up for a massive fail.

Logan had high-fived me when all of my brothers and I got together to play cards at my place Sunday night. I told him how it went at the nursing home, how Ruby Grace had agreed to be friends, to let me help her with the wedding, and how we'd spent the entire afternoon together.

I had to admit, at the time I high-fived my little brother and simultaneously got a glare from my older one, I was on a high. It'd been easier than I thought to get her to agree to still spend time with me — even with her fiancé in town — and I'd spent an entire afternoon with her. Even better, I'd spent an entire afternoon with her *in her element*. She thrived at that nursing home, and everyone there loved her. They could tell she was different. She cared. She gave a shit.

I was convinced that people like her made up not even one percent of the entire population. She was just too good, too kind, too giving. It was like she'd strip herself bare if it meant she could shelter even one other person.

So, yes, that first night had felt great.

But now, five days later, I was beginning to wonder if I was the biggest idiot to ever exist.

On Monday, I worked all day at the distillery and then met Ruby Grace for dinner. Her mother had tasked her with booking the rehearsal dinner venue, and Ruby Grace looked like she was about to have a complete meltdown trying to decide on a place that would fit and please everyone.

Then, on Tuesday, I'd been half asleep on my couch after a long day at work when she called me and asked if she could come over. She showed up with chalkboard signs in hand and an apologetic shrug. We stayed up until almost one in the morning making *welcome* signs and *seat yourself* signs and *cocktail hour this way* signs and *gifts here* signs. Chalk dust clouded my living room by the end of the night, but hugging a sleepy Ruby Grace goodbye on my front porch made up for it.

I'd thought I'd be relieved to hear I wouldn't see her Wednesday, but instead, I was gutted when I saw her at the nicest restaurant in town on my walk home from the gym — seated next to Anthony in a cozy little booth, him feeding her a fork full of decadent dessert while she giggled and the cameras around them flashed.

And now it was Thursday, and here I was, circling yet another rack of expensive dinnerware at some fancy department store I couldn't pronounce the name of. I had a register gun in my hand, a fake smile on my face, and a knack for pretending like I had any shot in hell of waking up the girl holding the gun next to me and convincing her she was making the wrong choice.

The gun beeped in my hand each time I scanned a potential gift, and it was like those beeps were tied to my frustration.

Sure, I'd played in the pool with her all day long on Sunday, but she'd gone home to him.

*Beep.*

And sure, it'd been me who helped her with the signs, with the rehearsal dinner, but it'd been him who got to kiss chocolate off her lips.

*Beep.*

And fucking *sure*, she told me over and over how much she appreciated me being here with her today, told me how much it upset her that Anthony hadn't been able to make it, told me how much it meant to her that she didn't have to do it alone.

But it would be *him* she'd tell she loved in less than four weeks. It would be him she'd vow to love forever, that she'd promise to be faithful to, that she'd build a life with.

And I would still be here.

The friend.

The fool.

*Beep-beep-beep.*

"You okay over there?" Ruby Grace asked, smirking at my aggressive scanning.

I blew out a breath, cracking my neck before I resumed a more casual pace. "Just wondering why one couple needs so many plates and bowls, I guess."

Ruby Grace mirrored my sigh at that, holding up the gun to scan a set of wine glasses. "Honestly, I thought this would be my favorite part. I've always imagined hosting dinner parties the way Mama does, entertaining a house full of guests, making a four-course dinner and custom cocktails." Her hand dropped, the gun loose between her fingertips. "Now, I just wish I could fast-forward a few weeks and have it all over with."

I watched her for a long moment, a sickening wave of nausea settling in at her words.

Weeks.

I had *weeks*, and only a few of them, to show this girl what her life could be if she'd only open her eyes.

Ruby Grace went back to scanning, running her fingertips along some tablecloth fabric before checking the price tag and giving it a scan.

*Beep.*

The farther she walked away from me, the more urgency I felt. And before I could think better of it, I rounded the other side of the table she was circling, meeting her in the middle.

"Let me take you on a date."

She nearly ran into me, and when my words spilled into the atmosphere, they might as well have been hands shoving her backward. She stumbled a bit, and I reached out, my hand finding the small of her back and steadying her before she crashed into a rack of crystalware.

Her eyes were big, golden suns as they flicked between mine, her plump ruby lips popping open, closing again, popping open, closing.

"Uh..." she finally managed.

My brain snapped into damage-control mode. "A friend date."

At that, one of her manicured eyebrows rose, the corner of her lips curving into an amused smile. "A friend date," she repeated.

"Look at you," I said, stepping back as if to hammer home the fact that I had completely innocent intentions.

Even if that was a lie.

"You're so stressed out with all the wedding planning. It's been consuming your every waking minute of every single day. Hell, I've only been helping for a few days and even *I* am overwhelmed."

"I'm okay," she insisted. "A little tired, I admit. But, this is all part of the process."

"Ruby Grace, you can't even make a decision on which stupid plates you want." I held up the gun, clicking through a few screens until I could see everything we'd scanned. "As of now, if everything on this registry is purchased, you'll have two-hundred-and-seventy-three of them. And I'm pretty sure you don't plan on hosting any parties *that* big."

Her face screwed up like she was certain I couldn't possibly be right. She snagged the gun out of my hand, studying the screen before she let out a long sigh, pressing one of her delicate hands to her forehead. She held it there for a moment before dragging it over her face on a groan.

"Okay. You win."

I smiled. "My favorite words to hear."

Ruby Grace shoved my gun back into my chest. "The problem is *when* are we going to go anywhere or do anything when I have so much to get done?"

"That's easy. We go now."

"*Now?!*" She gaped. "We still have so much to register. We have two more floors to cover."

"So?" I shrugged. "We'll get it done. We have time."

"My bridal shower is next Saturday. And the wedding is in less than four weeks."

I huffed, dropping my gun on an empty part of the table next to us before I grabbed her upper arms in my hands. "Ruby Grace, there is nothing that needs to be done in this moment. Everything will be okay. Everything will get done — and in time. I promise."

"But I can't go anywhere right now. I'm not dressed for anything, unless we're registering for wedding gifts at a department store or going to church," she pointed out, gesturing to her knee-length sun dress and wedges.

"That's half the fun. We'll figure out what we want to do and then buy the clothes we need to do it."

"But—"

"You are spreading yourself so thin, you're going to disappear completely by the time your wedding day gets here if you don't take a moment to just *live* a little."

Her little bottom lip poked out at that, and I had to fight against the urge to pull her into me, frame that beautiful face, suck that lip between my teeth...

"You're tired. You need a break. We *both* do." I paused, searching her worried gaze. "Trust me?"

"No."

I laughed. "Liar."

She smiled a little at that, and then let out another long breath, her little shoulders giving way with it. "Okay. I trust you."

My heart did a little flip at that victory. "Good."

"But... Noah?"

"Yeah?"

"Before we go, we have to at least eliminate these plates down to less than one hundred."

She held up her gun, cringing at the screen.

I chuckled, swiping my gun off the table and spinning it in my hand a few times before tucking it in the band of my jeans like a cowboy. "Lead the way, Bonnie."

"Does that make you Clyde?"

"Of course."

"You know that story didn't end very well, right?"

I smirked, stepping into her space and lowering my voice so only she could hear. "I guess we'll have to re-write an ending of our own."

I stood there a little too close, a little too long, eyes falling to her lips for the tiniest second before I caught her gaze again. And she didn't say a word, didn't swallow or step back. She just stood there, staring back at me, letting those words linger in the space between.

She still hadn't taken a breath when I finally walked away.

## RUBY GRACE

"No."

I crossed my arms, covering the new bathing suit top Noah had purchased me at the lake shop for our spontaneous "friend date." It was all I wore — that new swim suit — but Noah was sitting on a beast of a machine, holding up a lifejacket he wanted me to put on over it.

"Come on," he said on a laugh, holding up the bright pink jacket again. "You're wasting daylight, and I have more planned for this friend date."

"I'm not getting on that thing."

"It's a jet ski," he reminded me.

"I know what it is, and I'm not getting on it." I crossed my arms harder.

"It's just like riding a horse."

"No," I argued, eyeing the beast. "On Tank, I knew you wouldn't purposefully throw me off or do donuts or go sixty miles per hour."

"It tops out at forty-five."

I gave him a flat stare.

"Fine," he said on another laugh. "I'll keep it under twenty until you're comfortable. And trust me, by the end of the day, you'll be begging me to let *you* drive. It's fun. And it's safe. Wear the life jacket and pay attention to other vessels on the water. It's that simple."

I blew out a breath through my flat lips, making the same noise Tank made the night I met him as I stared at Noah, debating. It was a beautiful summer day, the sun high in the sky and beating down on my shoulders as a cool breeze drifted lazily over the blue water of Lake Stratford. It was only a half hour outside of town, and a resident favorite getaway — especially in the summer. Other boaters and jet skiers were already out enjoying the water, sunbathers lining the beach, fishermen dotting the rocky shores.

When I finally uncrossed my arms and swiped the life jacket out of Noah's hands, a victorious grin spread on his face.

"You better not try to throw me off this thing, Noah Becker, or so help me."

He laughed, scooting up on the jet ski as I fastened the belts of the jacket around my waist. When I was all buckled in, I hopped on behind him, the tops of my thighs lining up with the backs of his, my chest to his back — which was bare, since he elected *not* to wear a lifejacket.

I swallowed at the heat of him, the tanned, toned muscles of his back already glistening with water from when he jumped in the water before climbing onboard. His hair was a little longer than when I first met him, the ends of it dripping water down his neck, and I watched those little droplets of water with something similar to envy as I wrapped my hands around his middle, scooting a little closer.

"You ready?" he asked over his shoulder, pressing the red button on the jet ski that fired the engine to life. It rumbled softly underneath us, and my heart picked up speed at the noise.

"No."

He chuckled. "Hold on tight."

Without another word or warning, Noah pressed his thumb on the throttle, and we shot away from the shore.

I yelped, nearly falling off backward before I gripped his abdomen tighter. "Noah!"

I watched the speed climb the same way the grin on his face did. The numbers on the little screen increased too quickly — ten, fifteen, twenty, twenty-five. We flew over the soft waves of Lake Stratford, slicing through the water like a viper, and my heart threatened to leap out of my chest with each new acceleration.

"I changed my mind. I want off. I want off!"

Noah just laughed, his head tilting back a little before he reached with the hand not on the gas behind him. He squeezed my knee once reassuringly, glancing over his shoulder quickly before he turned back to the lake ahead.

"It's okay. I promise. Just trust me."

I stared at his hand on my knee, the warmth of it spreading over my entire leg before it dipped somewhere under the bottoms of my swim suit. He removed it just as fast as he had placed it there, and my heart raced in my chest for a completely different reason.

I tried to calm my breathing, to find assurance in his promise that it would all be okay as my hair whipped in the wind behind me. But when a large boat crossed in front of us, leaving a massive wake, and Noah didn't steer away from it, my eyes bulged.

"Noah," I said as a warning.

He kept going, aimed straight for the large waves the boat had made when it passed.

"Noah, don't you dare."

"Hang on!"

"Noah!"

But it was too late. We hit the first wave made by the boat, the nose of the jet ski skipping up a few inches off the water. I screamed, gripping onto Noah so tight I thought I'd cut off his breathing. The next wave was even bigger, and the jet ski flew into the air, the roar of the engine ebbing a little at the loss of water pressure as we went airborne.

I was still screaming, gripping, fearing for my life when we landed again, and this time Noah cut the wheel right, turning us along the edge of the waves instead of straight over them. We rode them fast and furious, catching another fit of air before we were out of the waves and back on the glassy water.

I was pretty sure my stomach was still somewhere back behind us.

Noah slowed down until we were stopped, floating in the middle of the lake to the tune of the soft, rumbling engine. He turned to look at me over his shoulder with a shit-eating grin.

"That was fun."

I smacked his shoulder, shoving like I was going to push him off while I fought against a smile. "That was *not* fun! That was terrifying!"

"Yeah? Why you smiling, then?"

"I'm not smiling!" I insisted, but even as the words fell from my lips, I couldn't fight the grin. I laughed, softly at first before it took over completely, and I laughed so hard I had to wrap my hands over my stomach, my forehead hitting the place between his shoulders as I tried to catch my breath.

When I looked up again, Noah just quirked one brow in victory.

I shook my head. "You're infuriating, Noah Becker."

"I believe I was the first one to say that about *you*, Ruby Grace Barnett."

I smiled wider, blowing out a breath before running my hands back through my damp hair. "Okay. Fine. I admit it. That was fun."

"Told you."

"What now?"

He grinned, thumb hovering over the throttle as he faced forward again. "Better wrap those beautiful arms around me again, sweetheart."

And I did, just in time for him to cut the wheel and floor it, spinning us in a donut circle that made huge, billowing waves around us. I was laughing and squealing, leaning into the turn with him when he cut the wheel again, and we went flying over the waves we'd made.

I didn't know how much time passed with him doing donuts and figure-eights and making waves bigger than the jet ski before he'd send us barreling over them, but I *did* know that the huge smile didn't leave my face the entire time. My cheeks hurt by the time we finally slowed again, and we were both breathing hard, chests heaving with the adrenaline and excitement.

"You're wild," I whispered on a laugh, trying to catch my breath.

"What's that?" he asked, grinning at me over his shoulder.

"You're wild!" I said louder, throwing my hands up in the air and turning my face to the sun. I closed my eyes, basking in the rays and the feeling of euphoria for a long moment. When I looked at Noah again, he was watching me, throat thick with a swallow as his eyes searched mine.

The sun that had felt so light and airy just moments before seemed to beat down on us then, the heat unbearable, our lips so close where he tilted his head toward me, where I leaned into him.

My hands slipped around his waist again, shaking a little as they settled over the ribs and valleys of his abdomen. I licked my lips, eyes falling to his before I caught his steel gaze once more.

There were so many words I wanted to say in that moment, so many words that would have completely annihilated our *friends only* agreement.

*Kiss me.*

*Touch me.*

*I don't feel this way with anyone else.*

Each new thought shocked me more than the last, and my lips parted, the effort to catch my breath lost somewhere in the wind that swept over us. I should have been thinking about Anthony, about our wedding, about everything I needed to get done for it, about everything we would do as a married couple in our life together.

I should have been thinking about *anything* other than how much I wished Noah would cross the line we drew between us and capture my lips with his.

He wanted me. I knew he wanted me. And I knew if I leaned in even another inch, he'd take me.

So, with every ounce of willpower I had, I backed away, eyes floating down to the seat between us before I looked at him again, wearing a fake, *everything's okay* smile.

And instead of saying all the words whirring through my mind, I settled on three safe ones, instead.

"Can I drive?"

## NOAH

The sun was a lazy ball of fire riding on the evening clouds later that day when Ruby Grace and I spread out a large blanket on the beach. She was lying on her stomach, her legs slowly kicking in the air as she popped another strawberry between her lips. Her focus was on the lake, on the jet skis and boats and fishermen and tubers and swimmers.

Mine was on her.

The back of her swim suit top had shifted, showing me the lines the sun had already made on her skin that day. Her hips were narrow, her small ass curved and toned, her legs still the epitome of every man's fantasy as she swung them gently in the air — back and forth, back and forth, ten manicured toes skating the sky.

I would have been perfectly content to stare at her, just like that, for as long as I lived.

Even if I couldn't have her, if I couldn't kiss her or touch her or pull her into me and shield her from every unwanted harm — just *looking* at her was a blessing. I felt her presence swell into my chest, filling me up in some way that I never would have realized before.

Because I didn't know I was empty.

Not until she poured into my life.

Ruby Grace's content sigh brought me back to the moment as she shifted, rolling onto her side and propping her chin up with one hand. "So, what made you think of Stratford Lake for our friend date?"

I took another bite of the sandwiches we'd bought from the lake's convenient store, speaking around the mass of meat and bread in my mouth. "My dad used to bring all of us out here. It's one of my favorite places."

Her face sobered. "And you brought me?"

I shrugged. "I thought maybe it could become one of your favorite places, too."

A soft breeze rolled over us, brushing Ruby Grace's wild hair back over her shoulders as a soft smile found her face. I marveled at the deep blue water of the lake behind her, the beige sand, the warm glow of the sun drifting in and out of the clouds. It was the kind of view an artist would stop time for, pulling out their easel or camera or pen and paper to capture the moment in whatever way they could.

"What was he like?" Ruby Grace asked. "Your dad?"

I smiled, stealing a strawberry from her plate and popping it in my mouth. "He was the original trouble maker. I remember Mom always yelling at him for something. But, not in a way that they were *actually* fighting. It was more like this adorable, *you annoy me but I love you anyway* kind of yelling."

Ruby Grace smiled, running her fingers over the sand at the edge of the blanket. "So, I guess we have him to thank for the notorious Becker brothers running amok, huh?"

"Oh, definitely. But, it's not like we go *looking* for trouble," I pointed out. "We were just taught from a young age not to put up with anything that's wrong. So, whether that means sticking up for ourselves or for our brothers or a friend or even a complete stranger, that's what we did. It's what we *do*." I shrugged. "Dad never raised hell unless there was something to raise hell about."

"Like the way Patrick Scooter was running the distillery?"

I blanched, heart stopping in my chest as I watched Ruby Grace in a new way. She was the mayor's daughter — young, affluent, *far* removed from the distillery. I knew everyone in the town had some sort of tie to Scooter Whiskey, but it surprised me that she knew anything about the inner workings of the place.

"Yeah," I finally managed. "Exactly like that."

"My dad hated it, too," she said, dragging her index finger in a heart shape over the sand before she erased it with her palm. "He said Patrick was tarnishing the brand, taking out all the honesty and down-home history that made the whiskey special. He said Patrick was going too mainstream, trying to be something Scooter Whiskey wasn't."

"That's how my dad felt, too. And he had all these ideas about how to keep the same traditions, but liven up the brand, too. He was smart. He had research and industry surveys. He knew what he was talking about."

"But Patrick wouldn't listen."

I nodded. "He seems to still have that problem."

Ruby Grace watched me for a long moment, her fingers paused in their current doodle in the sand. "The fire your dad died in... your family doesn't believe it was an accident, do they?"

I swallowed, watching a boat in the distance as I tried to figure out how to respond. The answer was easy — no, we didn't believe it was an accident. But, admitting that was admitting that we had conjured some conspiracy theory, that we thought the Scooters were crooked, that someone had it out for our dad. It was essentially admitting insanity, and I didn't want to do that — especially when Mom's reputation and heart was on the line.

"We believe there's a lot we don't know about that day," I decided on, and before she could respond, I changed the subject to her. "What's *your* dad like? It had to be kind of hard, growing up as the Mayor's daughter."

A sarcastic smile spread over Ruby Grace's face, and she rolled, splaying out on her back with her eyes on the sky above. "Let's just say my dad felt more like a father *figure* than he ever did a father."

I frowned. "Wasn't around much, I take it."

She shook her head, eyes tracing the clouds. "Don't get me wrong, he's a great dad to me and my sister. He provides for us, tells us how proud he is of us and how much he loves us. He's like me in a way that Mom and Mary Anne don't understand. He gets it when I need to hide away, when my anxiety spikes in a crowd. And if Mom ever needs help with parenting, he steps in, no questions asked. He helped me with my college application and essay, told me he would support me no matter what I decided to major in. And thanks to him, I've got the best golf game of any woman in Stratford, I'd bet."

She paused, regaling his *great dad* qualities like there was some list and as long as he had checked those boxes, she couldn't say otherwise.

"But," she continued. "Sometimes it just felt like he was this mostly silent bystander and Mom was both parents. Dad's *real* kid is this town, and everything that goes along with nurturing it. That's where his time goes. That's where his energy is spent." She chuckled. "Well, that and the casino or any gambling event he can con the council members into."

"And that doesn't bother you?"

"No," she answered quickly, biting her bottom lip before releasing it again. "I understand it, feeling so passionate about something that you'd want to dedicate your life to it. He really looked up to Grandpa, too, and I think he always wanted to take his place. This is just what makes him happy. And I love him, I want him happy." She rolled onto her side again. "Now, do I wish we had more time together growing up? Sure. But, I get him. And he gets me. At least, for the most part."

"For the most part," I mused. "Meaning, he probably wouldn't be cool with you going back to college after the wedding either."

A shadow passed over her face, and I internally cursed at myself, knowing I'd crossed over in the territory that always made her clam up and run away. She didn't like talking about *her* dreams, about sacrificing those for her soon-to-be husband.

And it seemed to be my favorite button to push.

I was surprised when she didn't yell at me or tell me to mind my own business as she stormed across the beach and away from me. Instead, she let out a long breath, eyes falling to the blanket we sat on before they found mine again. "I'm sure he wouldn't exactly be thrilled, no. But, it's more Mama than it is him. She knows what it takes to be a politician's wife, and she's been more than open with me about it."

"What exactly does it take?"

She shrugged. "Selflessness. Passion. Love and understanding that I won't always be the priority in his life. But, that was part of the reason I was so attracted to Anthony when we first met. He knows what he wants, and he's driven, and smart. I love that about him."

My chest tightened the more she talked about him. It was the first time she'd said it — that she loved him — where I actually believed it was true.

I hated it.

"I think it's amazing that you found a man like that," I finally offered, swallowing my pride like a jagged pill. "I really do. But, and I don't mean to say anything out of line, but I wonder if he wouldn't support *you* the same — if you told him you wanted to go back to school or volunteer with AmeriCorps. You could be there for him and still be there for yourself, too."

Ruby Grace nodded, but she wouldn't meet my eyes. "Yeah. I suppose."

"Can I ask you something?"

Another nod.

"If you could look twenty years down the road on a blissfully perfect day in your future life, what would it look like?"

She smiled, finally looking at me again. Her eyes were filled with wonder and curiosity, like I was some project she was assigned to but didn't know where to start.

"Hmmm..." she said, lying back again. She crossed her long legs, folding her hands over her bare navel as she watched the clouds. "It would be Sunday. After church. I'd have a huge, delicious supper spread, the table set for a family of five. My three kids would be out in the yard playing, and as I watched them from the kitchen window, my husband would come up behind me, wrap his arms around me, and ask me to dance."

I swallowed past the thick knot in my throat, visions of my own parents flooding my mind. And it wasn't lost on me that in her vision, she didn't mention *Anthony*, specifically.

"What else?" I asked.

She smiled wider. "We'd have a dog — a big one. One that would slobber everywhere and knock our toddlers down when he played with them. And our house would be country, but not like the *classic* southern style. It'd be eclectic, with art from all over the world, and bright colors and funky designs."

The more she talked, the more she lit up.

"I think I'd like a big entertaining space in the back yard, a place to host parties and barbecues, and I'd want a little vegetable garden that I could grow my own tomatoes and squash." She paused, her smile falling a little. "And I'd have a charity, one that supported something I cared about... maybe earth conservation, or education in rural locations, or quality of life for senior citizens, or mental illness support for our veterans. A way to give back. A way to save someone..."

I smirked. "I bet it'd be the most efficiently run charity in the world. Probably the most well-known, too."

She rolled onto her side. "Why do you say that?"

"Because it's you."

She watched me for a long moment, like she was waiting for me to continue, but I didn't feel the need. That was all there was to say. It was her, Ruby Grace, and we both knew that anything she set her mind to, she'd not only achieve it — she'd break records, too.

"Noah?" she whispered.

"Mm?"

"Can I say something... and you not ask questions when I do?"

I considered it, curiosity overpowering any hesitation I had. "Okay."

Ruby Grace sat up, then, sitting on her knees as she tucked her hair behind both ears. Those kneecaps brushed the tops of my thighs where I was lying on my side in front of her, nothing between us but a half-empty container of strawberries and two bottles of water.

She chewed her cheek, like she wasn't sure what to say or how to say it, and her eyes watched her hand — the one braced on the blanket just a few inches from mine.

"I don't know if this is stupid or... I don't know, pointless to say, but..." She blew out a breath, lifting her eyes to mine. "Thank you, for talking to me, for being my friend when you didn't have to be." Her brows bent together, a shade of pink tinging her cheeks. "I never feel more like my *real* self than I do when I'm with you."

My next breath lodged somewhere in my throat, stuck and swelling with every new inhale I tried to take. Her words broke me as much as they filled me with longing and hope. It should be Anthony she felt most like herself with, since he was the man responsible for the diamond glittering on her finger.

But it was me.

Her eyes searched mine, her body leaning forward, down, toward mine. She was so slight that even on her knees, we were nearly face to face with my head propped up on one elbow. The closer she got, the more I saw the strawberry juice stained on her lips, smelled the sweet scent of her breath as her lips parted, saw the sunburst in her hazel eyes under the glow of the sun.

I knew in that moment that all I had to do was move toward her even an *inch*, and I could kiss her. I knew that if I reached out a hand, wrapped my fingers up in her red hair and pulled her into me, she would submit.

But I didn't.

I *couldn't*.

I'd promised her — just friends. And I would respect those boundaries until the day she didn't belong to another man.

Until the day she was actually mine.

"We should go," I whispered with her mouth inches from mine, her lids fluttering shut.

She popped them back open, blinking several times before she pulled back, clearing her throat on a nervous nod of acknowledgement. "Yeah. Yeah, we probably should."

But before she could stand, I reached out, covering her hand with mine.

I smoothed the pad of my thumb over her wrist, the smooth palm of her hand, the shiny skin over her knuckles. I hoped the touch would say everything I couldn't.

*I feel the same way.*

*I want you, too.*

*I'm here, whenever you're ready.*

I stood, wrapping her hand in mine to help her up before I released her and put the space between us again, packing up our picnic without another glance in her direction.

The ride home in my truck was quiet, only the soft melody of my playlist and the wind whipping in from the windows the only sounds between us. Ruby Grace looked out the window the entire time, her eyes distant, mind somewhere far away.

I let her be.

When I pulled into the department store parking lot, parking next to where we'd left her convertible, she finally pulled her gaze inside the truck.

"We didn't get a thing done today," she said, unfastening her seat belt.

I smirked. "But do you feel better?"

At that, she sighed, a genuine smile coloring her lips before she nodded. "I do. I really do."

"Then it was a successful day."

The sun had already set, the department store long closed, and the light from the moon above and my headlights seemed to be the only ones in the world.

Ruby Grace reached for the door handle, but paused, looking back at me over her shoulder. "Thank you for today, Noah."

"Anytime, Legs."

She shook her head, pushing the door open and sliding out before she closed it behind her. She leaned her elbows on the edge of the window, her hair a mess, skin sun-kissed, smile lazy and sated.

"I'll see you around."

I nodded. "See you around."

Her smile slipped, eyes searching mine for something that I was sure she didn't find because she tore them away too quickly, crossing her arms over her chest and walking across the lot to her own car. She slipped inside, offering me one last wave before she pulled away, turning left down the main drag that would take her all the way home.

And I just sat there, hands on the steering wheel, eyes on my passenger seat, and heart somewhere down the road with a girl who didn't even realize she had it.

# Chapter Thirteen

**RUBY GRACE**

"**I** call bullshit."

I smirked, holding my cell phone between my ear and shoulder Saturday afternoon as I packed up all the supplies for the centerpieces Annie and I were going to make that day. Photos of Anthony and me throughout the year had been printed, frames of the same size waiting to be filled, flowers and jars that would hold floating candles rounding out the look.

We had a lot of crafting to do.

And apparently, a lot of talking, too.

"There is absolutely no way you spent an entire day in a bathing suit with Noah Becker and he didn't put his hands on you."

"Not even once," I assured her, hiding my own disappointment at that fact. I folded the top on one box before working on filling the next. "He's my friend, Annie."

"Friend, shmriend. He wants you. And the way you talk about him, I think you want him, too."

"This is literally the first time I've talked to you about him, other than when you *forcibly* left me alone with him that night at the Black Hole."

"Exactly. You don't talk about him, but you spend at least four days a week with him and have been since you got back into town. You never talked to him *before* you went to college."

"Yes, I did," I argued. "I sat behind him in church, remember?"

"Right. Must have been thrilling conversations between a nine-year-old and a senior in high school," she deadpanned.

I sighed, plopping down on my bed and surveying the half-packed boxes around me. I didn't know why I was trying to hide it from Annie. She was my best friend. She could see through me like a jelly fish.

But admitting I had feelings for Noah to her — to *anyone* — was dangerous.

It was impossible.

If I admitted it, I'd have to *do* something about it — and that something was either give *him* up, or give Anthony up.

I couldn't do the latter.

I didn't *want* to do the first.

It was like white water rafting. I was in the raft — cold, wet, terrified. Worst case scenario, I'd get dumped, hit my head on a rock and life as I know it would be over. *Best* case scenario, I'd make it to the end of the river.

Still cold and wet, but alive.

There *was* no easy way out of the situation I'd found myself in, and the best way I knew how to handle it was to just avoid making a decision at all.

Noah and I were friends. No lines had been crossed.

Everything was fine.

"He's just my friend, Annie," I told my best friend, and myself, keeping my voice low. Mama and Daddy were gone, but Anthony was downstairs, working in Daddy's home office.

Not that I was talking about anything he couldn't hear.

At least, that's what I told myself as I lowered my voice even more.

"We haven't done anything wrong."

"The fact that you have to say that..."

"I know," I said, sighing again. "I know. But, he makes me feel... like *me*. This summer has been so stressful with all the wedding planning, and when I'm with him, everything feels easier, lighter, more manageable. We have *fun*, even if we're just making stupid chalkboard signs."

"Do you feel that way when you're with Anthony?"

I didn't answer.

A long exhale came from the other end of the phone. "Alright. Just get over here so we can talk about this, okay?"

"I really would rather *not* talk about it and just make centerpieces."

"Well, you're going to have to do both. Text me when you're on your way."

I groaned. "Fine."

"I love you."

"Love you, too."

"Ruby Grace?"

"Yeah?"

Annie paused. "Everything is going to be okay. Okay?"

I nodded, ignoring the way my throat tightened at her words. "Okay," I whispered back.

When we ended the call, I finished packing up the last of the centerpiece ingredients, heaving the first box into my arms and carefully walking it downstairs. It was heavy, and I stumbled on a step, nearly crashing to the floor and taking the fragile contents of the box along with me.

"Shit," I murmured, balancing the box on the railing.

I was on the middle plateau between the two flights, and I didn't want to chance a tumble.

"Anthony?" I called out, still balancing the box on the railing. "Can you help me with these boxes for a second?"

No answer.

I frowned, looking around at my options. I didn't want to go back *up* the stairs, either, so I deposited the box on the floor of the square landing, trotting down the second flight of stairs and making my way back to Daddy's office.

"Anthony?" I called again.

No answer.

I heard his voice when I rounded the corner past the kitchen, making my way down the hall.

*Of course, he's on the phone.*

I hung my hands on my hips, pausing in the hallway to debate my options. I decided to just get a glass of sweet tea and wait for him to get off the phone so he could help me load up the car. I was in no hurry, anyway.

But before I could turn back toward the kitchen, I heard my name.

"Yes, it's been hectic being out here, but Ruby Grace has been great about it all. The crew filmed our dinner earlier this week, and she looked ravishing. She's everything I could have ever asked for in a wife."

I smiled, a mixture of guilt and love swirling in my stomach as I leaned my back against the wall, folding my hands over my heart. It was rude to listen in, and I knew it, but truth be told, I *needed* to hear that kind of thing from Anthony.

I needed to hear what I meant to him.

"I know, Dad. Yeah. Right. Ha! I know, you should have seen us at the barrel tasting event. I swear, this town lives and dies by that distillery."

I smiled. That was Stratford, alright.

"Oh, trust me, I can handle her father. With what we're doing for him, I don't think he could even pretend to not love me — even if that were the case," Anthony said, lowering his voice.

My stomach somersaulted, and I slid my back quietly along the wall, getting closer.

"It's not the only reason, Dad," he said after a long pause. "No. I know. I understand. Listen, being a politician is all I needed to do in his eyes. We golf, shoot the shit, gamble at the casino, talk about how the extremists are taking the country to hell in a hand basket. He dragged me to the casino last week." A pause. "I know. You think he would have learned after that, but... anyway. Her mom is a little tougher, but I play the perfect gentleman and she eats it up. Just have to open a few doors and call her ma'am and she lights up like a Christmas tree."

A pause.

An exaggerated sigh from Anthony.

"Dad, trust me, I get it. I know they're not exactly what we had in mind for the perfect in-laws. They're country bumpkins, *but*, they're in the political circuit — even if it's in a small way. This is what you wanted, right? The Barnett name is known in this town, and when we did the background check on Ruby Grace, we didn't find a single thing that could come up and bite us in the ass during the elections. She's clean. She's poised. She has no aspirations of her own." He paused again. "And, she's pretty, which is a bonus."

Another chuckle.

Another roll of my stomach.

"Her mom has trained her well to be the perfect politician's wife," he continued. "Her family isn't exactly the premier picture we had in mind, but they're pretty clean cut. They're reputable. And they need us to play our part, just like we need Ruby Grace to play hers."

I bit my lip against the tears stinging my eyes, confusion rolling over me and mixing with the betrayal. I didn't understand it — any of it. He loved me. He loved my family.

What part was he playing in our life?

What part was I supposed to play in his?

*This can't be Anthony. He wouldn't talk about me like this. It's all a misunderstanding.*

I tried to convince myself, fighting against the urge to hyperventilate as I pressed myself against the cold wall in our hallway.

But I couldn't lie to myself, not when I was hearing everything I needed to hear to know the truth.

"This was always our plan, Dad," Anthony said. "She's perfect."

A pause.

"I know," Anthony said. "The way I see it, Ruby Grace will be more than happy to take on the community projects. It'll be a good look for the campaign. And, hey." He lowered his voice even more. "Having her tied up in all of that will leave me plenty of free time for a little fun on the side... know what I mean?"

He full-on laughed at that, and even from where I stood in the hallway, I could hear the gusto laugh of his father.

His father, who had kissed the back of my hand when we met and told me how beautiful I was, how smart I was, how lucky Anthony was to have me.

And it was all a show.

It was all a lie.

*They need us to play our part, and we need Ruby Grace to play hers.*

A sob broke through my throat before I felt it coming, and I clamped my hand over my mouth, squeezing my eyes shut to force the tears back in.

"I gotta go, Dad, I think she's downstairs." A chuckle. "Okay, I'll call you later to discuss the speech."

I needed to move. I needed to get away from Dad's office, from Anthony, from this house and this entire town. But I couldn't move. The hardwood floor was quicksand, sucking me in, making it impossible to take even one step.

Anthony rounded out of the office on a sigh, running one hand back through his hair before he paused, eyes lighting up at the sight of me. "Ah, there's my beautiful wife-to-be. I was just coming to check on you." He smiled, pulling the shell-shocked board of my body into him and pressing a kiss to my forehead. "Need help with anything?"

I couldn't speak.

I just stared at him, at his hazel eyes — the ones I'd lost myself in for hours over the last year — at his perfect blond hair, his perfectly sculpted body, his perfect Superman chin.

And here I was, his perfect little abiding bride-to-be.

Anthony frowned, searching my face. "Baby? Are you okay?"

My stomach rolled violently at the nickname, and I blinked several times, awareness flooding back. "I'm fine. I just almost fell trying to get the boxes with the centerpiece stuff downstairs. Could you help me with them?"

Anthony smiled, thumbing my chin before he kissed my nose. "Of course, my little do-it-all-by-herself. You should have just asked me in the first place."

I faked the best smile I could, snaking my way out of his hold. "One of them is on the stairs. There are three more in my room. Can you load them into the car for me? I'm feeling a little lightheaded, think I need some water."

Anthony swept my hair away from my face, still wearing that stupid, sympathetic smile. "Of course. You go hydrate and rest. I'll be back."

He walked me to the kitchen, pouring me a glass of water before he disappeared up the stairs to retrieve the first box. As soon as he was gone, I took my first inhale, gulping down the entire glass of water before refilling it.

My mind was spinning, heart racing, rib cage closing in on my lungs. Every second that passed, my hands shook more, and the tears I'd managed to hold back flooded my eyes over and over before I'd blink and clear them away.

"All set," Anthony said, bounding back into the kitchen.

I didn't realize how much time had passed. Everything felt like a dream.

"Want me to come help? I can take a break from work. It is Saturday, after all."

"No," I said quickly.

Anthony frowned.

I swallowed, shaking my head and forcing another smile as I placed my hands on his chest. I wanted to beat my fists on it, scream at him, cry and kick him out and throw the ring on my finger in his face.

But even in my frantic state, I knew that wasn't the right thing to do.

I needed time. I needed space. I needed to think, to process, to figure out what to do.

Who to trust.

"Sorry," I said, still smiling. "I just, I haven't had much time with Annie since I got home, what with her being pregnant and me doing all the wedding stuff. I need some girl time."

Anthony returned my smile in understanding. "Of course. Well, you two don't get into too much trouble, okay?"

My smile was shaky, but I held it as long as I could, closing my eyes against the urge to vomit when Anthony leaned in for a kiss. I turned my head, offering him my cheek, and he kissed it sweetly before pulling back, still framing me in his arms.

"See you later this evening?"

I nodded. "Mm-hmm."

As soon as his hands were off me, I swiped my purse off the kitchen counter, bolting for the door. I practically sprinted across the drive to my car, hands shaking as I pulled the handle and climbed inside. The engine roared to life when I pushed the ignition button, and I threw it into reverse, kicking up gravel with my tires as I flipped it around and sped off down the old dirt road.

My heart kicked hard in my chest, picking up more and more speed with every inch I put between Anthony and myself. My eyes flooded with tears, ones I couldn't hold back any longer. They slid down my cheeks, hot and searing, my hands tight on the steering wheel, stomach lodged somewhere in my throat.

Halfway down the road to the Main Street drag, I pulled over, trying to calm my breaths before I had an all-out panic attack.

I needed to breathe. I needed an explanation. I needed someone to hold me and tell me it was all going to be okay.

I needed Noah.

The thought hit me as quickly and as unsuspectedly as everything else had that day, but it didn't make me panic more. If anything, the realization soothed me, blanketing me like a silky sheet of reassurance.

My heart rate slowed.

My breathing evened out.

My hands stabilized, the tears on my cheeks drying, no more falling from my eyes to join them.

For a long time, I just sat there with my hands on the steering wheel, staring at the swirling dust from the road between me and Main Street.

Then, I fished my cell phone out of my purse and texted Annie.

*Mom sprung something on me, we'll have to reschedule our super fun centerpiece building day. See you at church tomorrow.*

As soon as the text went through, I turned my phone off, put the car in drive, and floored it across town.

# NOAH

"Just a minute!" I called from the bathroom, cursing under my breath as I ended my shower prematurely and yanked a towel off the rack. I'd debated ignoring the knock at my door altogether — mostly because I was pretty sure it was someone trying to sell something or convince me to switch religions. But, there was a chance it was one of my brothers, or my mom, since all of them liked to stop by unannounced.

The knock came again, a little louder this time, as I swiped a pair of sweatpants from my bed.

"Yeah, yeah, I'm coming! Hold your horses."

I grumbled, putting on the first white t-shirt I saw hanging in my closet, even though I was still a little damp. As soon as I was dressed, I stormed across my house to answer the door, frustration boiling even more when yet *another* knock came. I frowned, blowing out a hot breath and ready to let whoever it was on the other side have it — unless it was Mom, of course.

When I swung the door open and saw Ruby Grace standing on my front porch, all the frustration died.

And was immediately replaced by the most powerful sense of protectiveness I'd ever experienced in my life.

Her fiery red hair was tied in a messy bun for the first time since I'd met her, little tendrils falling from the hair tie and framing her long, worn face. Her eyes were puffy and red, mascara smudged beneath them, bottom lip trembling as she watched me.

She looked so small — her arms folded over her middle, shoulders slumped, head hanging.

Someone had hurt her.

I swallowed, fists tightening at my sides, before I slowly pushed open the screen door between us. I didn't chance a single word when she stepped inside, and as soon as she was in my house, I shut both doors behind her, folding my arms over her like I could protect her from whatever or whoever had hurt her.

Ruby Grace melted into me, a little sob muffled by my t-shirt as she buried her face in my chest and twisted her hands in the fabric covering my abdomen. She pulled me closer, trying to fold in on herself as I surrounded her, hugging her tight, one hand finding the back of her head. I ran my fingers through her hair, pressed her closer to my chest, my lips finding the crown of her head as I forced a calming breath.

"It's okay," I assured her without knowing what *it* even was. "I'm here. I'm right here."

She cried harder at that, pulling at my shirt again like she needed me closer. There wasn't an inch of us that wasn't touching, but I tried, anyway. I tightened my grip, pulled long, calming breaths through my nose before gently releasing them, helping her to do the same.

It felt like hours that we stood there, just inside my front door, her wrapped up in my arms as I rocked her. With each passing minute, her sobs softened, her breathing quieted, and finally, she pressed her hands into my chest, lifting her head from that spot to lock her eyes on mine.

Her devastated, tear-glossed, achingly beautiful golden eyes.

"I'm sorry," she whispered, her bottom lip trembling with the apology. "I... I didn't know where else to go."

I ran the pad of my thumbs over her cheeks, wiping away the salty streams there before I framed her face in my hands. "You never have to apologize for coming to me. Ever. No matter what."

She closed her eyes, releasing two more parallel tears before she buried her head in my chest again.

I had so many questions — namely, who the fuck did I need to kill — but, I knew she'd tell me what happened when she was ready. So, instead, I held her, walking her over to my couch and pulling her down into the cushions with me. She curled up in a ball in my lap, and I covered us with a blanket, rocking her gently in my arms until her breathing quieted again.

"Do you want some water?" I asked after a while.

She nodded, sniffing and running the back of her wrist under her nose before crawling off me. I squeezed her knee before I stood, making my way into the kitchen.

Once I was alone, I cracked my neck, forcing a calming breath that was more for me than for her. I had the bad habit of jumping to conclusions, of letting my temper get the best of me, and I knew it was going to take every ounce of willpower I had to be calm and cool and collected when she finally did tell me what happened.

If it was Anthony, if he had cheated on her or broken her heart in any way, I *also* knew that "staying calm" would be a nearly impossible goal to accomplish.

With two glasses of water in hand, I made my way back to the living room. Ruby Grace hadn't moved an inch. Her eyes were blank, bottomless holes as she stared at my coffee table.

"Here," I whispered, handing one glass to her and setting the other on the table. She wrapped her hands around the glass, taking one small sip before resting it in her lap, her eyes focused on the liquid inside.

"Anthony doesn't love me."

She whispered the words, and not a single shadow of emotion passed over her face when she released them.

I didn't know how to respond. Half of me wanted to say *I fucking know that, I've been trying to tell you*. But, the other half of me knew there was a reason she thought he did before this moment, and there was a reason she thought he didn't *now*.

"That's not true," I finally offered, against the internal rolling of my eyes.

"No," she said, shaking her head. "It is. I heard him..."

I frowned, not understanding.

She closed her eyes, forcing a long breath before she spoke again. "He was talking to his dad on the phone, he didn't know I could hear him. And he... he said some *awful* things about me, about my family."

My throat tightened, and I reached for the other glass of water, taking a sip to cool myself down before I spoke. "What did he say?"

"That I was right for their *plan*. That I was pretty and I don't have any aspirations of my own and I've been *trained well* to be a politician's wife." She scoffed, eyes floating up to the ceiling as she rolled her lips together. "He doesn't want to marry me because he loves me, he wants to marry me because I fit the role." Her eyes fluttered shut again. "I'm a pawn in a game I didn't even know I was playing."

"He didn't say that."

Ruby Grace's eyebrows bent together in confusion, her gaze leveling with mine. "What?"

My jaw clenched along with my fists at my side. "Please, tell me he didn't say any of that. Tell me, so I don't get in my truck and drive across town and beat in his fucking face until no one recognizes him."

"Noah," she gasped, reaching out for me. "Please, don't. Don't hurt him." She swallowed. "Don't leave *me*."

The breath I blew out through my nose felt like fire and smoke, black invading my vision. That son of a bitch didn't deserve her in the first place, and now?

Now, he didn't deserve to breathe.

"Please," she said again, scooting closer to me. She placed her water on the coffee table, leaning into me, her small arms wrapping around my middle as she rested her head on my chest. "Please."

I blew out another breath, but this time, I let it out slower, wrapping my arms around her in return. There was nothing I wanted more than to drive across town and give that motherfucker exactly what he had coming.

Nothing, except to hold Ruby Grace and be the one who made her feel better, the one who showed her that what he did to her did not define who she was.

"I feel so stupid," she said after a while, her head still on my chest. "All this time, I thought I'd hit the jackpot. I had the perfect guy, the perfect ring, the perfect future. I didn't mind sacrificing my own dreams for his, because I knew he loved me. I knew that I'd be his partner, standing by his side, and he'd bend for *my* wants in the future." She paused. "I thought I'd found what my parents had. And that was all I'd ever wanted."

My heart broke with that admission, because I knew the feeling all too well. Ruby Grace had watched her parents grow in love just as I'd watched mine, and it was what we had pictured for *our* futures.

Now, her picture had been shattered.

I tilted her chin up, leveling my eyes with hers. "He's an idiot," I stated simply. "And I know that doesn't fix anything. It probably doesn't make you feel better, either. But, he is. And he's going to regret the day he lost you. He's going to regret that he didn't realize what he had when he had it."

She sighed, leaning into my hand. "I doubt he'll even care. He'll find someone else who can play the part, and he'll run for office just the same."

"He'll care," I promised her. "Trust me. And he'll regret it. There isn't a man alive who could be loved by you and not kick himself every single day for fucking it up."

A steady silence fell over us, her eyes on mine, those words between us.

"I don't even know how to *begin* telling my mom," she finally said, and those eyes watching mine welled up with tears again. "It'll break her heart."

"She'll understand. She loves you."

Ruby Grace shook her head, letting out a long, heavy breath. "Everyone is going to be talking about this, Noah. *Everyone*. Forever."

"Let them talk. They don't know you or the situation, and their judgment doesn't affect who you are." I held her gaze, running my thumb down the line of her jaw. "Do you hear me? What they think of you is not who you actually are. They do not have that power over you." I smirked. "Plus, someone else will fuck up and give them a change of subject. I mean, just leave it to me and my brothers. We've been doing it all our lives."

She chuckled, but it died quickly, sadness washing over her again. "I feel like a fool."

"It's *him* who's the fool," I assured her, searching her eyes with my own. "You are, without a doubt, the most caring, loving, passionate, intelligent, and classy woman I have ever met. You walk with a confidence unparalleled by anyone in this town, and you give without ever expecting anything in return, and you're brave." I shook my head. "You are *so* fucking brave."

Her eyes softened, her voice just a whisper again. "You didn't mention the way I look in any of those bullet points."

"You're beautiful," I said easily. "But that's not what makes you the woman I l—" I swallowed, throat constricting like her eyes held it in a vise grip. "That's not what makes you the woman you are. You are more than your eyes, and your hair, and your strawberry smoothie lips and long, lean legs. You're not meant to be a puppet in some man's sideshow, Ruby Grace. You're meant to be his entire world."

Ruby Grace let her eyes wander over every inch of my face, as if she was just noticing me for the first time.

And maybe she was.

"I love the way you see me," she whispered.

I swallowed, heart picking up speed as she leaned in closer, her hands fisted in my shirt, her eyes on my lips.

"I just see you with my eyes."

"No," she argued, her lips centimeters from mine, her sweet breath invading my senses. "No, you see me with your soul." She swallowed, eyes flicking up to mine before they fell back to my mouth. "And I feel you with mine."

Her lips touched mine tentatively at first — feather light, each of us releasing a shaky, anxious breath. I felt that tiny, almost non-existent touch in every inch of my body. A wave of chills rushed through me, our lips hovering, breaths hard and heavy with want.

With *need.*

Then, my hands slid into her hair, and I pulled her into me, claiming her mouth like it had never touched another man.

She moaned, melting into me as I deepened the kiss, my lips hard and hot on hers. Her hands twisted in my shirt before she let it go completely, sliding the warmth of her palms beneath the fabric and over my stomach. I shivered at the touch, groaning against her kiss and pulling her closer.

I felt stupid for ever thinking I could know, could fathom, what it would be like to kiss her, to have her in my arms like this.

Kissing Ruby Grace wasn't like kissing a normal girl. It was like kissing royalty, like kissing a goddess, like being hand-picked by the heavens to surrender your heart forever in exchange for just one, tender, earth-shattering moment.

I surrendered to that moment, to that sacrifice, letting my hands wander her curves, my lips savoring the pressure of hers, my tongue tasting the sweet taste buds of her own. I pulled her closer — tugging, reaching — until she straddled me on the couch.

But when the heat of her center rubbed against my hard-on, I bit her bottom lip, sucking in a groan and releasing her mouth on a panting breath that felt like I'd been sucked back down to Earth and landed flat on my back.

"Stop," I breathed, pressing my forehead against hers.

Ruby Grace's chest heaved, her hands still under my shirt, lips parted.

I swallowed. "I don't want you."

Her face crumbled at that, brows bending together as she pulled back to look at me.

"Not like this," I clarified. I reached under my shirt for her hands, folding them in mine and bringing her knuckles to my lips. "I have thought about kissing you since the day you showed up at the distillery, Ruby Grace. And I'd be lying if I said I'd never thought of doing more. But, I... I *can't*. Not now. Not when you're torn up over another man."

The level of hurt on her face in that moment was enough to make me wish I'd never opened my door in the first place. I knew that kind of hurt — it was rejection. And *God*, it killed me that I'd been the one to put it there.

But I couldn't lie to myself, or to her. I wanted her more than I could say, but that didn't change the fact that she still wore another man's ring on her finger.

I waited for her to curse, to slap me, to crawl off my lap and slam my door in my face as she stormed out of my house and maybe even out of my life completely.

Instead, she let out a relieved breath, shoulders folding forward as she squeezed my hands that held hers.

"Tonight has nothing to do with him and you know it," she breathed.

My heart was a stallion in my rib cage, thunderous and powerful, steady and strong.

"We've *both* known it," she continued. "And I've tried to fight it, tried to convince myself that what I felt when I was with you was wrong, that it wasn't real." She shook her head. "But it *is* real. I'm just sorry it took me so long, that it took *this,* for me to finally admit that to myself."

I searched her eyes, and when I found nothing but sincerity there, I didn't know if I wanted to jump and throw my fist in the air or curl into her and fucking sob.

Because I felt it — right then and there on my couch on a normal, summer, Saturday afternoon in Stratford, Tennessee — I felt it and I knew.

The ring on her finger didn't matter anymore.

She was *mine.*

And I was hers.

As if to hammer that point home, she kept her eyes locked on mine as she reached down, slipping the ring off her finger and leaning back to deposit it somewhere on the coffee table before she slipped her hands back beneath my shirt.

"Now," she said, rolling her hips just enough to elicit a stiff breath from me. "I'm going to ask you to kiss me again, Noah Becker. And I won't ask you twice."

My lips were on hers before she could even say the words.

# Chapter Fourteen

**RUBY GRACE**

Dark.

Everything was dark.

Outside, the sun was shining, another bright summer day in Tennessee. But inside Noah's bedroom, where he was currently kissing me and backing me up — slowly, step by step — it was all dark.

Dark walls. Dark comforter. Dark curtains covering the window and blocking the sun's light from sneaking through. Blind caresses in the black space between us — lips and necks and hands and sighs. Dark intentions, dark promises waiting to be fulfilled.

His dark hair in my hands, my dark heart in his.

He was just a shadow as he held me, his kisses touching me like a sweet, soft, summer midnight on a tropical island.

I didn't realize how much a kiss could feel like a vacation.

I didn't realize how much a person could feel like home.

"I've wanted to kiss you for so long," he breathed against my lips, breaking contact just long enough to whisper the words before his mouth claimed mine again. "And now, I don't think I'll ever be able to stop."

Every breath was a trembling, shallow sip of air. My body didn't know how to react with new hands on me, with new lips, a new tongue, a new feeling. I didn't want to think about another man in that moment, but I couldn't help it. Because I remembered my first kiss with Anthony.

And it was *nothing* like this.

Noah's hands held my face like I was the treasure he'd hunted for his entire life and finally found. He peppered me with kisses before holding me to him longer, slowing it all down, caressing my lips with passionate, silky kisses. He'd slip his tongue inside my mouth, taste me, draw my bottom lip between his teeth and release it on a groan that I felt all the way to my toes.

This wasn't just a kiss.

This was a dream, a fantasy — and every part of my body surrendered to the impossible realism of it all.

Noah backed me up farther, his hands sliding down to the small of my back to guide me, and when the back of my legs hit the edge of his bed, he stopped, holding me steady.

"Ruby Grace," he whispered, kissing me again before I could answer.

"Yes," I barely breathed in return.

"Can I take this dress off you?"

"*Yes.*"

The word was a longing sigh falling from my lips, and as soon as it had, Noah trailed his fingertips down my arms, hands rolling into fists at my sides and bunching the fabric of my dress up with it. He captured my mouth even harder, sucking in a breath on a passionate kiss before he broke away and lifted the dress up and over my head.

My arms were still in the air when he threw my dress somewhere behind him, and he reached up, meeting my hands with his own as he kissed me again. He wound his fingertips with mine, and somehow, what his hands did to mine was even more sensual than the kiss, than his t-shirt on my half-naked body, than his hard-on pressing through the fabric of his black sweatpants.

I didn't ask to take his clothes off. Instead, I trailed my hands down, his fingers following mine until I slipped them between us. His hands found my waist as mine dove beneath the band of his sweatpants. I trailed my fingertips from hip bone to hip bone, just under the band, and I groaned when I realized he didn't have briefs on beneath.

"You surprised me," he mused with a smirk. "Didn't have time for underwear."

"Would have just gotten in the way," I breathed. Then, I gathered the hem of his shirt in my hands and tugged.

Noah lifted his arms, letting me strip him before he reached around me and unhooked my bra.

I inhaled a stiff breath when he slipped the straps of it over my shoulders, the fabric eliciting a wave of chills as he dragged it down my arms and let it fall on the floor between us. His eyes dipped to my exposed breasts for just the smallest moment before he found my eyes again, his Adam's apple bobbing hard in his throat.

Then, his lips were on mine again.

My knees buckled when he pressed me back farther, and I fell into his sheets. His lips never left mine as he helped guide me up, crawling over me, every part of him towering over every part of me as he settled between my legs. I sighed when the warmth of his bare chest brushed my nipples, and the heat of him lined up with the heat of me, only his sweatpants and my tiny strap of a thong separating us.

Noah pulled back, balancing on his elbows above me as he searched my eyes, my hair, every centimeter of my face. He seemed to be tracing lines between my freckles — first with his eyes, and then with the tender tip of his finger.

"God, Ruby Grace," he whispered, shaking his head. "What are you doing to me? I feel like I'm under your spell."

I smirked, rolling my hips against his. "The real question is, what should I do to you *next*?"

Noah groaned at the contact, biting his lower lip and kissing me hard before he pulled back again, this time peppering my collarbone with kisses and shifting his weight.

"*You* aren't going to do anything to me. Not yet. Not before I get my turn."

The chuckle I meant to give in response was lost in my throat, kidnapped by a gasp that ripped through me at the shock of his mouth on my sensitive nipple. He sucked gently, rolling his tongue over the puckered tip before trailing over to the other. He massaged the weight of each breast in his hands, his mouth devouring me like I was the sweetest dessert.

And then, he trailed down.

His lips wandered like lost travelers over the hills and valleys of my rib cage, sliding down the middle of my abdomen, traipsing the freckles between my hips before he settled on his elbows between my thighs. His eyes were dark and hooded as he gazed up at me, and with that look of sin holding me captive, he pressed one, feather-light kiss to the wet center of my panties.

I moaned, back arching up off the bed as my fists twisted in the sheets. When he slipped his thumbs under the straps of my thong and slowly trailed it down my thighs, I couldn't help but watch, and I loved the way his eyes darkened even more when I was bare beneath him.

I'd never had anyone that up close and personal to my vagina.

Anthony never went down on me, and as far as I was concerned, it was just something that happened in the romance movies Betty loved to force me to watch. But the second Noah had my panties off my ankles and dropped somewhere off the bed, he dragged his tongue up the inside of each of my thighs, and then, he pressed that same brush of a kiss to the same spot.

But nothing was between us this time.

Every inch of me trembled at the warmth of that kiss, and even more so at the loss of it. I gripped onto the sheets again, like they could ground me, like somehow they could steady my shaking nerves.

"You're trembling, Legs," Noah whispered against the spot he'd just kissed, his breath hot and wet and sending another wave of chills over me.

"I'm so nervous I feel like I'm about to pass out."

The words flew out before I thought better of them, and Noah laughed, pulling away long enough to look up at me. "Why nervous? It's just me. It's just us."

"I know," I said, shifting until I was on my elbows and could meet his gaze. "I just... I've never..." I didn't even want to say it, so I just nodded to where he was between my legs. "You know."

His face sobered. "A man has never eaten your pussy before?"

A fierce blush shaded my cheeks at the *p* word.

*What, am I twelve?*

"Never," I think I said. I wasn't sure if I just moved my lips or if an actual sound came out.

"Not even your *fiancé*?"

I shook my head.

For a moment, anger flashed in his eyes, and he shook his head again, jaw muscles ebbing and flowing in tense little pops. Then, he let out a long breath and met my gaze again. "Well, just proves to me once again that he's a fucking idiot. And now I'm hell bent on devouring your pussy until you have the best orgasm of your goddamn life."

I swallowed, the blush on my cheeks paling immediately as my fists twisted in the sheets. Noah glanced at my hands, and a devilish smirk spread on his handsome-as-hell face.

"Hold on tight."

Without another tease, or so much as a warning, his mouth was on me.

*On* me — as in, his lips surrounded my clit, his tongue tracing the sensitive bud in a circular rhythm before he dragged it back and forth in slow, long rolls.

I fell back into the sheets, my entire body convulsing at the feel of his expert tongue. I couldn't wrap my head around anything he was doing, and as soon as I felt like I was used to the sensation, his tongue would start a new pattern, or he'd suck my clit between his teeth, or drag his tongue between my lips and dive inside me before returning to my clit.

Every second was a new feeling, a new reason to shake, a new thief of breath.

"Yep," Noah said, kissing the inside of my thigh as he ran his hand up over my knee. "He's a fucking idiot. Because you have the sweetest pussy, Ruby Grace."

I didn't have time to blush or moan or bite my lip because in the next breath, he slid one finger inside me, right up to the knuckle.

I was so wet, he slid right in, but I still felt every inch of him stretching me open. I gasped, head rolling back in the pillow, fists abandoning the sheets to fly back and hang onto the top of his headboard. I needed friction. I needed grounding. I needed *something* to keep me from flying out of this universe entirely at the feel of him inside me *and* sucking me at the same time.

My mind raced, trying to piece it all together as Noah worked between my legs. I'd never felt so cherished, so worshipped. Having a man between my legs was somehow the most powerful experience, and I reveled in it, letting every time I'd ever wanted to touch him or kiss him build up in my memory before I'd remind myself that it was happening. That time was now.

Noah Becker had his face between my legs, and I was like a prisoner surrendering willingly to whatever consequence lay before us after this moment.

It didn't matter. *Nothing* mattered.

Nothing but this man and this moment.

Noah stayed between my thighs for hours. I was certain of it. It *had* to be hours. After working me open, he slipped another finger inside me, his tongue rolling in a new way as he curled his fingers inside me. And I felt it building, like a slow, glowing ember that caught oxygen and exploded into flames with another flick of his tongue.

"Noah," I breathed, heart racing, legs trembling. "Oh, God. Noah. *Noah*."

His free hand gripped my ass, pulling me even more into him, the other working its magic inside me. And when he circled my clit faster, faster, giving me the friction I needed, I completely spiraled.

Sheets and headboard be damned. I flew into the atmosphere, every part of me alive and burning, stars invading my vision as I succumbed to the darkness and panted out each rolling, euphoric wave of my orgasm.

I was floating.

I was soaring.

I was nothing at all and everything I'd ever wanted to be.

My heart was still racing in my chest, breaths loud and heavy in the space between us as Noah slowly climbed his way back up, trailing kisses along the way. When he settled between my already sore legs again, he smirked, brushing my wild hair away from my face and kissing me.

I tasted me on him, tangy and sweet.

"That was hot," he said, his words reverberating through me. "*You* are hot."

"Noah," I breathed, threading my fingers through his hair and pulling his mouth to mine. I kissed him long and hard, feverishly, like my next breath had to be syphoned from that kiss. "I want you inside me."

He let out a shaky breath, pressing his forehead to mine. "Are you sure?"

I nodded, pulling at him again, nails on his back and in his hair and everywhere I could grab until he pushed off me, standing at the edge of the bed. He kept his eyes on mine, a hard swallow marking his throat as he reached for the band of his sweatpants. He bent, taking them down with the motion, and when he stood again, I forgot my next breath.

I just stared, mouth open, heart stopping along with my lungs before they both kicked back to life.

*Oh, God.*

I'd felt him against me when he was on top, his erection pressed into my stomach, but even that couldn't have prepared me for what I was face to face with now.

"Don't be scared," he said, worry etched in his brows as he stepped toward me. The monster between his legs was hard and thick in his hand, and he stroked it once, twice, three times before he rounded the bed and sat down next to me. His back was against the headboard, his legs out in front of him, and I edged my way up until my back was against the headboard, too.

He was pumping, swallowing, watching my expression.

I was still staring between his legs.

"Come here," he said, voice low and raspy. He reached for my hand, and when I met his fingertips with my own, he locked eyes with me, moving us both until my hand was on his shaft.

His eyes closed at the touch. My mouth fell open again.

And slowly, carefully, I wrapped my hand around him and slid it down, down, all the way to the base before I rolled it back up.

A heavy breath broke through his nose, and his hand left mine, reaching for my thigh, instead. He squeezed, letting me explore, letting me stroke him — gently, slowly, his erection growing harder and harder with each pump.

I wanted him inside me.

I knew it would hurt. I knew I likely wasn't ready to fit all of him in me. But, I wanted to try. I *needed* to know what it felt like to be connected with him in that way — nothing between us, no beginning of him or ending of me — just one, blissful being.

I swallowed past the knot in my throat as I released his shaft, his eyes creaking open at the loss of my hand. He watched me with that heated stare as I crawled into his lap, my hands balancing on the headboard behind him as I lowered down.

His thick shaft slipped between my lips, and I rolled my hips, sliding my wet core up and down his erection. Each time I rolled, the tip of his shaft would rub my clit as the rest of him floated between my soaked lips, and I moaned, letting my head fall back at the sensation and gripping the headboard even tighter.

"Jesus Christ," he cursed. Prayed? "That feels so good. I'm not even inside you yet. How does that feel *so* fucking good?"

I moaned in response, still rolling my hips, coating him with my orgasm and feeling another one building in the process. When he was nice and wet, I reached down, bringing my gaze to his as I wrapped my hand around his cock.

"Condom?" I breathed.

Noah wrapped one arm around me, holding me in his lap as he leaned over and dug in the drawer of his bedside table. His hands disappeared behind my back when we were righted, and I heard the tear of the wrapper, felt him pull his shaft from my grip and cover it with the latex, and then, his hands were on my hips again, his eyes on mine, all the control in my hands.

I swallowed, forcing a shaky breath before I reached back again. He pulsed in my hand, hard and ready, and when I lined up the tip of him with my entrance, we both stopped.

Our breathing stopped.

*Time* stopped.

And I lowered, just an inch, just enough for everything in the universe to snap back into action.

We breathed a sigh of ecstasy in sync, and I lifted my hips before sliding down even farther, taking him a little more. Each time I lifted, each time I sank down on him a little more, our breathing accelerated. Noah groaned when I swallowed him whole, feeling the stretching burn from the inside out, and for a moment I just stayed there — him completely inside me, his hands bruising my hips, the moment branding my heart.

I lifted, sank back down.

Rolled my hips.

Rubbed my clit against his pelvis.

"*Fuuuuck,*" he groaned, wrapping his arms around me as he sat up a little more. We were chest to chest, and he held one strong arm around me while the other slid up my back, his hand cradling my head and pulling it into him. He pressed his forehead to mine, closing his eyes as he flexed his hips, and I whimpered, feeling the extra inch of him I couldn't reach on my own.

I didn't know sex could feel like this.

I didn't know anything in the *world* could feel like this.

It wasn't a hard, pounding fuck, the way Anthony loved to take me. It wasn't minutes of panting and then a heady, quick release and roll off of me.

This was art.

This was Noah, the painter, his hands the brushes, me the canvas.

This was me, the muse, feeling every breath of his like the fire that fueled my existence.

We were slick with sweat, rolling and slipping over each other as I rocked and he flexed, his mouth finding mine, kissing me with reverence as sighs and moans mingled between us. They seemed to dance in time with our movements — a thrust, a sigh, a flex, a kiss, a roll, a moan.

It was a beautiful waltz.

And we danced for hours.

I came again, rolling my clit against him as he flexed into me, and then he rolled us until I was on my stomach, my face in the pillows, back arched up off the bed and ass up in the air — waiting. He entered me from behind, and the sheer sensation of that new depth of penetration shocked both of us.

I sucked in a breath.

He groaned out my name.

And in the next breath, he came, pulsing his release inside the condom as he pumped in and out of me, over and over, until every drop was expelled.

For a long moment, he stayed there, balanced on his hands above me as I released my grip on the sheets. Our breaths slowed, chests aching with the release of air, and he gently withdrew, discarding the condom in the trashcan by his bed before he collapsed back onto the bed.

I didn't have time to even reach for my panties before he pulled me into him, surrounding me with his arms, his legs, hands weaving into my hair, breath skating over the skin of my neck.

And I didn't know how to fight what happened next.

My eyes welled with tears, nose stinging as the dam broke loose, and as soon as those tears hit Noah's chest, he pulled back, worried eyes searching mine.

"I'm sorry," I whispered, wiping at one before Noah took my place, his thumbs brushing over my wet cheeks. "I don't know why I'm crying."

"It's okay," he responded, voice just as low. "I do."

My brows pulled together, eyes flicking back and forth between his. "You do?"

He nodded. "I felt it, too, Ruby Grace," he said, pulling me back into him and surrounding me with his heat, with his weight. "I felt it, too."

I closed my eyes, two more tears slipping free as I pulled him closer, wanting more, needing to seam us together in every way possible. It didn't feel real, the whole experience morphing in my mind like a dream I was suddenly aware of, a dream I was about to wake up from.

So, I held on tight, willing it to be true, willing *him* to be real.

My body succumbed to the darkness, my mind following quickly, every part of me slipping into the promising black space around us like it was the open arms of a long-lost friend.

If he was a dream, I would sleep, just so I could keep him a little longer.

I'd sleep, and maybe — just maybe — I'd wake on a day where I got to keep him forever.

## NOAH

*God, I don't want to wake her.*

It was all I could think the next morning as I sat on the edge of my bed, watching Ruby Grace sleep. Her hair had fallen out of the tie she'd fastened it in at some point in the night, and wild, red tendrils splayed over my pillow like flower petals. Her mouth was open just a bit, one leg kicked out of the sheets, eyes fluttering a bit behind her lids.

She was dreaming.

I hoped it was of me.

I sighed, watching her with a sinking feeling in my gut. She hadn't stirred since we fell asleep together, which was late afternoon yesterday, other than when I'd woken her up somewhere around midnight because her sweet ass was rubbing against my erection. We'd slowly made love, both of us on our sides, our eyes still closed, and as soon as we'd both reached our climax, she'd passed out again.

But my body woke me again at five — craving her, craving so, *so* much more of her.

So, I crawled out of bed — begrudgingly — and got a workout in.

I needed to do *something* with all the pent-up energy.

And the entire time I did my calisthenics, I thought about the girl in my bed. I ran over my memories of the night, searing into my mind what it felt like to touch her so I'd never forget it. And beneath all of that, I worked through the heavier feeling in my chest, the one that was as foreign as it was somehow familiar.

It was deeper than sex.

Now that I'd had her, I knew I couldn't live in a world where I *didn't*.

I wanted to let her in, let her see all of me, and I wanted to see all of her, in return.

While I'd spent the morning working out and planning every word I wanted to say to her, and knowing exactly *where* I wanted to take her to say it all, she'd been here, in my bed, sleeping. Knocked out. Completely exhausted.

After everything that had happened yesterday, I knew she needed rest, and I didn't want to take that from her.

But it was Sunday in Stratford, and there wasn't an excuse outside of being dead that could get Ruby Grace Barnett out of going to church.

I was still a little sweaty from my workout as I swept a strand of her hair from her face, running my fingertip down the line of her jaw. She stirred a little, stretching her arms up above her head and pointing her toes before her eyes fluttered open.

The moment they locked with mine, she smiled.

And my heart nearly burst at the sight of that sleepy smile.

"Well, good morning," she said, voice raspy. "You're sweaty."

I chuckled. "And you're sleepy."

She groaned, rubbing her eyes. "I really am. I feel like I could sleep for years."

"Here," I said, offering her the cup of hot tea I'd made her. "Earl Grey. Just a little bit of caffeine, but it should help."

She took it in thanks, scooting up until she was seated against the headboard, and after her first sip, she hummed.

"That's good," she said, wrapping her hands around the warm mug.

My sheets pooled at her waist, but her breasts were bare, exposed, just sitting there right in front of me in all their perky glory. Ruby Grace followed my gaze and gave me a knowing smirk.

"Whatcha thinking about, Noah Becker?"

"Just you, Ruby Grace," I mused, meeting her gaze again. "Always you."

Her eyes softened, one hand leaving the mug and reaching out for mine. She folded her palm over my knuckles, lacing her fingers with mine, a thumb brushing my wrist.

"Tell me last night was real," she whispered.

I swallowed, squeezing her hand in mine. "It was real," I promised her. "It was perfect."

She nodded, closing her eyes on a smile before she took another sip of her tea. For a while, we just sat there, eyes wandering over the other, gentle smiles on our lips. There was so much I wanted to tell her in that moment, so much I wanted to make known, but I knew it wasn't the right time. Or the right place. There were things I needed to do before I made my big gesture, before I showed her the way it could be, if she were to choose me.

If she were to give me the honor of being the next man she called her own.

"I want to take you somewhere," I said after a while, smoothing my thumb over her palm. "Will you go somewhere with me?"

"Where?"

I shook my head. "I don't want to tell you. Not yet. But... will you go with me?"

She leaned up, placing her mug on the bedside table before she took my face in her hands. "Anywhere."

I smiled.

"But, not today," she said next. "Today, I need to deal with... all of *this*." She gestured to the space around us, as if her former fiancé and her family and the rest of the town were right there in my bedroom with us. Then, she turned my hand over, checking the time on my heart monitor watch with another groan. "Starting with church. In like an hour."

I chuckled. "I understand."

Reaching for her hand again, I squeezed it in mine, frowning as I watched her. She was so young — *too* young to be faced with the hardship she was about to endure. It wasn't going to be easy to break off an engagement, especially not in this town.

And *especially* not with her family.

"Why don't you take a few days?" I offered. "I'll be right here, but you do what you have to do. Okay?"

Her lips formed a brief smile before it fell again. "Okay. Yeah. I think that's best."

"Do you want me to come with you? To be with you for any of it?"

She sighed at that. "No," she said, rubbing her free hand down her face. "As much as I know it'd be easier that way, this is something I need to handle on my own."

"I get that," I said, lacing our fingertips together. "How about you save Friday for me, then?"

"Friday," she mused.

I nodded. "Gives me some time to get everything together."

At that, she cocked a beautiful eyebrow. "What are you planning, Noah Becker?"

"That's for me to know and you to find out, Ruby Grace Barnett," I retorted, kissing her nose, her cheeks, and then capturing her lips. She inhaled at the connection, breathing into me, a sigh leaving her lips when I finally pulled back.

Her mouth curved into a playful smile. "Last night, you said I have strawberry smoothie lips."

"You do," I said, running my thumb over said lips. The bottom one stuck to my skin, pulling down to expose her teeth before it popped back up.

That sight shot electricity straight down to my cock.

I groaned, shaking my head and readjusting myself in my shorts as I slid my hand back into her hair. "I thought that the first time I saw you back in town. And every day since, I wondered if they tasted like a strawberry smoothie, too."

"And do they?"

I shook my head, leaning in to kiss her and elicit another breathy sigh.

I decided it was my new favorite sound.

"Better," I murmured against her lips. "They taste even better."

# Chapter Fifteen

## RUBY GRACE

Church felt like the Gravitron from the Tennessee State Fair that morning.

One minute, I was smiling like a loon, stomach flipping as I replayed every moment with Noah the night before.

The next, that stomach flip would turn into more of a roll, and I'd lurch forward, feeling like I was going to vomit any minute.

In the course of twenty-four hours, everything had changed.

I glanced down at the ring on my finger — the one I'd put back on before leaving Noah's — and bile rose in my throat again. I couldn't wait to take it off. I couldn't wait to shake off the weight of the wedding to a man who didn't love me, who didn't care about anything other than what I would look like on his arm, what my family could do for his campaign.

I felt like the biggest fool, but soon, it would be *him* who felt that way.

Still, I knew my stomach wouldn't stop turning — not until it was all said and done, and maybe even then, too. I didn't know where to start, who to tell first, and I didn't have any way of knowing what to expect once our house of cards crumbled.

Our friends would be shocked.

The town would gossip.

Mama's heart would be broken, no doubt.

And Daddy? I had no idea how he would take the news. Part of me wondered if he'd disown me, if I'd even be able to call myself a Barnett by the end of the week.

Part of me didn't care, as long as I was free of the man who had lied to me for the past year.

And maybe that was what upset me most — that under all the anxiety over what was to come, I was still heartbroken over what had happened. The man I had promised my forever to wasn't the man I thought I knew at all, and as much as I wished I didn't hurt over that fact, as much as I wished Noah being with me the night before fixed everything, it didn't.

I had still been betrayed.

My heart fluttered at the thought of Noah, a small smile curving on my lips. I reached up, smoothing my fingertips over the bottom one, remembering how it felt when his tongue swept across the sensitive skin.

The way he touched me, the way he made love to me...

It was unlike anything I'd ever experienced.

How could I feel more passion and care in one night with that man than I felt in an entire year with the one I promised to marry?

As if he could sense I was thinking of him, Noah stretched his arms up over his head, resting them on the back of the pew before he did a casual scan of the congregation like he wasn't just trying to look back at me.

But he did.

When our eyes locked, every shred of doubt, every fear faded.

He smiled.

I smiled.

And then I counted down the minutes until I could be in his arms again.

"Mama, can we talk?"

She was in the kitchen, baking her famous lemon squares for her meeting with the women's circle at church the next day. Her auburn hair was up in a messy bun — which Mama never did, unless she was stressed, cleaning, or baking.

Sometimes, it was a combination of the three.

"Sure, sweetie. Just let me get these in the oven and we can pull up the seating chart again."

I shifted. "It's actually not about the seating chart."

"Oh," she said, opening the oven and sliding the baking sheet of squares inside before she popped it closed again. "Is it the registry? I know we're a little behind, but we can get it all done before next Sunday. Most people wait until the last minute to buy gifts for the shower, anyway."

"Mama," I said, taking a seat at the kitchen island. "It's important."

I set the ring Anthony had given me on the counter with a gentle *clink*, metal hitting granite, and it was as if that sound alone stopped Mama in her tracks.

She stopped right in front of the sink, one hand under the faucet and the other ready to turn it on, but she never did. Instead, she just stood like that, glancing at the ring, at me, back at the ring, at me again.

Her face paled, and she turned back to the sink, kicking on the faucet with her wrist before running her hands under the water. "We still need to decide what readings you want to do during the ceremony. I was thinking we should do something fresh. Corinthians is so overdone."

My heart squeezed.

"Mama."

"And you know, maybe we *should* do the twine like you wanted. Instead of the coral ribbon." She dried her hands haphazardly on one of the towels hanging from the oven, immediately launching into clean up. "You were right, that would look so much classier."

"Mama."

"And we need to go in for your final fitting on Friday. Don't forget that."

"Mama!"

She winced, shutting her eyes and hanging her head between her shoulders with the sponge in her hand. She shook her head, eyes still closed, and I knew in her mind she was praying to God that I hadn't actually taken my ring off.

"Please," I begged her, my own throat tightening. "Can you please sit down?"

She sniffed, dropping the sponge on the counter and sitting at the stool across from me. She wouldn't look at me. She kept her eyes on her hands, which were folded now, her right fingers playing with the ring that adorned her left.

I inhaled a deep breath once she was seated, once the ball was in my court. Dad and Anthony had gone out for the evening, back to the casino, and after talking to Annie first, she'd helped me decide that Mom was the first person

I should tell in the family. From there, I could make a plan to talk to Anthony, to Dad, and figure out how to break the news to our close friends and family — and to the town.

If there was one thing Mama excelled at, it was damage control.

"I need your help," I finally said.

She lifted her head a little, her worried eyes finding mine.

"I overheard Anthony on the phone yesterday," I explained, and tears flooded my eyes, the shivers too much as I tried to steady my shaking hands by stuffing them between my thighs and the barstool. "He said some really awful things."

"Men say awful things all the time," she replied quickly. "They're stupid. And half the time, drunk."

"He was sober."

"Whatever he said, I'm sure he didn't mean it."

"I'm calling off the wedding."

Her eyes closed, and she shook her head, inhaling a deep breath before she opened her eyes again. This time, she held her shoulders back, her chin high, eyes locking with mine. "No, you most certainly are not, young lady."

"I am. And I need your help, because we both know this is going to take a lot of damage control."

"You're not calling off the wedding!" she hissed, whispering as if someone might overhear. "You can't," she said, voice calmer.

"He said he fully intends on cheating on me," I said, as gently as I could with those being the words coming from my mouth. "He said I'm perfect to fit the *role* he needs his dutiful wife to play. He said I was *bred for this*."

"And you were."

My mouth fell open. "I'm not a horse, Mother."

"No, but you *are* the daughter of the Mayor of Stratford, and you *are* a Barnett. Do you understand the implications of what you're saying? If you called off this wedding, the entire town would have something to say about it. You'd make our family a laughingstock. You'd bring us *shame*."

"And if I *don't* call off this wedding, I will be miserable for the rest of my life."

Mom threw her hands up, rolling her eyes. "Oh, for heaven's sake. So what, he wants to have some girls on the side. You think he's the only husband to ever have that thought? Your father has had many a secretary in his day, and you know what? It never mattered to me. Because it was *me* who had the house, and the kids, and the life I always wanted. Those girls, those *hussies*?" She shook her head. "They were just sex, sweetheart. It means nothing."

My mouth fell open wider. "Dad cheated on you?"

She waved me off. "Don't be so dramatic. It's not a big deal. And neither is any of that stuff Anthony said. He cares about you, Ruby Grace. He wants to provide for you, give you a home and a place to raise your children. He'll make sure you never want for anything."

"He doesn't love me, Mama," I whispered.

"What does love have to do with marriage?"

My heart broke again, this time by the realization that the love I thought my parents had was a sham. My father had cheated. My mother had stayed anyway. They weren't in love, they were in a business agreement.

But I would not do the same.

"Everything," I said. "It has *everything* to do with marriage. I refuse to marry a man who doesn't love me, who sees me as a prize or another tick on his list of things to get done in order to make it to a run for president someday. I'm a human being. I'm a woman. I deserve a man who will love and honor and cherish me, just as I do him."

"Anthony will do all those things."

"While he cheats on me? While he tells his father that I have no ambitions and I'm *pretty, so that's a bonus*?" I scoffed. "Mother, do you hear yourself?"

"You are not calling off this wedding," she said, ignoring me and shaking her head. She stood again, crossing to the sponge and picking up where she left off cleaning.

"I am."

"You are not."

"Mama, I—"

"You can't!" she screamed, turning in place. The sponge fell to the floor and her hands flew to her face, sobs racking through her in the next instant.

It was just like I'd thought

I broke her heart.

"Oh, Mama," I said, rounding the island and sweeping her into my arms. I held her tight, holding back my own tears. "I'm so sorry."

"No, no," she said, sniffing and swiping at the tears on her face as she pulled back from my embrace. "You don't understand. You *can't* call off the wedding." Her eyes found mine. "We made a deal, Ruby Grace. With Anthony and his father."

My blood ran cold. "A deal?"

Anthony's words swam in my head.

*They need us to play our part, just like we need Ruby Grace to play hers.*

Mom winced, her face screwing up before a few more tears were let loose. She swiped them away. "Honey, your father was in trouble."

"Trouble?" I asked. "What kind of trouble?"

"Well," she said on a sigh. "You know him and his card games. At the casino, he's fine. Once he runs out of the money he came to play with, that's it. And I keep a tight leash on what he's allowed to piss away." She let out a breath, brows quivering again. "But, I didn't know. I didn't know he'd been playing at the underground casino, the one the Scooters run out of their basement. I knew he went sometimes, just to show face, network, but I never thought..."

"Mom," I interrupted. "What kind of trouble?"

She sniffed, running the back of her hand under her nose. "He was taking loans from them at the casino for cards, sure he would win and pay them back. But he kept coming up in the red. Over and over again." She shook her head. "He didn't even tell me until the Scooters threatened to expose everything if we didn't pay up."

I covered my mouth.

*No.*

"We were going to lose *everything*, Ruby Grace," Mom said, reaching forward to grab my free hand in hers. "The house. The cars. *Everything*. He was in an amount of debt we couldn't even dream of repaying."

"But, he's the mayor," I said, lip trembling. "He's always made good money. We're fine."

Mom shook her head. "He never made money like this."

I dropped my hand from my mouth, shaking my head. "I don't understand."

"We were in deep, trying to figure out what our options were, when Anthony came to your father to ask for your hand," she explained. "And... well... we saw an out. We saw a way to make our problem disappear, and Anthony saw a way to get what he needed, too."

My blood ran cold.

*It couldn't be.*

It couldn't possibly be my mother standing across from me, speaking about me as if I was some old antique china cabinet or a prized hog to be bartered with.

But it was.

And suddenly, the betrayal I *thought* I'd felt from Anthony was nothing.

"How could you?" I whispered, shaking my head as tears flooded my eyes.

"I'm so sorry, baby," she said, reaching for me.

I yanked away.

"It was our only choice. We would have lost everything."

"Yeah? Well, now you lose *me*," I spat, turning on my heels. "I'm calling off the wedding."

"Ruby Grace! Please!"

She grabbed me from behind, spinning me around to see the devastation in her eyes — the *desperation* in her eyes.

"This is your family," she said through her tears. "This is your father, and your mother, and your sister. This is your family's legacy, the Barnett name, our entire reputation. This is more than just a wedding. This is the only way to save our family from complete and utter wreckage." She stood taller. "And I understand it isn't fair. I do. And I am so, *so* sorry that you are in the middle of this." Mama swallowed, like she didn't like the taste of the next words she was about to speak. "But, you are a part of this family. And that means that when a fire happens, you do whatever you have to do to put it out."

My next breath felt like the fire she spoke of. It was hot in my lungs, searing every fiber of muscle and organ around it. I whimpered at the feel, at my mother's hands on my arms, at the plea she was giving.

"You cannot walk out on this family," she said, tears building in her eyes once more. "We are a unit. We stay together — *always* — and we will get through this together. But we need you, Ruby Grace. Your father needs you. Your sister needs you. *I* need you."

I couldn't speak, couldn't think, couldn't *breathe*. Every muscle in my body was locked in place, heart racing, pulse heavy in my ears.

"You can call off the wedding," she finally said. "But if you do, you're calling off this family, too."

My mother's eyes searched mine in a way they never had before, in a way I never knew they could. I'd never seen my strong, commanding mother look so broken, so desperate, so on the verge of losing it. She looked at me like I was the key to everything, and I realized in that moment that I was.

She was right.

This wasn't just about me anymore.

And bile rose in my throat at what that meant.

We both jumped a little when the front door opened, Dad calling in from the foyer that he and Anthony were home. Mom's eyes doubled in size when they looked back at me, her pupils dilating as they flicked back and forth.

She needed an answer.

She needed to know what I would do.

She needed to know if she was safe, if our family was okay, or if everything was about to be blown to smithereens.

"Mmm, are those lemon squares I smell?" Dad asked, his voice closer now. He and Anthony would round into the kitchen at any moment, and either everything would be exactly as they left it, or nothing would be the same again.

Time was up.

And I had to make the hardest decision of my life.

Mom sucked in a breath when I pulled out of her grasp, but I didn't meet her eyes again as I made my way to the island.

Just as Dad and Anthony swung into the kitchen, I slipped the ring back on my finger.

# Chapter Sixteen

## NOAH

I could barely contain my excitement when Friday finally came around.

All week long, my thoughts had been tied up in Ruby Grace.

When I was working, I'd watch my hands make whiskey barrels, but in my head, I remembered the way they looked like making Ruby Grace squirm in my bed. When I was at home, I saw her everywhere — on my couch, in my bed, in my shower. When I visited Mom in the middle of the week for a surprise dinner, I thought of Ruby Grace, of how one day I would dance with *her* in *our* kitchen.

I was in too deep, too fast. I knew it. I tried to hold myself back, but it was pointless.

I'd had a taste of her, and now, I wouldn't rest until I had all of her, too.

To pass the time that work didn't take up, I worked on my surprise for Ruby Grace. I knew exactly what I would say to tell her what I'd done, and where I'd take her to do it.

That's why, on Friday night, I asked her to meet me at Tank's stable at dusk.

I was getting him ready, brushing him and giving him a snack before I got him saddled up, when I saw a pair of familiar legs making their way down the hill.

The sun was setting, the clouds turning orange and pink and purple, casting a fairytale glow over the field of wildflowers Ruby Grace walked through to get to me. I paused where I was petting Tank, breath catching in my throat at the sight of her. She had her hands in the back pockets of the tiny jean shorts she wore, her long hair an illuminated orange and floating on the breeze behind her as she walked. She was so tanned from the summer, and the white, flowy tank top she wore just accentuated that bronze glow even more.

I swallowed, watching her take each step.

The closer she got, the more my heart raced.

I let out a whistle when she was close enough to hear, and as soon as I did, a grin split her face.

"Damn, Legs," I said, crossing my arms and not bothering to hide my eyes as they scanned her. "You should come with a warning label, you know that? *Warning: this woman will knock any unsuspecting man dead upon first glance. Proceed with caution.*"

She chuckled, shaking her head and stopping a few feet away from me. She crossed her arms to mirror mine. "You say that like you would have heeded the warning."

"Oh, I one-hundred percent would have disregarded it entirely," I said. Then, I opened my arms. "C'mere."

A tinge of sadness touched her eyes as she stepped into me. When I wrapped my arms around her, she rested her head on my chest, a deep sigh leaving her lips.

"Long day?" I asked.

"Long week," she answered, and her hands fisted at my back, twisting my flannel shirt in her grasp like she was in danger of me floating away. "Can you just hug me for a while?"

"For as long as you want," I answered easily.

She sighed again, turning her face until her forehead was buried in my chest. She held me tight, and I held her tighter, gently swaying us as the sun set. And though she seemed content there, *happy*, even — I couldn't shake the feeling that something was wrong.

It wasn't until Tank neighed, annoyed at the lack of attention, that Ruby Grace finally let me go.

"I see you, too, Tank," she said, voice soft as the smile on her face as she slipped out of my arms and over to him. She ran her hand over his neck, fingers touching his mane. "You look like you're ready for an adventure."

"I think he knows where we're going," I said. "It's one of his favorite places, too."

"And where exactly is it that we're going?"

I smiled, patting Tank's saddle. "Hop up and you'll find out."

We were both quiet on the trail, the only sound the rhythmic, soothing sound of Tank's hooves hitting the dirt and the soft buzzing of the insects coming alive as the sun set. I let my eyes wash over the lake, the tall weeds and flowers in the fields, the tall trees, their branches hanging over and shading the trail from time to time. And Ruby Grace rested her cheek between my shoulder blades, her arms wrapped around me, breathing soft.

Something was on her mind.

We hadn't talked much all week — mostly because I was honoring my promise to let her have her time to sort everything out. I had no idea what had happened since we parted, how she had broken the news to her family, to Anthony. I imagined they were still figuring out how to handle the fall out, since I hadn't heard anyone gossiping about it yet.

I knew that time would come. And I'd be there for her when it did.

"I think there's a storm coming," she mused, pointing to some building clouds in the distance. As if on cue, a soft roll of thunder made its way over the lake.

"Don't worry. We'll have shelter."

The sun had just dipped below the horizon when we reached our destination, and I pulled Tank to a stop, hopping down before tying him up to his favorite tree. It was right by the edge of the lake, and he could graze the grass next to it and get as much water as he wanted.

"Good boy," I said, rubbing his neck as I fished out an apple from my saddle pack.

"A treehouse?" Ruby Grace asked as I helped her down. She slid her hands in her back pockets as soon as her boots were on the ground, and I inhaled a stiff breath.

I was so jealous of those goddamn hands...

"This isn't just *a* treehouse," I told her. "This is *the* treehouse. It's in the best location, made from the sturdiest wood, and it has the absolute coolest hangout inside. It's award-winning. And usually, girls aren't allowed. But, you know, I'll make an exception just this once."

She smirked, nudging me with her shoulder as she scanned the treehouse.

It was nestled in an old, sturdy oak, with planks of wood hammered to the trunk that led all the way up to the door. It wasn't a luxurious treehouse, like the fancy ones that had plumbing and a bed. There were folks in town who built those kinds, mostly with the purpose of renting them out to tourists. But no, this was a *true* treehouse — built by a father with love for his sons.

Ruby Grace seemed to be taking in every corner of it, from the different-colored wood to the small windows and tin roof. Her hazel eyes swept over every inch.

And my eyes stayed on her.

"Can we go inside?"

I scoffed. "Of course. Why do you think we're here?" I unhooked my saddle bag, tossing it over my shoulder before I held my hand out for hers. "M'lady."

I helped Ruby Grace up the stairs first, popping the latch on the bottom door and keeping my hand on the small of her back as she climbed inside. When she plopped down on the floor and looked around, I reached up and to the right, flicking on the generator, and with it, all the string lights hanging inside.

And that's when Ruby Grace gasped.

"Wow," she breathed as I climbed the rest of the way up. I still couldn't take my eyes off her, not with her eyes wide like that, her mouth hanging open.

The inside of the treehouse was where the real magic lived.

There were eclectic rugs covering every space of the floor, collected over the years from places Mom and Dad traveled together. Four, giant bean bags large enough for at least two people each sat in every corner, and the corners were decorated to fit different styles — one for each brother.

Michael's had his old guitar leaned up against the wood, posters of his favorite southern rock bands taped to the walls. His corner used to be a lot younger, since he was only four when the house was first built. Over the years, he'd added to it, decorating it to fit his style the more he came into himself.

Logan's corner was two walls of very neatly organized bookshelves — his favorites and others that Dad bought for him to read throughout the years. They were ordered by author last name and then by color.

Jordan's had football legends ranging from last year all the way back to the early fifties, complete with a shelf of limited edition trading cards and a signed Tom Brady pig skin on a gold holder.

And mine was decorated with sailboats and constellations, with globes of all shapes and sizes, and a world map that spanned the entire wall behind my bean bag.

In the center was a large, square table where we would play board games, do puzzles, and have arm wrestling competitions. And above it all was a giant skylight window, revealing small branches of the tree and the now dark purple sky above.

"This is yours?"

I nodded. "Mine. And my brothers'. We all share it."

"I never knew this was out here," she mused, still taking it all in.

"Most people don't, not unless we bring them out here. And trust me when I say we don't bring many people out here. In fact, you're only the third guest outside of the family. At least, that I know of."

A smile bloomed over her face, eyes shining as they met mine. "Really?"

"Really."

"I feel special."

Her smile was sad, eyes worn.

I couldn't wait to get her mind off everything that put that sadness there.

"Good," I said, standing before I offered my hand down to her. "You are."

I helped her stand, and when she did, we were chest to chest, breath to breath, eyes dancing over lips. She swallowed, and that sadness she'd worn before crept back in, shading her eyes as she watched me.

I stamped down the feeling that something was off, choosing instead to slide my hands into her back pockets and pull her into me. She took a deep breath as my palms slid against the denim, and I cupped her gently, tugging her close.

"I'd like to kiss you, Ruby Grace," I whispered. My eyes flicked between hers, but her gaze was locked on my lips, her hands resting on my chest.

She didn't answer, just nodded, hands fisting in my shirt and pulling me closer as her chin angled up. I slipped my hands from her pockets, trailing my fingertips up over her arms before I slid my hands into her hair, cradling the bottom of her head, thumbs framing her jaw. She closed her eyes, a soft breath escaping her parted lips and touching mine before I closed the distance and kissed her.

Part of me wondered if the magic would fade, if now that we'd crossed the lines between us and taken each other when we knew it was wrong, if the chemistry would die. Maybe it was just lust. Maybe it was just me wanting someone I couldn't have.

The moment our lips touched, I knew it was more.

We both inhaled, like we'd been under water until our lips locked, and that was our first breath of oxygen in days. We drank each other in, hands roaming, pulling, touching, pleading. The kiss was gentle at first, just one long press of her lips to mine, but then we moved, lips opening and closing, tongues sweeping, teeth grazing the flesh tenderly.

She was shaking.

I was, too.

And when I pulled back, pressing my forehead to hers, we both let out a trembling exhale.

"I've wanted to do that all week," I confessed.

I thought she'd smile, or laugh, but if anything, her face seemed to crumple more. "Noah..."

"It's okay," I told her, pulling her into me. I wrapped my arms around her, resting my chin on the crown of her head. "I know it's been a long week. We don't have to get heavy yet. Here, let me show you something."

I grabbed her hand, leading her over to the aqua blue bean bag that was mine.

"Sit," I said, patting the giant chair. "You have to sit to get the full effect."

Ruby Grace obliged, a curious smile on her face once her cute butt was in the chair and her eyes were on me again. "Okay. Now what?"

I smiled. "Look up."

When she did, she gasped, eyes widening. "Whoa."

I plopped down in the chair next to her, shifting us until she was under my arm and we were both reclined back, our eyes on the tin ceiling. It was covered in pin-hole-sized dots that mirrored stars, building constellations that were illuminated by a light hanging outside the treehouse. The holes were covered by glass, shielding any outside weather, and Dad had painted the tin roof above my section a dark, navy blue to make it look like the night sky.

"Is that the Big Dipper?" she asked, pointing to the constellation.

I nodded. "Mm-hmm. And Orion's Belt, Scorpius, Lyra," I said, pointing to them as I called out their names. "There are more, but I can't remember them. Dad knew them all."

"Why are they only in this corner?"

"This is my corner of the tree house," I explained. "Dad built this for me and my brothers, and when he did, he tried to put a little bit of each of us in our own sections. At the time that he built it, I was hell bent on sailing around the world one day, and I had a big fascination with space and the constellations."

She smiled, eyes tracing the man-made stars. "Do you still want to? Sail around the world?"

I shrugged. "I mean, I think it'd be cool, but I think that desire shifted more to just traveling, in general. I'm so tied to this town, to the distillery, that I never leave. I want to change that in the coming years, get out and see the country, the world."

"I get that," Ruby Grace whispered. She opened her mouth to say something more, but paused, closing it again, instead.

I swallowed.

"My dad built this for us with the intention of us always having a safe place to run to. He never got upset if we wanted to take time out here, and he told us whenever we got angry, to come here and think it all through first before acting. And I mean, it wasn't *all* for angsty teenage boys," I said on a smirk. "We came out here just to have fun and hang out, too. But, it's been a safe place. For all of us. And I knew one day I'd bring someone out here, that I'd share it with them, I just didn't know who. Or when." I shifted, looking down at her in my arm. "I wanted to wait until it was the right time, the right person."

She pulled her gaze to mine, then, and her brows bent together. "Noah..."

"I know this has probably been one of the hardest weeks of your life," I said. "I can't even imagine what you've gone through in the days since I last held you. But, I'm so glad you came tonight."

Thunder rolled deep and heavy through the treehouse, and gentle rain began tapping on the tin roof, giving me the background music for the declaration I'd been preparing all week.

"Noah, we need to talk."

"I know," I said, thumbing her chin. "I know we do. But, can I go first?"

She frowned, but nodded in concession.

My stomach flipped a little as I sat up, turning until I could face her completely. "You aren't the first girl to come into my life, Ruby Grace, but you are the first girl to come into my life and leave a mark." I swallowed, searching her eyes with mine. "I've never experienced this kind of... feeling. It's selfless. I can't stop thinking about you, about all that you are, all that you *will* be. My thoughts are consumed with the way you make me feel, with the sound of your laugh, with the colors of your eyes, with the passion flowing from your heart for everyone you care about." I shook my head, taking both her hands in mine. "I thought it was impossible to ever make you mine... *truly* mine. And I would have settled on being your friend if I had to, but *God*, I'm so glad I don't have to."

Her eyes watered, and she bit her bottom lip, shaking her head and letting her gaze fall to my chest. "Noah..."

"I did something this week," I said, heart racing a little faster now. "And I know it's going to probably be a lot to take in, and you have time to consider everything, but..." My smile was so wide, I could barely speak through it. "I applied to AmeriCorps for you."

Her eyes snapped back to mine. "You... you *what*?"

"I only did it for two positions," I said quickly. "And only for two that I thought you would be perfect for, two that I knew you'd love. They're both out west. One of them is working in a center focused on mental health and substance abuse victims, and the other is on a Native American reservation working with senior citizens." My hands started shaking the more I spoke, my excitement growing. "I had to do some digging for your community service history, and I wrote a motivational statement on your behalf, but... well... yeah. I applied for you."

She gaped at me, and my heart raced more.

"Obviously, you don't have to go," I said, trying to gauge her reaction. I thought maybe she was in shock, or maybe she didn't think it was possible, that this was something she could do. I aimed to show her that it was. "And you can apply to different ones if those don't interest you. I just... I wanted you to know that you can do whatever you want. If you want to go into the Corp, you can. If you want to go back to school, you can. Because even if your parents cut you off, AmeriCorps will help pay for your education. And I'll go with you," I said, but as soon as the words left my lips, I paled. "I mean, if you want me to. Or I can stay here and wait, whatever you want. But what I'm trying to say is... we're a team, Ruby Grace." I smiled, smoothing my thumbs over her wrists. "We're in this together, and it's not just about me and my dreams. It's about you and yours, too."

The rain picked up, the *ting ting* on the roof the only sound between us as Ruby Grace opened her mouth, shut it again, opened it, shut it. She searched my eyes with a look I couldn't decipher — something between awe, love, shock, and hurt. All of those emotions existed in equal measure in those hazel eyes, and my stomach knotted tighter, my thumbs still rubbing her wrists.

"Can you say something, please?" I said on a soft laugh.

Ruby Grace rolled her lips together before closing her eyes, and she shook her head, as if the next words she was about to speak were burning her tongue but she was holding her mouth closed to try to keep them in anyway.

And when she finally spoke, I understood why.

**RUBY GRACE**

My throat burned as I tried to sort through the thoughts in my head.

Every fiber of my heart urged me to throw myself into Noah's arms, to wrap myself up in him and cry tears of thankfulness. Here he was, the man I'd always dreamed of, showing me the kind of love I'd wanted all my life — the kind of love my fiancé would never give me.

And I had to walk away from it.

I had to walk away from *him.*

Tears stung my eyes when I finally opened them. Noah stared back at me, hope lit up in his cobalt blue irises, and he waited for me to speak.

*You're amazing.*

*No one has ever cared for me this way.*

*I feel more like myself when I'm with you than I ever have before.*

*You're everything I want.*

*I love you.*

"How could you?" I said, instead, and all the color drained from Noah's face when the words were in the air between us.

"I..." He closed his mouth, swallowing. "What?"

The tears I'd been holding at bay broke free, sliding down each cheek in parallel lines as I formulated the lie I had to tell him.

It didn't matter that I felt the same about him that he felt for me.

It didn't matter that I wanted him, that I wished more than anything in the entire world that I could kiss him and hold him and say, *"Of course, I want to go, and of course, I want you to go with me!"* I wished I could leave this town behind, leave my family obligations and expectations in the dust and just take on the world with him at my side.

But this wasn't a movie.

This was my life.

And in *my* life, there was more to think about than just my own selfish wants. I had a mother depending on me, a father in trouble he couldn't get out of on his own, a sister who was oblivious to the peril — and I wanted to keep it that way.

I came here tonight to give myself one last evening with Noah, one last time in his arms, one last kiss... and then, I knew I'd have to let him go. I knew I'd have to tell him something — *anything* — to get him to stay away from me.

If I told him the truth, he'd tell me it wasn't my problem. I already knew he would. But, he couldn't possibly understand. This was my family at stake — our name, our reputation. Generations of Barnetts were watching me from above, expecting me to do what was right to save the family name.

And I wouldn't let them down.

I couldn't let them down.

"I can't believe you would do this," I said, sniffing back tears as I stood, leaving Noah in the bean bag. He scrambled up after me. "You applied for a *job* without asking me, Noah. A job that requires years of commitment."

He gaped. "But... this is what you said you wanted."

"No," I corrected, even though my heart screamed *yes*. "It's what I *used* to want."

Noah furrowed his brows, taking a step toward me. "Baby, please. Come here."

He held is arms out wide, and my heart squeezed tight at the sound of the nickname rolling from his lips. I wanted to be his baby. I wanted to be *his*, period — and I cried harder at the cold reality that I never would be.

Life wasn't fair.

This was one lesson I'd never forget.

"You're treating me like a child," I said against the sobs. "Like you know what's best for me."

"That's not what I—"

"Stop trying to save me when I didn't ask to be saved."

His mouth popped shut at that, and he blinked several times, digesting my words as he watched me like I was someone else entirely.

In that moment, I was.

"Don't do this," he finally whispered, shaking his head. "Please. Don't do this."

"I'm not doing anything," I said, crying harder. "*You* did this." I shook my head, swiping the tears from my face as I made my way toward the treehouse door. "This was all a mistake. I stepped out on my fiancé after one stupid misunderstanding without even talking to him. And I'm sorry I did that, I'm sorry I went to you, but this?" I gestured to the air between us. "This *thing* that you're trying to make happen between us? It's just a fantasy. It's not the real world."

"Stop it!" Noah said, crossing the treehouse and stepping in my pathway to the door. "Stop pushing me away because I'm the first person in your life to actually give a damn about you."

I covered my mouth with my hands, closing my eyes and willing myself to calm down, to stop crying — but I couldn't.

"Look at me," he said, framing my arms, but I kept my eyes shut. "This isn't a fantasy and you know it. This? What *we* have? It's real. It's that bullshit man who only wants you to play a part that's not real. It's your parents who want you to be a prop in their life instead of an actual daughter that's not real."

I couldn't respond, not with my heart ripping itself to shreds inside my rib cage with every word he spoke. All I wanted was to wrap my arms around him, bury my face in his neck and tell him everything. I wanted to hear him say I didn't owe them a thing, that this wasn't my mess, and more than anything, I wanted to believe that myself.

But as much as I wanted those things, I wanted to be there for my family more.

I loved them, no matter what had transpired between us, and I couldn't let them go down in flames. Not when I knew I held the fire extinguisher in my hands.

"Look at you," he said, squeezing my arms as another sob ripped through me. "You feel it, too. You don't want to leave right now. You don't want to fight with me."

I shook my head, pressing my hands into my face more to soak up the tears as they fell.

"What are you not telling me, Ruby Grace?"

Another wave of sobs tore through me, and when I could finally force a breath, I let my hands fall, creaking my eyes open to look up at him through my damp lashes.

I still couldn't speak.

"What is it?" he whispered, hands framing my face as he searched my eyes.

I shook my head. "You don't understand," I whispered.

"So help me," he begged.

My face twisted, more tears breaking loose as I shook my head over and over again. "But, that's just it," I said, pulling free from his grasp. "You don't understand. And you never could."

"Ruby—"

"I have to go," I said, sniffing back the last of my tears with a new resolve. I skirted around him, flinging the door open and climbing down the ladder on the tree without another glance in his direction.

Noah called out to me the entire way down, calling my name and telling me to wait — *begging* me to wait. I swore my chest would explode any moment if I didn't put distance between us, and the cool rain splattering against my hot skin was the only welcome relief I found in the meantime.

"Wait," he said again when we reached the bottom. His hand caught the inside of my elbow and he spun me around, his eyes wild now, frantically searching mine. "Please. Don't do this. Don't leave, don't walk away from this, from..." He swallowed. "Don't walk away from me."

I let out an audible sob at that, ripping away from his grasp.

"You can't walk all the way back," he said when I turned. "It's raining. It's at least a mile."

"I'm fine," I said through my tears, through the rain, through the rolling thunder. I took out my phone, using the flashlight app on it to light my way.

"Damn it, Ruby Grace!"

Noah ran to catch up to me, blocking my path as the rain pelted down on us. His hair stuck to his forehead, his eyes transitioning to my favorite steel color as a crack of lightning sprawled across the sky.

"I love you."

The words knocked the breath from my chest, and I shook my head, trying to move around him.

"You love me, too," he said. "And you don't have to say it for me to know it. But what you do have to do is stay. Right now. You have to be brave, and you have to *stay*."

"I can't," I whimpered.

"Why not?" He stepped into me, hands reaching forward, and this time, I didn't rip away when his hands found my arms. "Just tell me why. Tell me the *real* reason why, and I swear, I'll leave you alone." His hands trailed up, framing my face. "If that's what you want."

Noah swallowed at that, like the words tasted as bad as they sounded. He lowered his forehead to mine, and both of us inhaled a breath that sounded like a roar of thunder.

"I promise I will," he said again, this time softer. "But I don't want to. I want you to stay. Please, Ruby Grace. *Stay*."

His lips found mine, hard and pleading, and I melted into him, my hands tugging at his wet shirt as another crack of lightning split the sky. I took that kiss selfishly, eagerly, opening my mouth and letting him slide his tongue inside as I moaned and leaned into him even more.

I wanted him to brand me.

I wanted to brand *him*.

For as long as I lived, I knew I'd never forget that last kiss with Noah Becker.

But when the lightning was gone, the thunder rolling behind it, I broke free, panting, and I didn't meet his eyes when I said the last words I'd ever say to him.

"Don't follow me."

With that, I was gone.

# Chapter Seventeen

## NOAH

Two weeks.

Those words were on repeat in my head Sunday evening as I sat with all my brothers on Mom's front porch, holding a full beer in my hand, knowing I couldn't stomach even one sip of it. I hadn't touched anything Mom had made us for dinner, either.

Two weeks.

I counted the days, the hours, the minutes and seconds that fit inside that time period.

It was only fourteen days. Three-hundred-and-thirty-six hours. Twenty-thousand-one-hundred-and-sixty minutes. One-point-two-million seconds.

And then, she would be Ruby Grace Caldwell.

My fist tightened around the can, a bit of the beer spilling over the side as I fumed at that fact. I knew I shouldn't have gone to church, shouldn't have put myself in her vicinity where I could stare at her and sit in my misery like a masochist.

But I *had* to see her.

After she left that night, I followed her even though she told me not to. I had to make sure she made it back to her car okay. But, I stayed back, gave her space, and once she was in her car, I did as she asked me to.

I left her alone.

I thought she'd call, or text, or send a fucking smoke signal. *Anything*. Something to tell me that she'd just had a moment, but she was okay now.

But it never came.

And earlier, at church, our pastor announced that the wedding was just two weeks away.

Which meant it was still happening.

Which meant I didn't mean *shit* to Ruby Grace.

I sighed, releasing my grip on the can a bit as my eyes wandered over Mom's garden. I felt so many things in equal measure — betrayal, longing, confusion, anger, heartbreak. But more than anything, I felt foolish.

I was the biggest fool.

I'd chased a woman who had another man's ring on her finger, a woman out of my league by any standard, a woman younger than me, a woman who, in reality, was still just a girl in so many ways. I'd wanted to save her, to be her partner in everything, to fill the emptiness in my life with her and be the one to do the same in her life.

I'd ignored all the warning signs.

And now, I was paying the price.

"You okay over there?" Mikey asked from where he was strumming on his guitar at the opposite corner of the porch. He kept his eyes on the strings, plucking away. "You sound like a dragon with all that huffing."

"Fuck off, Mikey."

His head popped up at that, brows tugging together. "Hey..."

"Oh, don't mind him, Mikey," Logan said. "He's got his panties in a wad over Ruby Grace and clearly he just wants to sulk *around* us, but not actually get our advice."

"You don't know what you're talking about," I spat.

"I know I don't. None of us do. And we *won't* until you tell us."

"Leave him alone," Jordan said from his rocking chair, sipping on the old fashioned he'd made. It was like his word was final, Mikey giving me one last look before he started strumming again, and Logan sighing before he drained his beer and stood, walking inside to be with Mom.

Jordan didn't look at me, but I silently thanked him, anyway.

I had so many questions running through my mind, so many things I wanted to talk about and work through. But at the end of the day, I knew it was pointless.

It didn't matter *why* she'd run from me, or why she was still marrying Anthony.

All that mattered was that she *did*. And she was.

End of story.

I felt her hands on my shoulders before I even realized she'd joined us on the porch. Mom gave my traps a gentle squeeze, holding me in place while she spoke to my brothers. "Can you guys give us a minute?"

Mikey stopped playing abruptly, hopping up before trotting down the stairs to his car. "I'm going to Bailey's. I'll be back in a bit."

Jordan stood next. "I'll go see what Logan is up to." He paused, finally looking at me. "For what it's worth, I'm here. If you need anything."

Just saying that was hard for Jordan. I knew, because he hadn't approved of my plan to try to get Ruby Grace in the first place. But as he passed, he put a hand on my shoulder next to Mom's, squeezing once and leaning in to kiss her cheek before he left us alone.

That was a brother's love. It was resilient, and always there — even when we didn't deserve it.

When it was just me and Mom, she rounded my chair, sitting in the empty one next to me. For a long while, she was silent, just rocking next to me with her eyes on the yard.

It was crazy sometimes, looking at Mom. She'd aged in the years since Dad had passed, and I wondered what he would look like now. Would his hair be gray? Would the wrinkles around his eyes and lips be deeper? Would he still be stout as ever, or would he be thin, with a beer belly and a balding head?

Mom was still the same woman I remembered from being a toddler, even though her hair was shorter, a little grayer, her eyes a little more worn. She was still the same superhero I'd always seen when I looked at her.

"So," she said after a long moment, still rocking gently. "You better have a reason for not touching your brussel sprouts tonight. Those have been your favorite since you were a teenager. And your brothers hate them, so you know I made them just for you."

I tried to smile. "And you know I love you for it. I'll take some home, reheat them for lunch tomorrow."

"I'll pack them up for you. But that doesn't get you off the hook for telling me why you can't even drink your beer right now."

I glanced at the offending can, like it'd given away my secret even though I knew I was doing that well enough on my own.

I'd always sucked at hiding my emotions. Jordan was the best at that, Mikey was perhaps the worst. But, I wasn't much better than him. When I was angry, I lashed out. I got into too many fights. I shut out those who tried to help me. I would brood and sulk in my thoughts, but never share them with anyone.

Maybe because I knew no one could help.

Maybe because I was too scared to admit I needed it.

"Ah," Mom said after a long pause. "It's a girl, isn't it?"

I sighed, running my finger along the edge of my beer can. "That obvious, huh?"

She chuckled. "Well, I've seen you bent out of shape about many things over the years, Noah. But this... that misery on your face... it's the kind only a broken heart can bring."

When I didn't say anything more, Mom rolled her lips together, considering her next words before she spoke again.

"You know, I always knew that when you did fall for someone, you'd fall hard. You used to watch me and your dad so closely, and I had a feeling that you'd be the one who held out for the right one. Now, don't get me wrong," she added with a wry smile. "I'm not naïve enough to think you've never dated and broken a few hearts of your own. But, I guess I just knew that you wouldn't really give your heart away. Not until you felt like it was right."

I shook my head. "How do you do that? Do all moms have some sort of superpower where they can just see right through their children?"

She laughed. "Oh, I wish. I think you were just a little easier for me to read," she said on a shrug. "You're like me, in a lot of ways. And I think we've had a special connection ever since you were born." She chuckled again. "Your dad was always jealous of it. He wanted you to be a daddy's boy, but you were always on my hip when you were sick or down about something."

I smiled, heart aching at the mention of Dad.

"Now," she said, patting my knee. "Tell me about her."

I sighed. "You'll be disappointed in me if I do."

"Try me."

"She's engaged," I said first, ripping the Band-Aid off.

Just like I thought, Mom's face paled. "Noah Emmanuel."

"I know, I know," I said, pinching the bridge of my nose. "Trust me. I tried to stay away, to keep a boundary between us. But, I swear to God, Mom — she was like a magnet. The harder I tried to stay away, the more she pulled me in. And I have no idea why or how. I just know that I was powerless to resist when it came to her."

Her eyes softened at that. "Well, if I've learned anything when it comes to love, it's that it rarely follows all the rules we set in place for it." She sighed. "It's Ruby Grace Barnett, isn't it?"

I didn't answer.

I didn't have to.

"You know, when you were younger, I used to have to wait days for you to finally open up to me about what you were upset about," she said. "I mean, your younger brothers would break in minutes, and Jordan would take it to the grave. But you?" She smiled. "All you needed was time."

I nodded, knowing it to be true.

"And I understand if that's what you want now. I just hate seeing you like this, and I want to help." Mom reached over and squeezed my forearm. "But, I can't if you don't tell me what happened."

I sighed, looking up to the sky before I met her eyes. "I don't even know where to begin. I don't know how we ended up here, or how it all started. It just... happened."

"When did she stop being the annoying girl who kicked the back of your pew?"

I scoffed. "When she showed up at the distillery wearing a dress that made her look more grown than me, and heels that made her legs stretch on for days, and lips painted as red as the paint on Dad's old Camaro."

Mom smiled. "How about you start there, then."

So I did.

And before I knew it, the sun had set, the half moon and stars above our only light as Mom and I rocked side by side. I talked, and she listened, nodding her head and chiming in from time to time. But, for the most part, she was silent, and the night was silent — other than the faint sound of music coming from inside, where I assumed my brothers were eavesdropping and pretending to be busy.

When I'd finished, telling her about the treehouse and how Ruby Grace had left, I fell quiet.

I had nothing more to say.

Mom reached over, squeezing my hand where it rested on the arm of my rocking chair before she folded her hands in her lap again. She rocked, eyes on the stars, and a long moment passed before she finally spoke.

"There was another man before your father."

I cocked a brow. "What do you mean?"

She sighed. "I mean, before I fell in love with your father, there was another man who had my interest. And I had his. I would say we were in love... but, it's not the same love I had with your father. It was younger, wilder, not as steady."

"Did Dad know?"

She smiled. "He did. He didn't want to know much, to be honest. But I told him, just because I wanted to be honest with him."

I nodded, wondering why she was telling me this after all these years.

"When your father and I announced our engagement, that other man came back into my life. It had been years," she said, her eyes distant, a sad smile on her face. "And he'd been dating someone else... someone I was close with before. But, when he heard about your Dad and me, he came to me. He confessed his love, and he begged me not to get married."

My jaw fell slack. "Wow. Did Dad know about *that*?"

She chuckled. "He did. I told him when it happened, but again, he didn't want to know much. That was the special thing about your father. I was always open with him, and he was always trusting of me. I think that's how I knew our love was real. There was no jealousy, no fear of being betrayed. We just... we just *knew*. We were a fact, you know?"

My heart squeezed. "Yeah. I know."

Mom smiled my way. "Anyway, the reason I'm telling you this is that... there was a part of me — a very, *very* small part — that still had feelings for that man. I did. And I knew it was wrong, but when he came to me, I was faced with all those old emotions that we'd had together. And if I weren't stronger, if the love between your father and me wasn't as it was, I might have fallen. I might have given into him and done something I would have regretted." She paused. "But, as it was, I told him I was happy with your father and that he should leave me alone. Not just for now, but forever."

I swallowed. "Which is exactly what Ruby Grace said to me."

Mom sighed, gently nodding. "Yes. And I know it hurts to hear, Son. I know it does. And maybe she really *is* your first love. But, our first love doesn't usually tend to be our last. We learn from it, grow from it, and move forward. And I think that's what you have to do here."

My chest twisted, head shaking involuntarily. I didn't want that. It was the absolute last thing I felt like I could do — walk away from her — even if it was the right thing to do.

"I know you don't want to hear that," Mom said. "But, the way I see it, whether she cares about you or not, she obviously cares about Anthony more. She's still engaged to him, regardless of what happened between them. That tells me she wants to work on it with him. She wants to see this through. And if you love her — if you *truly* love her — you will respect that wish, and you will leave her be."

"If you love them, let them fly, huh?"

Mom's smile was soft, apologizing. "Something like that."

She reached over to grab my hand again, squeezing it once before she stood and clapped her hands together. "Now, I have peach cobbler inside, and you're not allowed to leave until you eat at least one piece."

"Mom..."

"Ah!" she said, holding up one finger as she turned her back to me. "No excuses, Noah Emmanuel. Inside. Now."

I smirked, shaking my head as I stood. And before Mom could open the screen door, I called out to her.

She turned, and in that moment, I swore I saw Dad standing next to her — maybe as a memory from long ago.

"Thank you," I said, holding my arms open.

She smiled, eyes glossing over as she stepped into my embrace. She rocked me like she had all my life, and I kissed her forehead, releasing her on a sigh.

"Always, baby boy," she said, reaching up to pinch my cheek. "Always. Now, come on. Pie awaits."

Jordan watched me a little too carefully as we ate pie at the dinner table, Logan filling Mom in on the latest from the distillery. I gave him what I could in terms of a reassuring smile, and he just nodded in understanding.

*I'm here*, he was saying.

*I know,* I said back.

As much as my stomach protested, I choked down Mom's pie — along with the advice she'd given me. It was the absolute last thing I wanted to hear, and part of me hoped she'd say something else.

*Fight for her!*

*Object at the wedding!*

*Steal the bride!*

But that wasn't who my mother was. She was sound, peaceful, logical, and patient. She was the most nurturing and intelligent woman I knew — and what she'd told me to do was the right thing.

I had to let Ruby Grace go.

Now, I only had to figure out how.

## RUBY GRACE

I wondered if I should just stay there at the bottom of the pool.

It was quiet down there — peaceful. The sun's rays only barely reached me, and the water was thick and blue, my hair floating around me like a red tide. My chest was burning, thirsty for air, but I starved it a little longer.

I could just stay there.

I could stay there until I ran out of air, and then I'd never have to get married. I'd never have to rise to the surface and face the life I had cornered myself into.

I'd never have to look into Noah Becker's devastated blue eyes again.

It had been the absolute worst week of my entire life.

At home, everything went on as it would have. Mom made last-minute wedding adjustments, Dad worked all day and told me each night how excited he was for me, and Anthony held me like he loved me, kissed me like he cared — and remained completely oblivious to what I knew about his true feelings.

And I hadn't seen Noah.

In so many ways, he felt like a ghost to me now. I wondered sometimes if he was even real at all, if I'd imagined the events of the entire summer. But the bruises were there on my heart, the scars on my lips where his had burned mine — I felt him everywhere, like he was a permanent part of me, though I'd never see or speak to him again.

I closed my eyes, my heart all but convinced to succumb to drowning. But, my feet kicked without permission, forcing me toward the top of the pool as my lungs set a fire inside my rib cage. When I broke the surface of the water and inhaled, my body rejoiced while my heart cried out against the injustice.

I opened my eyes.

"Trying to break your third-grade record?" Annie asked, swinging her feet in the water and rubbing sunscreen on her exposed belly.

"Looked more like a poor suicide attempt to me," Betty chimed in, floating her arms up overhead before leaning to one side. It was part of the warm-up in Noah's water aerobics routine he'd been teaching there, and my heart squeezed at the memory, urging me to go back down for another try.

"Ding-ding-ding," I said, pointing at Betty. "We have a winner."

Annie frowned, exchanging a glance with Betty before she let out a sigh. "Okay, you're not even allowed to joke about that."

"I'm sorry," I said, swimming to the edge where she sat. I laid my head on my arms, letting the sun warm my back. "I must be so miserable to be around right now."

"You're not," she assured me. "But, I do hate this for you. It's four days before your wedding. You should be glowing, and happy, and have literal heart eyes popping out of your head like a cartoon."

I nodded. "I know."

"She also shouldn't be marrying that no-good, two-timing prissy son of a dirty politician."

Annie laughed at Betty's remark, and I tried to smile, but it felt like trying to run fast under water — impossible.

"Seriously," she said when I didn't respond. "What exactly is your plan here? You're just going to marry this man and then... what? Divorce him after your father's debt is paid?"

I shook my head.

"Annul the marriage?"

I shook my head again.

Betty was adjusting her swim cap, and she let it snap against her forehead, lowering her goggles and blinking several times as she watched me. "Wait... you're not actually planning on *staying* with him... are you? As in, marrying him, having his babies, being the dutiful politician's wife he wants you to be?"

When I didn't answer, Annie cringed and Betty fumed, shaking her head and holding up one old, wagging finger. "Oh, hell no."

"What would you have me do?" I asked.

"Call off the wedding like you were planning to," she said, as if it were that easy. "And run to that boy who *really* loves you."

"Betty..." Annie tried to warn, but I was already pulled into the argument.

"My hands are tied," I said, standing to face her. "My father's reputation, his job, our house, our entire *life* depends on me marrying this man. I can't just feed my father to the wolves."

"So, you'll feed *yourself* to one, instead?"

I opened my mouth to respond, but no words came. So, I just shut it again, eyes falling down to where my fingers skated over the water.

Betty sighed, making her way to the ladder at the edge of the pool before she slowly climbed out, Annie holding one hand behind her just in case. "Come," she said, not even looking back at me. "Walk with an old woman, would you?"

Water was still dripping off each of us as we walked in our towels, first around the tennis court and then back to the garden, where a path wound through each little corner of it like a snake. It was shaded, a nice reprieve from the sun, and it wasn't until we were within those garden walls that Betty finally spoke.

"I want to start by saying that no matter what you choose to do, I will love you through it," she started, tugging off her swim cap and pushing her goggles up on her head. "Because you are like a daughter to me, Ruby Grace. Like the daughter we never had."

Her eyes shined at that, and I knew she was thinking about Leroy.

I reached over, threading my arm through hers.

"And maybe that's why I feel compelled to say this to you. I know you already have a mother, but, the way I see it, you can never have too many moms in your life. And, if I'm being honest, I don't agree with the guidance your true mother is giving you right now."

I swallowed.

"I know it's complicated. I know it feels like your hands are tied, like there's no choice for you in this matter — but I want to be the one to tell you that there is. You're young, Ruby Grace. Right now, it feels like you have to do what is expected of you, that there is a standard you must meet, that in order to be happy, you have to follow this list of rules and guidelines and you have to marry a certain kind of man and live in a certain kind of house and raise certain kinds of kids." She sort of laughed, sort of scoffed. "But, honey? That's all bullshit."

I smirked.

"Can we sit?" she asked, a little out of breath as she pointed to a bench near the bed of Indian blanket sunflowers.

When we were both seated, she took a few breaths, dabbing at the sheen of sweat on her forehead with her towel before she sat back.

"There comes a time in your life when you look around you and you realize that you don't want to play the game anymore," she said. "You realize you don't want the fake friends, or the toxic relationships, or the people telling you how you should live *your* life when they can't even run their own. Some find it in their thirties. Some in their forties. Some, like the old woman beside you, not until most of their life has passed."

I frowned, reaching over to hold her hand. "You've had an amazing life," I argued. "A man who loved you, a town that cherishes you."

"That's just it, though," she said. "Leroy wanted to stay in this town, whereas I wanted to flee from it. I wanted to travel, to see the world, to talk to strangers from other cultures and learn more than just what's here in Tennessee. But I never did." She held up a finger. "Now, I don't want you thinking I wasn't happy, because I was. I loved Leroy. I *still* love that man — even though he broke our pact to let me die first, the bastard."

I chuckled, eyes glossing over.

"But, aside from his love, I never fulfilled *myself*. And that's one area where Leroy couldn't help me. He would have supported me, if I would have stood up for *myself* and said out loud what I wanted. But, I never did. Instead, I found my adventure by watching movies and living through *other* people — through celebrities. I waited until Leroy was gone from my life, until my legs were too old and tired, my lungs not capable of feeding me enough oxygen, my heart not steady enough to pump enough blood into my brain. It took me too long to speak up for myself, and I regret it. Truly, I do. I could have seen the world, could have experienced so much more with the man I loved, if I only would have stood up and spoke."

I sighed. "And that's what you want me to do."

"No," she said, shaking her head. "*I* want you to do what you want to do — regardless of if I agree with it or not. Like I said, you're my daughter in my eyes, and I will support you through anything." She paused, running her bony, silky finger over my wrist. "But, let's just say I'm speaking to you on behalf of future Ruby Grace. I'm speaking as Ruby Grace at seventy-four, in a nursing home of her own."

My heart kicked up a notch as I tried to imagine it — an older version of me, looking back on my life, on what I'd built, what I'd leave behind.

What hurt the most was that I couldn't even picture it.

"All I'm saying is that I know it feels like you're tied to a railroad track with a train coming straight at you. It feels like it's this or nothing. But, I'm telling you, you have a giant pair of scissors in your hands that you can cut that rope with."

"Betty..."

"It may be difficult," she said, cutting me off. "You might get rope burn and you may cut yourself and bleed a little. You may let some people down. Hell, you may uproot everything you knew about your life before, about what you thought it'd be, and you may walk into something completely different, something you never expected." A smile bloomed on her pale lips, then. "But, my dear, isn't that the best part of being young? The possibilities are endless, the paths limitless, and you have so many different directions you can walk." She shrugged. "You just have to decide if you want to walk the path of least resistance, the one where you are merely another traveler on the road. Or, if you want to forge a new path with those scissors, bit by bit, limb by limb, and discover something you never could have imagined."

"It sounds selfish."

She scoffed. "Selfish. What a silly word. Should you give to the ones you love? Absolutely. But should you lose yourself in order to better *their* lives at the expense of your own? Never."

With that, she stood, stretching her arms above her head with a yawn before she started walking.

I frowned. "You're leaving?"

"I'm going to take a nap, like an old woman should," she said, glancing back at me over her shoulder. "And I'm going to leave you alone to think. To *really* think — without your mom in your ear, or your sister, or Noah, or Annie, or me. I just want you to sit here, on this bench, in this garden, and I want you to ask yourself the tough questions."

"I know the questions," I said on a sigh. "It's the answers I'm having trouble with."

She smiled knowingly. "Well, then, sit here until they come."

"And if they don't?"

"Then you didn't sit long enough," she tossed over her shoulder.

Then she rounded an old oak tree, and she was gone.

Later that night, I knocked on my father's office door before letting myself inside.

He looked up at me from where he sat at his desk, his reading glasses low on his nose and hands still typing away on his keyboard. "Hey, pumpkin."

I swallowed, letting myself in and closing the door behind me with trembling hands. Anthony and Mom were out on the front porch, drinking sweet tea like Mama loved to do after dinner, but just in case, I wanted another barrier between us.

"I need to talk to you," I said when I was inside.

"Okay," he answered, but his eyes were back on his screen now, fingers flying over the keys. "I'll be out in an hour or so, just have to finish this up."

I ignored his request and sat down in one of the chairs on the opposite side of his desk, folding my hands in my lap.

Dad glanced up at me, and I watched the concern wash over his face when he saw me — when he really *saw* me.

I had to look as tired as I felt. I knew it. I knew there were bags under my eyes, that my blotchy skin had to be betraying the fact that I'd cried all evening after leaving the nursing home. I had barely eaten at dinner, which Mama covered up by saying I was worried about fitting into my wedding dress.

Ever the damage control.

But now, sitting across from my father, I didn't want to hide it anymore. I didn't want to pretend like everything was fine.

Dad swallowed, pulling his hands from the keyboard and steepling them together as he sat back in his chair. "Or we can talk now."

My next breath was a shaky one, one that burned as much as it brought relief in the form of fresh oxygen. I looked down at my hands, at my manicured nails, at the engagement ring on my finger.

"I know about the deal you made with Anthony and his father."

I couldn't look at my father, then.

I couldn't glance up from my nails and see the man I'd admired my entire life paling at the realization that his little girl knew about the debt he owed, about the way he planned to pay it.

My gaze stayed fixed in my lap, and that was the only way I had the courage to keep talking.

"I want you to know that I understand why you did it. I understand that, sometimes, sacrifices have to be made to keep a family afloat. You and Mom have taught me that." Tears flooded my eyes, and the next words choked out of me with less steadiness. "But, I also want you to know that I have never been so hurt in my entire life. And I never thought my father would ever be capable of selling me to the highest bidder."

"Pumpkin..."

"No," I said, shaking my head, effectively letting the first two tear drops fall into my lap. "I'm not finished."

Silence.

I sniffed, wiping the back of my hand against my nose with my heart thundering hard in my chest now. "Anthony doesn't love me. I know that now, and I also know that it doesn't matter. You and I both know that at the core of my heart, of who I am — I am a giver. Just like you. Just like Mom. We sacrifice for others, and more than anything, we put this family first."

My heart ached, Noah's face the only thing I could see as I shut my eyes and freed another set of tears.

"I will do this for you," I whispered, breaking with the admission. "For our family. Because it would kill me to do anything that would ever hurt you, or Mom, or Mary Anne." I sniffed, finally pulling my gaze up to meet my father's.

When I saw the tears on his cheeks, his eyes red and glossy, I broke again.

"But, you will do something for me in return," I choked out on a sob. "You have to get help, Daddy. You can't keep doing this — not at this expense. You have to go to Gamblers Anonymous. You have to stop with the casinos, and the card nights, and the horse tracks. It may have been all fun and games at one point, a way to pass the time and wheel and deal with the good ol' boys in this town, but now, it has affected not just your life, and not just my life, but our entire family's."

Dad rolled his lips together, two tears streaming parallel down his cheeks as he watched me. He was quiet for a long while, the air in his office stuffy and suffocating.

"I'm so sorry," he finally whispered. "I know... I know I'm sick. I know I have a problem. I... I never thought it would get to this point, I never thought..."

He paused, face crumpling as a sob broke through. In all the years I'd been alive, I'd never seen my father cry.

Not once.

But that night in his office, he broke, reaching for a tissue on his desk and wiping the tears away, wiping his nose before his gaze sat miserably somewhere in the distance between us.

Now, it was *him* who couldn't look at me.

"I don't know when it got this bad," he said. "I used to have a hold on it. I'd walk into the casino with what I was okay to lose, and if I lost it, I left. But, when I started going to Pat's club... I don't know. Everything changed."

Pat was my father's affectionate pet name for Patrick Scooter.

The man he now owed so much money to that he couldn't pay his own debt.

"When my money ran out, I'd just hang around, drink, smoke cigars with the other city council members. But, Patrick would entice me, tell me to get in on the next hand, that he had me, he'd lend me the bet. It was innocent at first, and I easily paid him back. Somewhere along the way, though..." Dad shook his head. "I don't know. I got pulled into something I didn't even realize. It was bigger than I could have ever known. And when I started losing more, I would ask for more — small, at first, but bigger and bigger as time went on. I just thought *one more hand, and I'll win it all back.*" A shadow passed over his face, like he was trying to pinpoint the exact moment it all happened.

Like if he could, he could go back and change it all.

His mouth hung open for a long pause before he continued. "Before I knew it, I was in over my head in a debt I couldn't even wrap my head around."

I swallowed, trying my best to find sympathy somewhere in my heart for my father, for the man who raised me.

I came up empty handed.

"Your mom didn't even know until it was too late," he said, his voice low and cracking. "We were going to lose everything... and then... Anthony came to ask for your hand."

Just the sound of his name made my stomach roll so violently I nearly vomited what little bit of dinner I could choke down. Tears flooded my eyes again, so fast I couldn't even try to stop them before they rolled down my cheeks.

"That's enough," I whispered, voice shaking through the shallow breaths I managed to sip. "It doesn't matter. What's done is done."

Dad opened his mouth, but after one look at me, he shut it again.

"I just needed you to know," I said definitively. "I needed you to know that I'm aware of what you did, and I needed you to know that as much as it hurts *me*, I will do what needs to be done for this family." I shook my head. "Even if I wasn't given the opportunity to make my own choice in the first place."

Dad didn't say anything else, which was wise, because I was in perhaps the most unstable state I'd ever been in in my entire life.

I nodded, the conversation over, and then I stood and walked to his office door, taking a moment to wipe my face before I opened the door. I glanced back at the big, broken man at that desk, and in that moment, I didn't recognize him at all.

"For the record," I said, standing tall. "Even if you do get help — and you will — I will never forgive you for this."

And with the most painful decision of my life made, I turned my back on my father and shut the door on everything I ever thought my life would be.

# Chapter Eighteen

**NOAH**

I wasn't going to go.

I swore on my father's grave, on the *Bible* that I was not going to go to the wedding.

There was no reason to go. My mom was right — I needed to walk away from Ruby Grace, from what we had, what we could *never* have, and leave her behind. I had to let her start her new life with another man, because that was the decision she had made.

It was set in stone.

*I* was set in my resolve.

And for the past two weeks, I'd told myself I wasn't going to go to that wedding — no matter what.

But all of that changed last night.

I had stayed late at the distillery, working overtime for as long as Gus would let me before he finally kicked me out and made me go home. I'd been at the distillery more than anywhere, trying to throw myself into work so I could take my mind off the impending wedding. I couldn't go ride Tank, couldn't go to the treehouse, couldn't go *anywhere* I used to find solace — because now, all I found in those places were memories of her.

When I finally made it home, it was well past sunset, and I noticed a white envelope half tucked under my front door as I twisted my key in the lock.

I bent to retrieve it with a frown, and that frown had deepened when I read in small, neat script on the front of it:

*Read this before tomorrow. It's important.*

My heart had leapt into my throat, and I instantly thought it was a letter from Ruby Grace.

I'd flown inside, thrown my shit haphazardly on whatever surface was nearby, and torn into the envelope with greedy hands, greedy eyes, a greedy heart. But, the letter wasn't from Ruby Grace at all.

It was from Betty.

And in that letter, she'd revealed the missing piece to the puzzle I'd been trying to solve since the moment Ruby Grace left me in the rain at the treehouse my father built.

That letter was tucked into the inside pocket of my tuxedo, and as if it possessed the courage I needed to walk through the church doors, I brushed a hand over my chest where it was hidden, taking a deep breath. My eyes scanned the large wooden doors of the church — the ones I had walked through nearly every Sunday morning since I was born — and I wondered how they could look so foreign.

Inside those doors, there was an aisle lined with flowers and twine — both of which I'd helped Ruby Grace pick out.

Inside those doors, there were hundreds of people, nearly the entire town of Stratford, and then some.

Inside those doors, there was a man waiting at the end of the aisle for the woman I loved.

And inside those doors was the woman I couldn't let go of.

My breath was surprisingly steady as I finally found the will to open those doors, like I knew what I was going to do when the reality was I didn't have a fucking clue. But, I extended one steady hand for the wedding program being offered to me, took my seat at the end of the back left pew, and I waited.

I was practically invisible to everyone inside, and in that moment, I was thankful my entire family had declined the open invitation to the wedding. I knew they had done so on my behalf.

None of them knew I was here today.

The other wedding guests were all chattering with their friends or families or dates, commenting on the beautiful decorations or the stunning music coming from a harp player near the organ at the front. It was a shushed sort of chatter as we all waited for the ceremony to begin.

And it would.

In less than ten minutes.

*It's too late*, the realistic part of my brain warned me as I sat there, both hands on the wedding program, eyes cast toward the altar. *She's marrying him. Today. There's nothing you can do.*

But, there was something more powerful floating inside my chest, calming my breaths, easing my racing heart. It fluttered and filled me from the inside out with an inexplicable anticipation, like something epic was about to happen.

*Hope.*

I recognized it faintly as time warped and faded. I couldn't even be sure I was truly in the church — that's how detached I felt from my being. It wasn't until the moment I noticed a familiar pair of eyes watching me from the third pew that I came back to the moment.

Betty smiled, casting me a wink. I returned her smile, and it was as if that notion alone brought on all the jitters I'd been surpassing. My heart thundered to life in my chest, my hands shaking where they held the program, and I swore my feet were about to move without permission from my brain to hightail us out of there just as the harp died and the organ began to play.

The same camera crew that had followed Anthony and Ruby Grace around the Soirée was scattered throughout the church, cameras pointed in all different directions, with one free moving around the church and capturing the chatter before the ceremony. That camera moved to the center of the aisle, crouched low and out of view once the familiar hymn filled the air.

Pastor Morris stood at the altar now, smiling, his eyes scanning the crowd as he nodded silent hello's. Ruby Grace's mother was escorted down the aisle by an usher, but Anthony's parents were nowhere to be found. I frowned, wondering where they were, but didn't have time to process it much before a door opened to the right.

Anthony walked through it, along with some guy I didn't recognize. He stood next to Anthony and Pastor Morris at the altar, which told me he was the best man, but I couldn't keep my focus there for very long.

Because it took every ounce of willpower I possessed not to fly down the aisle right then and pummel Anthony's grinning face with my fist.

He stood tall and confident at the altar, wearing a light gray tuxedo with a coral pocket square and bow tie. His hair was neat and styled, his jaw freshly shaved, and to anyone else in that church, he looked like the perfect groom. He looked like what every girl had ever dreamed of when they pictured their wedding day.

But I knew the truth.

I knew the evil things he'd said about the best woman in the world, knew the pain he'd caused her, the way he'd treated her like some pawn in his game of life.

And now, thanks to Betty, I knew about the deal he and his father had made with Ruby Grace's parents.

That was what upset me the most. Anthony may not have owed Ruby Grace anything, but the fact that her parents could trade her hand in marriage in exchange for some debt to be paid off made me physically ill.

My fists tightened around the wedding program, all but crushing it. A couple I didn't recognize in the same pew as me eyed the crumpled up piece of paper in my hands before casting me a worried glance, to which I just offered a tight smile, relaxing my shoulders a bit.

*Breathe, Noah.*

A flower girl was the first down the aisle, and she sprinkled daisy petals behind her, smiling shyly at everyone in the pews.

Next was Mary Anne. Even though she'd been gone for a few years, it was impossible not to recognize her. She had the same red hair as her mother and sister, the same button nose, the same freckles dotting her cheeks. She was taller than Ruby Grace, though, and her features were less bold, somehow. She looked older than she actually was, but when she smiled, I saw the resemblance like they were twins.

The last one down the aisle before the bride was Annie, the flowers in her hands balanced on the swell of her belly in the creamy, coral dress that she wore. Her smile was sad, though she tried to brighten it as much as she possibly could as she scanned the pews. I kept my eyes on her, heart thundering as I realized who would be the next down the aisle.

When Annie reached the altar, she turned.

And her eyes locked on me.

She paled, her pink-painted mouth popping open just as the organ changed tune and the congregation stood.

All the blood rushed to my face before draining completely as I numbly rose to my feet, turning to face the back of the aisle along with everyone else. The organ played, and I adjusted my tie, forcing one calm, cooling breath as the doors to the church swung open.

The first thing I saw was a long, slender hand clutching the grey fabric of a tuxedo-clad arm. Her nails were painted a neutral pink, the tips white, and she held onto that arm like it was the only thing holding her to the Earth.

One step, and then I saw the long, flowy, cream skirt of her dress, outlined by the leg she'd taken the step with.

Another step, and the bouquet I'd helped her decide on came into view — a brilliant gathering of daisies and roses, surrounded by fresh baby's breath and dusty miller.

Three steps.

That was how long I was able to keep breath flowing into my lungs.

That was how long I was able to keep blood pumping to my organs.

Because on the fourth step, Ruby Grace came completely into view, and everything stopped.

The time that had stretched and warped as I waited in the church before the wedding began paused altogether, the music fading, lights dimming except where they shone on her. I didn't even notice her father, the arm that she clung to — not when she was in full view. It was all I could do to take all of her in, every inch of her glowing beauty wrapped in that silky, cream wedding dress. Her cheeks were high and rosy, her lips painted a dusty rose, the freckles from our days in the sun breaking through the foundation that powdered her face. Her long, copper hair was braided on each side, the length of it twisted and tied in a knot at the back just below where her veil sat like a halo. Those hazel eyes I'd loved to stare into all summer were as bright and golden as the sun that peaked in behind her before the church doors shut again, and it was as if that sound slammed me back to reality, slammed time back into motion, slammed my heart back into its race within my rib cage.

I didn't even notice her dress.

I didn't care.

Because it was that woman I was here for, not the dress she wore — and if I had it my way, if everything worked the way I hoped, that dress wouldn't mean anything after today, anyway.

Ruby Grace wore the same solemn smile as Annie had as she walked down the aisle, slowly, her father rubbing his hand over where she held his arm in assurance. With his face ashen and long, I wasn't sure if was assuring her or himself.

Ruby Grace didn't notice me as she walked by. In fact, she seemed to be in some sort of daze, some sort of dream.

Or nightmare.

The crowd *ooooh'd* and *awww'd* as she passed them, women dabbing at their eyes with handkerchiefs as the men smiled in wonder and awe.

I had no doubt she was the most beautiful bride to ever walk down that church aisle.

When she reached the end, Pastor Morris asked who gave her hand in marriage, to which her father responded that he did. He kissed her cheek, made an attempt at a smile that fell flat, and then, carefully, he passed her hand to Anthony.

Ruby Grace handed her bouquet to Annie, and Annie whispered something, nodding back toward me. My heart fell to my stomach as Ruby Grace turned, and just as Pastor Morris told the congregation they may be seated, she found me.

She blinked.

I blinked.

Her lips parted.

I smiled.

And then, I sat along with the rest of the crowd, and her eyes stayed glued on me.

Pastor Morris was already speaking, launching into what a beautiful day it was for such an occasion, but Ruby Grace couldn't take her eyes off the back pew. She blinked, over and over and over, her bottom lip trembling, and it wasn't until Pastor Morris said her name that she tore her eyes away, swallowing as she turned her focus to Anthony.

"Anthony," Pastor Morris said, smiling at the groom before he turned his eyes to the bride. "Ruby Grace. It is with great joy that I stand here with you today, surrounded by your loved ones as we celebrate the unity of two hearts becoming one."

Anthony smiled at Ruby Grace, but she couldn't muster so much as a grin. Her eyes floated back to me once more. She blinked. Then, she faced Anthony again.

"Marriage is an honorable sanction, instituted by God," Pastor Morris continued, but his words faded out when Ruby Grace looked at me.

Again.

Annie nudged her from the back, but she kept her eyes on mine, her brows folding together, lips parting.

Anthony frowned when she took too long to look back at him, and he followed her gaze. When he saw me in the back pew, he scowled, lips flattening into a tight line. He cleared his throat, squeezing Ruby Grace's hand in his own to pull her attention back to him.

She seemed to do so reluctantly, and even when she was facing him again, she wore the same worried look.

*Come on, Noah,* I silently pleaded with myself. *Stand up. Say what you came to say.*

I didn't know what I was waiting for — a sign, perhaps. Or maybe the classic line from Pastor Morris — *Should anyone have just cause why these two should not be wed, let them speak now, or forever hold their peace.*

But those words never came.

Because in the next breath, Ruby Grace shook her head, pulled her hands from Anthony's, and whispered something that looked a lot like *"I can't do this"* from where I was sitting at the back of the church. She looked at her father in the front pew, words no one could hear exchanged between them in that weighted gaze.

Then, she reached down, bunched her dress in her hands, and turned to face the congregation.

She locked her gaze on mine, and my heart kicked hard and painful in my chest.

She took a step.

I stood.

Then, amidst the gasps and murmurs of four-hundred Stratford residents, Ruby Grace Barnett was a runaway bride.

And I was her getaway car.

## RUBY GRACE

Chaos.

It was all chaos as I ran down the aisle, as best I could in my designer heels, with my veil flowing behind me and my eyes locked on Noah Becker in the back pew.

Somewhere in the distance, I heard my mother scream out my name. I heard Anthony call out for me. I heard the gasps, the *oh my's*, and, somewhere through it all, the distinct melody of Betty's signature laugh.

None of it mattered.

The only thing that *did* matter was the man, now moving out of his pew to stand at the opposite end of the aisle, with a smirk on his face and his hands tucked into the pockets of his navy blue suit. Those hands slipped out of his pockets just in time to catch me as I threw myself into his arms, and then my hands were in his hair, and my mouth was on his.

And everything went silent.

Somewhere in my consciousness, I knew there was still chaos all around us. There had to be a flurry of gasps and screams coming from every which way. The Mayor's daughter was kissing Noah Becker at the back of the church she was supposed to be marrying another man in. But in that moment, all I could hear was the drumming of my heart in my chest, the relieved sigh from Noah's lips as they met mine, the steadying of my own breath. I wrapped myself around him tighter, and he pulled me in closer, as if to tell me it was all okay now, that we were safe, that it was all over.

But it was far from the truth.

"Noah," I whispered, pulling back and pressing my forehead to his. "I'm so sorry. I'm so sorry. I never should have left, I never should have done that to you. I was lost. I was confused and scared," I explained, shaking my head as my eyes glossed over, the tears breaking loose before I had the chance to stop them. "I didn't know what to do. And there was so much I couldn't tell you, or at least, I *thought* I couldn't tell you. But I can't walk away from you. I can't walk away from us."

Noah quieted my words with another kiss, sliding his hands up to frame my face before he locked his eyes on mine. "You never have to."

I smiled, but the tears kept coming, and I leaned into Noah's touch as he thumbed them away. "I can explain," I said pathetically. "My father…"

"I know," he interrupted, searching my eyes. "It's okay. I know."

I frowned. "You do?"

He nodded.

"How?"

Noah smirked, looking somewhere over my shoulder, and when I followed his gaze, Betty smiled at me from the crowd of horrified faces.

*Sneaky old woman.*

I turned back to Noah, eyes glossing over again. "I'm sorry it took me this long to be brave."

He scoffed. "Please. I'm sorry it took *me* so long to stand up and say what I needed to say here. You beat me to the punch. Didn't even let them get to the part where they ask if anyone objects to the marriage so I could stand up and steal you away like they do in the movies."

"Betty would have loved that," I said, one tear slipping free. "But you can't steal something that's already yours."

Noah wiped that tear with his thumb before it could fall past the apple of my cheek. With a gentle smile, he slid his hands back into my hair as he angled my chin up. But, before he could press his lips to mine again, he was ripped away from me as a fist crashed violently into his jaw.

"Noah!" I screamed, covering my mouth in horror as he fell backwards into the pew. People scattered away from him, from where Anthony now stood towering over him, chest heaving, eyes wide and terrifying.

"You sonofabitch," he seethed, pointing one hard finger down at Noah. "How *dare* you kiss my fiancé on our wedding day? Are you insane, or do you just want me to kick your ass in front of this entire town?"

"Now, now," my father said, joining us all at the end of the aisle. He placed his hands on Anthony's shoulders. "Language, son."

Anthony shrugged him off, his eyes wild, but he blinked several times, then, as if he remembered we were the center of attention for the entire town.

He turned to me, then, straightening his bowtie before he reached for my hands. "Come on, sweetheart. Let's get back to the altar."

"No," I said, tugging my hands away.

His eye twitched, but he smiled, looking around us nervously. "Baby, this is madness. Come on. Everyone came here for a wedding today."

"Well, they won't be getting one from us."

Anthony's eyes narrowed, his voice a low whisper as he stepped into my space. "Ruby Grace, you're embarrassing yourself."

"No, I'm embarrassing *you*," I corrected. "But, I don't care anymore."

"Get your ass back up to that altar," he seethed, pointing to Pastor Morris, who was watching us like we were all demons personified.

Dad's brows rose at that, and Mom reached for me from behind, tugging me close to her and Mary Anne. She said something under her breath, something that sounded a lot like *what did you do?*

"Alright now, that's enough. I think we all need to go our own way for now, cool down, catch our breaths."

"No, what we *need* to do is get your ungrateful daughter back up on that altar," Anthony seethed once more, stepping into Dad's space until they were nose to nose. "This family has been nothing but a pain in my ass since this wedding was announced. Now, I've had enough of this. We can edit this all out of the tapes, but your daughter is marrying me today." He turned on Noah again. "And *this* sonofabitch will be kindly escorted out by my team."

The security that traveled with Anthony as he filmed his documentary stepped forward from the back on that cue, grabbing Noah by the lapels of his jacket where he still laid sprawled on the ground and ripping him up to stand again.

"Leave him alone!" I cried.

I heard the flurry of gasps and murmurs as Anthony exposed himself to the congregation. He couldn't keep his cool any longer, and I didn't have it in me to care about keeping his cover anymore, either.

"He'll be fine," Anthony murmured, smoothing out his tuxedo as Noah struggled against the security. "Now, let me escort you back down the aisle."

The entire town of Stratford watched with rapt attention as the scene unfolded. I was surprised no one had popped popcorn and started passing it out. Of course, no one had left, no one had done *anything* but stare and hold their hands over their mouths, some even had their camera phones out filming this shit show.

They loved the scandal — no matter the cost.

"You don't even love me, Anthony!" I tried to reason, shaking my head and pleading with him. "I heard you say so yourself on the phone with your father. I'm a trophy, a piece of your perfect political puzzle. Please," I said on a whimper. "Just let me go."

"That's absurd," he said, shaking his head like I'd made it all up. "I would never say any of that."

I stood taller. "I'm not marrying you."

"Oh, yes, you are," he said, grabbing my arm.

"Don't touch my daughter," my father interjected, stepping between us and peeling Anthony's fingers off my arm. "I think she's made her decision very clear."

"Oh, has she now?" Anthony asked, lowering his voice. "And what about our deal? What about the debt you can't pay, Mayor Barnett? Maybe you should fill her in on *that* before you let her make a decision."

"She already knows," Dad answered.

His voice was strong, loud and steady, as if he didn't hear the growing murmur of the congregation over what Anthony had just revealed. My father looked at me, then, his eyes determined, and he nodded.

That nod told me more than any words could.

"What's he talking about?" Mary Anne asked from somewhere behind me. I turned, seeing the confusion on her face, and my heart broke for my older sister. She'd been in the dark, living in Europe with no clue of the chaos going on back home.

I'd explain everything to her later.

For now, I had a dad who needed me.

Anthony's face was unreadable as I reached forward, threading my arm through my father's. "I do," I reiterated. "I know everything — including your plans to cheat on me as soon as this whole wedding was over, if you haven't already," I spat. "Classy, by the way."

He narrowed his eyes.

"And as far as my father's business goes, we'll handle that together. As a family," I said, squeezing my father's arm. "*Without* your help."

Anthony scoffed. "You daft woman. Clearly you don't understand anything about the amount of money your father owes to some very important people. There's no way you'll ever be able to pay it without us."

"That's where you're wrong."

The voice came from the front of the church, and Betty stood slowly, balancing herself with one hand on the back of the pew in front of her. She leaned against it, a victorious smile on her face.

"This old lady's got some savings that she can't take with her when she goes. I'll gladly contribute to the cause, if it saves Ruby Grace from marrying the likes of you."

The church was silent, every person inside it so still I wasn't sure any of us were breathing.

Anthony chuckled. "You clearly have no idea the amount of shit he's in."

That earned a gasp, and a flurry of whispers began again.

My poor father stood there like he'd seen a ghost.

"I'll help," Noah said, shaking the men off him as he readjusted his tuxedo jacket and tie. He stepped toward me, reaching out for my hands, and when I placed them in his, he squeezed tight. "I don't care how long it takes or what we have to do to settle it, we'll handle it without you," he said, eyes hard on Anthony. "But, let me make this crystal clear. There is no way I'm letting the woman I love marry a monster — especially not to pay a debt that was never hers to begin with."

A collective sigh rang out, and I swore I heard some girl cry out her injustice that Noah Becker was in love with someone who wasn't her.

I smiled at that.

"This has gone on long enough," my father said, standing between me and Anthony once more. "The debt is *mine*, and *I* will pay it. If you haven't noticed, I have a house and cars and plenty of equity to figure out my own solution." He swallowed, turning to face me then. "I'm just sorry I ever put you through this, Ruby Grace. I'm sorry I didn't step up sooner."

My heart squeezed, and I nodded in thanks. It was a wound I knew wouldn't heal for a long, long time.

But my father showed up for me in that church.

And for that, I was thankful.

Anthony growled, launching his fist into the side of a pew before he pointed one finger straight at me. "This is ridiculous. Get your ass back to that altar. *Now*."

Noah's face hardened as he turned, guarding me from Anthony. "What aren't you getting here, buddy?" he asked. "It's over. And you can leave now."

"*Excuse me?*" Anthony stepped into Noah's space, but not before my father laid a hand hard on his chest.

"You heard him, son," he said. "I think you should leave now, before you do something you regret."

Anthony's mouth popped open, and he watched my father incredulously before turning to me, and then to my mother. He pointed at her next. "You're really going to let this happen?"

Everyone looked at Mom, then — who was pale, her eyes wide as a doe's, lips trembling. I waited for her to cry, or yell at me, or scream for everyone to look away so they could start the whole ceremony over. I waited for her to kick into crisis mode, to say it was all one big show, that it was a joke. *Haha, we got you!*

Instead, she swallowed, pulled her shoulders back, and lifted her chin up high as she stared directly at Anthony. "I don't think my husband stuttered when he said it's time for you to leave."

A few whistles rang out at that, some laughter and some clapping, and Mom fought back a smirk as Anthony's mouth fell open wider.

"No," he shook his head, running to the men holding the cameras. "No, no, no. Turn them off. Cut the tapes. Turn them *off*." He was spiraling, raking his hands back through his full head of hair as he shook his head. "My father... he'll kill me... he'll disown me... I can't..."

And suddenly, it all made sense.

The man who had gotten down on one knee and asked for my hand in marriage was under pressure from his *own* father. Did he even want to be in politics at all? Or was *he* just a pawn in his father's game, the way he wanted me to be one in his?

His father wasn't even there, on his son's wedding day. That told me more than words how important he was in his life.

Just like he wanted me to play a part, that's what he wanted Anthony to do, too.

My heart ached for him, for the man I thought I knew, for the friend I'd found in him over the year we'd spent together. I stepped forward, wanting to comfort him, but the instinct died as soon as he leveled his cold, hard eyes on me again.

He shook his head, a disgusted look on his face. "After all I did for you, all I *could* have done for you... you ungrateful bi—"

The curse didn't even leave his mouth before Noah got his chance to return the favor from Anthony's sucker punch earlier. His fist landed hard against Anthony's eye, busting it open as he flew backward, the crowd gasping in horror again.

"Sorry, your warnings are up," Noah said, shaking out his hand. "Now, if you won't leave, then we will." He turned to me, then, offering his arm out for me with a smirk. "I've got your getaway car parked out front. What'dya say, Ruby Grace? Want to give this town something to talk about?"

My heart swelled in my chest, and I stepped forward, threading my arm through his as I leaned up and pressed my lips to his.

"Bonnie and Clyde," I whispered.

"Except a way better ending," he replied, and then he kissed me again — this time to the tune of four-hundred clapping hands and a frenzy of cheers.

Noah broke the kiss long enough to bend down and scoop me up into his arms, which earned us another loud cheer as I laughed, head back, eyes cast up to the church ceiling. I looked back at the congregation as Noah walked us toward the doors — at my parents, who both had tears in their eyes; my sister, who smiled at me reassuringly, though I knew she was hurt in her own way by what had happened that day; my best friend, who threw her fists into the air in victory; my town, who wore expressions ranging from excitement and scandal to confusion and anger.

And when I found Betty, I smiled, waving and blowing her a kiss.

*Thank you*, I mouthed.

She just winked, waving me off as the church doors swung open and Noah carried me out into the Tennessee heat.

I didn't know what came next.

I didn't know how my father's debt would be paid, or how Anthony would react once the dust had settled, or where Noah and I would go from here. I didn't know if my mother would ever forgive me, or if I would ever forgive *her*. I didn't know what the future held, but there were two things I knew for sure.

Everything would be okay as long as I had Noah.

And that day was a day that the town of Stratford, Tennessee, would never forget.

# Chapter Nineteen

**NOAH**

Staring up at the stars my father had made in the tin roof of our treehouse with the weight of Ruby Grace's head on my chest, I decided there wasn't a single moment in my life that anything had felt more perfect than it did right now.

I ran my fingers through her long, silky hair, still wavy from the braids I'd unfolded slowly before I slipped her out of her wedding dress. That dress now hung from a limb outside the tree house, and her bare chest rested against my rib cage, her arms wrapped around my middle, legs tangled with mine under the flannel blanket that covered us both where we lay.

The crickets sang a song outside the house, the sound mixing with the smooth, steady breaths Ruby Grace and I exchanged. She drew lazy circles on my chest with her manicured nails, and I could feel the curl of her smile against my chest as I let her hair fall from my fingertips before reaching back down for her scalp to start the trail all over again.

It was a dream.

It had to be.

It didn't seem real — the church, the wedding — or rather, the *not* wedding. I wondered if I'd imagined Ruby Grace running toward me in her dress, if I'd dreamed her into my arms now.

But the soreness of my jaw told me that sucker punch from her former fiancé was real. The dozens of missed calls from my family and half the town on my now-dead cell phone told me it had all really happened. Ruby Grace's hair in my hands, her breasts against my skin, the sweet, sated euphoria we both bathed in after spending the entire evening making love told me it was far, far from a dream.

It was the best reality I'd ever existed in.

I sighed, wrapping her in my arms tightly before pressing a kiss to her hair. She squeezed back, and after a moment of silence, she chuckled.

I felt the vibration of it through my chest, and I smirked, cocking one brow as I looked down at her mess of red hair. "What's so funny, Legs?"

She shook her head. "Just thinking about the look on Pastor Morris's face when you scooped me up and high-tailed me out of the church."

A short exhale of a laugh hit my chest. "I think he might need therapy after today."

"I think the whole *town* might."

"Any regrets?"

She leaned up on one elbow, then, resting her other arm over my chest as she faced me with bent brows. "Not a single one. You?"

I pressed my lips together. "Come on, now."

Ruby Grace smiled, leaning her cheek down on top of where her hand rested. Her golden eyes searched mine before they trailed over every inch of my face, like she was about to paint it, or like she was memorizing every detail.

"I feel like there's so much to talk about, but I don't know where to start."

I twirled her hair around my knuckle, letting one strand fall before I picked up the next. "Why don't you start with the first thing on your mind."

"How did you find out about the real reason I left that night we were here?"

"Oh, that's easy. Betty."

She rolled her eyes. "Well, I know *that* — at least, now I do. But I don't understand how, or when."

"She wrote me a letter," I explained. "Slipped it under my screen door while I was at work."

"How in the world did she get away from the nursing home… and did she *walk* to your house? How did she even know where you live?"

"She said something about having *a little helper*," I offered.

Recognition lit up in her eyes, then. "Annie."

"Maybe," I said. "Anyway, she — or *they* — left it the night before the wedding. Otherwise, I would have come a lot sooner."

"Why do I have a feeling she did that on purpose," Ruby Grace said, smirking as she shook her head. "That woman lives for the movie-like drama."

I chuckled. "Yeah, well, she got some today."

"That she did." Ruby Grace was still smiling, but it slipped as another moment passed between us, her fingers trailing up and down my chest. "I wish I could tell you all the hell I've been through these past three weeks, from the moment my mother told me about my father's debt. I know it probably doesn't make any sense to you, but… I felt this obligation to my family, to my father. I couldn't abandon them, couldn't walk out on them when it seemed I was the only way we could save our home, our possessions, our reputation, our... everything." She sighed. "I feel foolish saying it out loud, but, it's who I've always been. It's the way I was raised."

"Hey," I said, tapping her chin until she looked at me. "I understand. I promise, I really do."

"How can you, when I don't even understand myself?"

"That's easy," I offered with a shrug. "I would have done the same for my family."

Her brows rose. "You would have?"

"I understand that family tie. Blood is thicker than anything. And no matter what knucklehead in my family gets in trouble, we all rally behind them to make it okay again. There is no judgment, no pointed fingers — only love and understanding and, like you demonstrated, sacrifice."

She smiled. "I'm thankful you understand... but I think you and I both know what my parents did goes a little past what's acceptable."

I swallowed. "Yeah... it does." I paused, heart stopping on my next question. "Do you think you could have really gone through with it? Marrying him?"

"No," she answered immediately. "I thought I could. I had the decision made, solidified, and I was walking to the grave of what I thought my life could be as I walked down that aisle. But when I saw you... I knew I couldn't. I knew there was no path I could take that didn't lead to you in the end." Ruby Grace bit her lip. "And, honestly, I knew even before I saw you. I was walking down that aisle in a fog, trying to figure out what to say, when to say it, how to get myself out of that church and that dress and that whole situation. When I saw you... well, it was just the last kick of courage I needed."

I smoothed my knuckles down her cheek, over her jaw. "You surprised the shit out of me when you came barreling back down that aisle."

She chuckled. "I think I surprised *everyone*. Well, except for maybe Betty, who seemed to be plotting it this entire time." She shook her head. "I can't believe she stood up like that and offered to pay part of my father's debt."

"She loves you," I explained. "Plus, according to the letter she wrote me, she insisted that she couldn't take it with her when she goes, anyway. And she doesn't have any kids... other than you." I smiled when Ruby Grace's brows bent together. "Those were her exact words."

She frowned. "Wait... so you were both talking about paying off my father's debt even before today?"

I shrugged. "We didn't have a plan or anything... but, I think both of us knew we would do anything to keep you from having to be responsible for a debt that wasn't yours. Like I said, Betty loves you." I paused, eyes searching hers. "And so do I."

Ruby Grace melted into me, and my heart galloped and stuttered as she swept a hand through my hair, wiggling her way up my chest until her face hovered over mine.

"I never said it back," she whispered, hazel eyes dancing in the light from the makeshift stars. "And I'm sorry I didn't. Because you were right, when you said it the first night you brought me here. I love you, too."

Her eyes watered as I swallowed down the lump in my throat.

"I do, Noah," she said, shaking her head. "I'm so sorry it took all this for me to admit it out loud. I was scared. I was... *lost*. As much as the wedding planning and pressure from my family was smothering me, I chose to hide under that rubble instead of trying to break free. I think a part of me was worried about what I'd find on the other side..."

I nodded, understanding completely. I knew what it was like to have the town talk about you, to have your entire life uprooted in one single day. And I was sure that if I'd had a choice in the matter, I would have avoided it at all costs.

"But, that worry was unfounded," she continued, her plump lips spreading into a gentle smile. "Because I should have known from the very start that as long as it was you, as long as it was *us*, together?" She shook her head again. "There's no way life could be anything but perfect."

I smirked, capturing her chin in my hand. "It's okay," I whispered. "I'd be embarrassed to love me, too."

That earned me a laugh and a swat on the chest, but I killed her laughter when I pressed my lips to hers.

We both breathed into the kiss, inhaling each other, and when she let out a soft, longing moan, all the blood rushed to where her leg rested between my legs.

I groaned, rolling my hips to let her feel me. "It hasn't even been twenty minutes, and I want to bury myself in you again."

She bit her lip on a smile. "What are you waiting for?"

"Energy," I confessed honestly.

Ruby Grace laughed, kissing my nose before she balanced over me again. For a while we just stared at each other, listening to the insects, fingers trailing lightly over each other's skin.

"I think I want to do it," she whispered after a while.

I groaned. "Me, too, woman, but I need water. And a protein bar. And, like, at least thirty more minutes."

"Not that," Ruby Grace said, wide grin splitting her face. I counted the freckles that dotted her cheeks as she shook her head. "I mean AmeriCorps."

My heart stopped at that. "Yeah?"

She nodded. "Yeah. I can't believe you applied for me. I was so overcome with emotion when you told me... I just wanted to throw myself into your arms and thank you and thank *God* for sending you into my life. It was the first moment I realized you loved me... before you even told me. Because no one had ever done anything like that for me before. Ever."

I ran my hand down her cheek. "So, you want to go?"

"I do."

"Good," I said, smirking. "Because an email came through to my inbox yesterday. They want a phone interview for the position in Utah."

Her lips parted. "What?"

"They want—"

"AN INTERVIEW!" Ruby Grace screeched, throwing her arms around me and rolling until she was on top, surrounding me in every way with every limb as she squeezed and squealed. "Oh, my God. Noah!"

I laughed. "If this is the reaction I get, I'm going to apply for every job that exists in AmeriCorps."

Ruby Grace just squeezed me more before sitting up. She straddled me now, her legs around my waist as she pressed her hands to my chest. Her eyes searched mine, worry etched in the creases. "And you'll wait for me? If I go?"

"Are you kidding?" I asked, maneuvering until I was sitting up, too. We were chest to chest, then, and I wrapped my arms around her, pulling her close. "Anything, Ruby Grace. I'd do anything for you."

She kissed me, long and slow, our bodies melding together again before she fluttered her eyes open once more.

"I'll go, if they hire me. But only on one condition."

"And what's that?"

"Well, *two* conditions."

I chuckled. "Okay. You going to tell me what they are or just keep adding on?"

"One, you have to come visit me. Every chance you get. And I'll come home when I can, too."

"That's a given."

"And two," she said, trailing her finger down my chest and tapping it once. "When I'm done, we sail around the world together."

I threw my head back on a laugh. "It takes a lot of money to do that, Ruby Grace. And a sailboat."

She frowned. "Fine. Then when I'm done, we go sailing. Period. We can drive down to Florida, or up to Maine. Charter a boat. Whatever we have to do to get you on the open seas."

I smiled. "Why is this a condition?"

She shrugged, adjusting herself in my lap. "Because you're making one of my dreams come true," she whispered. "I want to make one of yours come true, too."

I swore, if any of my brothers could feel the way my heart melted at her words, they'd punch me in the arm and call me the biggest wuss in the world.

But I didn't care.

When it came to Ruby Grace, I *was* the biggest wuss in the world.

"You already did," I whispered back, brushing her hair from her face. "I dreamed of finding a woman like you, of finding a love like this." I smirked. "And here you are."

"Here I am," she said, giggling. Then, she rolled her hips, eliciting a sharp inhale from me as she painted on a face of innocence. "So, what do we do now?"

"Oh, I can think of a few things," I said, devouring her lips and pulling her back down into the bean bag.

"I thought you needed water. And a protein bar. And *at least thirty minutes*," she teased.

"Shut up and let me make love to you."

She giggled louder when I flipped her over, kissing her neck and pinning her arms above her head. And for the rest of the night, and well into the morning, we sealed our promises with every inch of our bodies, with every ounce of our souls, with every beat of our hearts.

When you hear the word *Tennessee*, what do you think of?

Maybe your first thought is country music. Maybe you can even see those bright lights of Nashville, hear the different bands as their sounds pour out of the bars and mingle in a symphony in the streets. Maybe you think of Elvis, of Graceland, of Dollywood and countless other musical landmarks. Maybe you feel the prestige of the Grand Ole Opry, or the wonder of the Country Music Hall of Fame. Maybe you feel the history radiating off Beale Street in Memphis.

Or maybe you think of the Great Smoky Mountains, of fresh air and hiking, of majestic sights and long weekends in cabins. Maybe you can close your eyes and see the tips of those mountains capped in white, can hear the call of the Tennessee Warbler, can smell the fresh pine and oak.

Maybe, like I used to, you think of whiskey.

But after that summer, Tennessee only conjured up one thing in my mind.

A girl.

No, a *woman*.

One who flipped my entire world upside down in just six weeks' time. One who gave Stratford the biggest scandal they'd seen since the distillery fire. One who would change the world — because she was destined to do so.

And one I knew I'd spend my forever with.

What a lucky sonofabitch.

# *Epilogue*

## NOAH - *Four Months Later*

"Thank you again for having me over for Thanksgiving," Ruby Grace said to Mom as she helped clear the table. "And for having it a little earlier in the day on my behalf."

"Are you kidding?" Mom asked, stacking plates. "I've been the only woman at this table for years. It was a blessing to have someone else to help wrangle these heathens."

"Hey," Logan said with mock offense.

"Besides, you're family now," Mom continued, pausing long enough to smile at Ruby Grace genuinely. "And we're all so proud of you for chasing your dream."

My heart swelled at that, because it was true. My brothers had adopted Ruby Grace like she was the sister they never had, and Mom was happier than I had seen her in years when Ruby Grace was around — even if it was just for dinner or an after-church lunch. She hadn't just filled *my* life with light and love, but my entire family's. And now, on my favorite holiday, it was almost impossible to fend off emotions watching her clear the table with my mom.

Today was the day Ruby Grace would start her drive across the country to serve her first full-year term in AmeriCorps.

It was hard to believe the day had finally come, that in less than an hour, my girl would slide into the driver seat of her loaded-up convertible and head out west to Utah. My chest had been tight all day with the effort it took to fight off tears, but I swore to myself that I wouldn't cry — no matter how much I would miss her.

Because this was her dream, and I stood by my word that I'd help her achieve it.

"Are we excused?" Mikey asked from the end of the table.

An uncomfortable hush fell over the family, and Mom glanced at me and Jordan before she smiled at her youngest son. "I was going to get the pie."

"I don't want any."

Mom nodded, her eyes worried and sad. "Oh. Okay, then. Yes, you're excused."

Mikey didn't say another word, just shoved back from the table, the legs of his chair scraping against the wood before he stood and pushed it back in. He was down the hall and shutting the door to his bedroom before any of us even looked up again, and he didn't say a word to any of us — not even Ruby Grace, who he knew was leaving.

He hadn't said a word all day.

I sighed, reaching over to squeeze her hand. "Forgive him. He's still not okay after the whole Bailey thing..."

"It's okay," she assured me, squeezing my hand back.

Just like we had all feared, Bailey ended up taking the record label in Nashville up on their offer earlier than she'd promised. And, along with that change, she'd also broken up with Mikey. She'd told them it wasn't forever, it was just for a while, so she could focus on her music.

But to Mikey, it was the ultimate betrayal.

He hadn't been the same since then, and where he usually showed his emotions willingly, opened up to us and let us help, he had shut down completely at this. Since that cold, rainy day in October when she landed the blow, my little brother had been a zombie version of the kid who existed before.

I hoped we'd get him back soon.

Jordan and Logan finished clearing the table as Ruby Grace and I did the dishes, and once the chores were done, we all gathered one last time for pie and wine. The time passed too quickly, and before I was ready, we were all standing on the porch saying our goodbyes to the woman I loved.

Jordan gave Ruby Grace the first hug — along with a AAA card he'd set up without telling any of us. "For emergencies," he told her gruffly. She smiled and thanked him, giving him one last hug before he moved out of the way to let Logan in next.

"Stay safe, and have fun," he said, wrapping her up in a hug. "And for God's sake, try to call home at least once a day so I don't have to watch my brother mope around without you here."

I punched his arm.

Ruby Grace chuckled, giving me a knowing smirk. "I promise, I'll text him an annoying amount in an effort to avoid that very thing."

"Thank you," Logan said, pressing his hands together in mock prayer as his eyes floated up.

"And you have fun with your new trainee," she said, lifting one brow at Logan. "I heard she's quite the firecracker."

"Ugh, don't remind me," Logan murmured. "The only reason she got the job at *all* is because of her father."

"Doesn't change the fact that you're responsible for her now," I pointed out.

"Who knows, maybe they'll have you train her just so she can take your place as the lead tour guide," Jordan chimed in.

Logan paled at that, mouth gaping like a fish as he looked at Mom first, then at me and Ruby Grace, and finally back at Jordan. "Don't even joke about that."

We all chuckled, but I knew there was a part of Logan that might actually be scared that could happen. After all, Mallory Scooter was the black sheep of the Scooter family. She had tattoos and piercings and purple hair and a bad attitude that had tainted her family's image for years. It seemed her father had finally put his foot down, forcing her to be the distillery's latest tour guide addition. It was an extremely valued job, and one that other employees fought hard for. No one was happy she'd been the one to be hired — least of all her.

Her first day was Monday, and Logan had just found out he would be her trainer.

"You'll be alright, little bro," I assured him, clapping him hard on the shoulder.

Mom stepped up next, her eyes glossy as she folded her arms around Ruby Grace. She held her tight, swaying a little. "I know I said it before, but we are all so proud of you," she said, pulling back and holding Ruby Grace's arms in her hands. "I know you'll call Noah, but don't forget to call me from time to time, too. Okay?"

"Of course. And you promise to check in on Betty from time to time?"

Mom waved her off with a smile. "Are you kidding? Visiting that wild old woman is the highlight of my week, now."

We all laughed at that. Mom had started volunteering at the nursing home with Ruby Grace to get to know her better, and in the process, she'd fallen under the same magical spell Betty weaved on all of us. Now that Ruby Grace was leaving, I had a feeling they'd become even closer.

"Alright," Mom said, dabbing at the corner of her eyes. "Come on, boys. Let's leave these two alone. Drive safe, dear, and let us know when you make it. Okay?"

"Will do," Ruby Grace assured her, and with one last wave from each of them, my Mom and brothers went back inside, leaving just the two of us on the porch.

Ruby Grace turned to me with a sad smile. "I guess this is it, huh?"

"I guess so."

My heart squeezed violently in my chest as I reached for her hand, walking with her in silence off the porch and out to her car. It was loaded up with boxes and piles of clothes still on the hanger. I didn't think she'd be able to fit everything she wanted in that little convertible, but she'd surprised me.

We both stopped next to her driver side door, and tears flooded Ruby Grace's eyes as soon as she faced me.

"Hey," I said, pretending like I wasn't on the verge of crying myself as I pulled her into me. I wrapped my arms around her tight, resting my chin on her head as I felt her tears dampen my long-sleeve shirt. "None of that now. It's not permanent, okay? Plus, this is your dream, this is what you've wanted for *so* long. You're doing it, Ruby Grace," I said, pulling back to look into her shining eyes. "You're going to *AmeriCorps*."

"I know," she whispered, sniffing back more tears. "But, I'm leaving *you* in the process."

"Just for a little while," I reminded her. "I'll come visit for Christmas, and every other chance I get."

"And I'll be back after the summer."

"Exactly."

"And then?"

I smiled. "And then, we find some poor sucker willing to let us on their sailboat for a month."

Ruby Grace laughed through her tears, burying her face in my chest again with a little whimper. "I'm going to miss you so much, Noah." She lifted her head again. "I love you. You know that?"

I chucked her chin. "I do. And I love you. You know that?"

"I do."

Silence fell over us, and for a while, I just held her there in that quiet space, the sun above breaking through the crisp fall air.

"So, any other stops on your way out of town?"

She shook her head. "Nope. My family did our dinner last night, and I can't go through Mom holding me in a vise grip and sobbing all over me again," she joked, but I didn't miss the underlying stress in her voice.

She and her parents had been working on their relationship since the not-wedding day, but I knew she was still far from forgiving and forgetting.

"And I said goodbye to Annie, Travis, and baby Bethany earlier this week."

"I bet they're all going to miss you."

"They will," she agreed. "And I'll miss all of them. But, I'm ready." A genuine smile bloomed on my favorite strawberry smoothie lips, then. "This is it, isn't it? I'm going. I'm really going."

I returned her smile. "You're really going, Legs." I pulled her closer, sweeping her hair from her face before lowering my voice to a whisper. "I am so proud of you."

My fingertips found her chin, and I tilted it up, pressing my lips to hers. It was a kiss I never wanted to end, one that was slow and easy and felt like the most natural thing in the world. That's how it had been for us since that night in the treehouse — effortless.

"Don't find another girl while I'm gone," she said when we finally broke the kiss.

"Yeah, right. More like you finding a hot AmeriCorps hippie with long hair and hemp clothes."

She snorted. "You're ridiculous."

"And you're amazing." I framed her face, kissing her again. "This isn't goodbye. It's see you soon. Okay?"

Her eyes glossed again. "Okay," she whispered.

I could have held her forever, kissed her over and over and over until she missed her check-in time for her new job in Utah. But, I forced a heavy sigh, breaking away from her hold and opening the driver side door for her to climb inside. Once she was seated, she rolled the window down, leaning out of it and pulling my mouth to hers once more.

"Woman," I chuckled between kisses. "Go. Now. You've got a long drive to Kansas City and it's already noon. I don't want you driving when you're tired tonight."

She sighed, pulling back and pressing her forehead to mine. "Okay. Okay. I'm going." She ran her hand over my jaw, like she was memorizing my stubble. "I'll call you when I stop for gas and food."

"And I'll call you every morning to remind you how much I love you."

She smiled at that. "You better."

With one last, longing kiss, she let me go, and I stepped back, sliding my hands in my pockets as she fired the car up. She checked the directions on her GPS, set her phone on the dash, and waved at me with tears in her eyes before pulling out of Mom's driveway.

I watched her take the left, watched her stop at the stop sign down the road, watched her take the left that led out of town. And when I couldn't see her taillights anymore and she was really gone, I let the first tear fall.

I cried because I'd miss her. I cried because I'd never wanted to let someone go as much as I'd wanted to keep them forever. But I didn't cry because I was sad.

I cried because I was thankful.

I was thankful I could finally show her what I'd wanted to all along — that she could be in love and *be* loved while she had a life and dreams of her own. I was thankful for the two-week vacation I had coming up in a month so I could fly to Utah and spend Christmas with her. I was thankful for my family inside the house behind me, for the group I had to support me while Ruby Grace was gone.

And more than anything, I was thankful I'd found the woman I was sure didn't exist.

More than a thousand miles couldn't separate us — not really. She was still here with me, and I knew she took me with her, too.

For now, I wiped my tears and headed back inside to celebrate Thanksgiving with football and leftovers and time with my family. After all, I had one little brother stressed over his new trainee at work and the other holed up in his room over a girl we all knew was trouble.

I was needed in Stratford, and she was needed in Salt Lake.

So, I counted down the days until she'd be in my arms again, until she'd be back in Stratford, until we'd make our plans for where we'd go next.

Until I'd get down on one knee and give her the ring stashed in my bedside dresser drawer.

And though my ring wouldn't be the first to don her delicate finger, I had no doubt it would be the last.

The Becker Brothers will be back this fall.

# Acknowledgements

This is my sixteenth novel.

Saying that out loud makes me laugh, and makes me tear up, and makes me sigh with happy butterflies in my heart. It also makes me realize that no book – EVER – will come without the help and support of my amazing team.

Staci Brillhart. You're almost always first in my acknowledgements, and that's because you truly are a part of EVERY single piece of my writing process. From the time the idea pops into my head until the final word of the acknowledgements are written, you're there. With this one, you were absolutely instrumental in providing crucial feedback that took this from a book that would have been great to a book that I'm more proud of than I ever have been before. You loved these characters the same way I loved them, and together, we really hammered them down and created something magical. Thank you. I love you MTT.

Momma, as always, I could never do this without you. Not only did you raise me to embrace creativity and believe I could do anything I set my mind to, but you've also shown me throughout your entire life – even more so in this past year – just how strong the women in our family are. Whenever I hit the hard days, I hear your voice in my head. One step at a time, baby girl. And I know it's because of you that I'm able to write "the end" on yet another book. I love you.

To my amazing team of beta readers: Kellee Fabre, Trish QUEEN MINTNESS, Kathryn Andrews, Sarah Green, Danielle Lagasse, Ashlei Davison, and Jess Vogel — thank you for reading along the way and for doing such a comprehensive read at the end of it all. We had a lot of loose ends to tie up, a lot of problems to think through and figure out solutions for, and you all were AMAZING. I don't know how I would do this without y'all. Please don't ever leave me! Love you all.

There is an angel walking on Earth with us. I'm convinced, because that's the only explanation for everything that is my personal assistant/close friend/ beta reader/all-hat-wearer – Christina Stokes. You are the most thoughtful and most hard-working individual I know. You are also the kindest, and I am so thankful to have you in my life. Thank you for thinking of me, of how to make my life easier, and for doing so with that dazzling smile on your face. I am more thankful for you than I could ever put into words, and I want you to know that you bring a special light to my life and to this community. I love you.

Shout out to Sasha Erramouspe for being my final eyes on this one. I cannot believe it earned the title of YOUR FAVORITE BOOK OF MINE YET. **\*sobs\*** That's like winning the gold medal in the Olympics in my eyes. Thank you for always making time for me and for your crucial feedback. I love you!

Elaine York of Allusion, THANK YOU for always working with my ever-changing deadlines and for always polishing my manuscripts up to sparkle pretty. I'm so happy to have you on my team.

Shout out to my PR team – Social Butterfly PR. Nina, Hilary, Brooke and the rest of the team, I am always so thankful for your help and attention to detail.

To Flavia Viotti and the rest of the crew at Book Case Agency, I can't thank you enough for all you do for my books. From foreign rights to audio and more, you get my words into the hands (and ears) of readers I couldn't otherwise reach. Thank you!

A huge shout out to Lauren Perry of Perrywinkle Photography and to the incredible models who helped bring my vision of Ruby Grace and Noah to life. This cover is absolutely beautiful and it wouldn't have been possible without y'all!

Thank you to all the bloggers, authors, and readers who make our book community go round. Special shout out to Angie Doyle McKeon for being the best bumble bee in all the land. I swear, I fill half my Kindle because of books you recommend, and I will never be ungrateful for when you recommend MY books. Thank you!

KANDILAND! Oh, Kandiland. You are my special little corner of the internet world, and every time I write, it's YOU who I think about. I think about your excitement, about your love and passion for reading, and it lights me up inside. Let's do this forever. Thank you!

And, as always, thank YOU, wonderful reader. You decided to pick up a romance book. Not just that, but an INDEPENDENTLY PUBLISHED romance book. And I'm so lucky (and happy and thankful) that it was mine. Thanks for coming on this journey with me, and I hope you will join me for more in the future.

Move from Kandi Steiner

### The What He Doesn't Know Series
Charlie's marriage is dying. She's perfectly content to go down in the flames, until her first love shows back up and reminds her the other way love can burn.

### The Wrong Game
Gemma's plan is simple: invite a new guy to each home game using her season tickets for the Chicago Bears. It's the perfect way to avoid getting emotionally attached and also get some action. But after Zach gets his chance to be her practice round, he decides one game just isn't enough. A sexy, fun sports romance.

### On the Way to You
It was only supposed to be a road trip, but when Cooper discovers the journal of the boy driving the getaway car, everything changes. An emotional, angsty road trip romance.

**A Love Letter to Whiskey**
An angsty, emotional romance between two lovers fighting the curse of bad timing.

**Weightless**
Young Natalie finds self-love and romance with her personal trainer, along with a slew of secrets that tie them together in ways she never thought possible.

**Revelry**
Recently divorced, Wren searches for clarity in a summer cabin outside of Seattle, where she makes an unforgettable connection with the broody, small town recluse next door.

**Black Number Four**
A college, Greek-life romance of a hot young poker star and the boy sent to take her down.

**The Palm South University Serial**
Written like your favorite drama television show, PSU has been called "a mix of Greek meets Gossip Girl with a dash of Friends." Follow seven college students as they maneuver the heartbreaks and triumphs of love, life, and friendship.

Rush (book 1)
Anchor (book 2)
Pledge (book 3)
Legacy (book 4)

**Tag Chaser**
She made a bet that she could stop chasing military men, which seemed easy — until her knight in shining armor and latest client at work showed up in Army ACUs.

**Song Chaser**

Tanner and Kellee are perfect for each other. They frequent the same bars, love the same music, and have the same desire to rip each other's clothes off. Only problem? Tanner is still in love with his best friend.

# About the Author

Kandi Steiner is a bestselling author and whiskey connoisseur living in Tampa, FL. Best known for writing "emotional rollercoaster" stories, she loves bringing flawed characters to life and writing about real, raw romance — in all its forms. No two Kandi Steiner books are the same, and if you're a lover of angsty, emotional, and inspirational reads, she's your gal.

An alumna of the University of Central Florida, Kandi graduated with a double major in Creative Writing and Advertising/PR with a minor in Women's Studies. She started writing back in the 4th grade after reading the first Harry Potter installment. In 6th grade, she wrote and edited her own newspaper and distributed to her classmates. Eventually, the principal caught on and the newspaper was quickly halted, though Kandi tried fighting for her "freedom of press." She took particular interest in writing romance after college, as she has always been a die hard hopeless romantic, and likes to highlight all the challenges of love as well as the triumphs.

When Kandi isn't writing, you can find her reading books of all kinds, talking with her extremely vocal cat, and spending time with her friends and family. She enjoys live music, traveling, hiking, anything heavy in carbs, beach days, movie marathons, craft beer and sweet wine — not necessarily in that order.

## CONNECT WITH KANDI:

NEWSLETTER: bit.ly/NewsletterKS
INSTAGRAM: Instagram.com/kandisteiner
FACEBOOK: facebook.com/kandisteiner
FACEBOOK READER GROUP (Kandiland): facebook.com/groups/kandischasers
GOODREADS: bit.ly/GoodreadsKS
BOOKBUB: bookbub.com/authors/kandi-steiner
TWITTER: twitter.com/kandisteiner
WEBSITE: www.kandisteiner.com

Kandi Steiner may be coming to a city near you! Check out her "events" tab to see all the signings she's attending in the near future:

www.kandisteiner.com/events

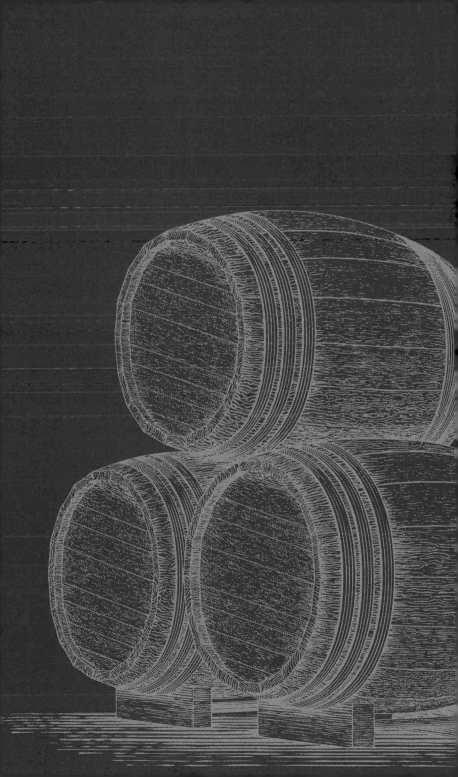